How Can I
Be Down?

How Can I Be Down?

Brenda Hapmton

www.urbanbooks.net

Urban Books, LLC
300 Farmingdale Road, NY-Route 109
Farmingdale, NY 11735

How Can I Be Down

ISBN 13: 978-1-62286-539-0
ISBN 10: 1-62286-539-1

First Mass Market Printing October 2017
First Trade Paperback Printing May 2015
Printed in the United States of America

10 9 8 7 6 5 4 3 2 1

Distributed by Kensington Publishing Corp.
Submit orders to:
Customer Service
400 Hahn Road
Westminster, MD 21157-4627
Phone: 1-800-733-3000
Fax: 1-800-659-243

INTRODUCTION

Playa-hating, backstabbing, stupid-ass bull-shit was what was going down in Los Angeles. The fellas and me packed up our bags five years ago and jetted to St. Louis. We figured since didn't nobody know much about us, everything would go smooth. And as for now, things are on the down low. What's behind us is truly behind us. But things didn't always go as smooth as they are now.

Years ago Papa Abrams, my daddy, used to run the show. He'd done six years in prison for drug trafficking, money laundering, and racketeering. He knew his time was just about up so he taught my brother, Kareem, and me the game remarkably well. By the time he got out, I was eighteen years old and things were running smooth. Money was flowing and everybody in the hood gave Papa Abrams the utmost respect. Even the police. They didn't trip with us and we didn't trip with them. That wasn't until some new fools moved in the hood trying to run the show, and things started to take a turn for the worse.

I remember it like it was yesterday. After coming home from my senior prom, getting ready to get down to business with Jada, my girlfriend, I opened the door and Daddy lay in the middle of the floor, stripped naked, smothered in blood with a gunshot wound to the head. I yelled for Kareem to come help but he was somewhere getting his mack on. By the time the police and the coroners came to haul Daddy's body away, Kareem heard the news and ran down the street trying to stop them from taking Daddy's body away. Kareem was only fifteen at the time and didn't understand what was destined to go down. Retaliation was the only thing on my mind, but shit took mega planning and preparation to do it how I wanted it done.

It didn't take the fellas and me long to figure out who was responsible, so as soon as things chilled, we went on a mission. Cleaned muh-fucking house. My boy Rufus was usually the one who pulled the trigger, but since it was Daddy who we were talking about, the pleasure was all mine. Shortly after, people started talking and the cops started coming around more and more every day asking questions. I'm sure they knew who was responsible, but we left no evidence. Six dead bodies and no one to blame. Not that the police cared, especially since I had a feeling we did them a favor anyway.

But after that, shit just wasn't the same without Daddy around. Our respect in the hood went to no respect. Rufus was thrown in jail for eight years on a simple-ass carjacking case, and Donovan moved to St. Louis for a fresh new start. When he offered for us to move with him, I told him I wasn't running from anyone. Daddy always taught Kareem and me that running was for cowards and said he'd done enough time in prison for the whole damn family. Including Mama, who was incarcerated for stabbing her boyfriend to death. Two weeks in there, she committed suicide. We were hurt like hell, but Daddy said we'd just have to make it the best way we could. If anything happened to him, he made me promise to take care of Kareem and told me to do whatever I could to keep my ass out of prison.

So, less than a year after his death, it was hands off for Kareem and me. Daddy had hookups all over the place, and his connections turned out to be worth thousands and thousands of dollars. Without a doubt, he had definitely paved the way for us. And after three more years in the game, we called it quits. Had enough money to set us out for a while. I washed my hands of the situation and never looked back.

When Donovan called and said everything was hooked up for us in St. Louis, Kareem, Quincy, and me rolled out. I knew Kareem wouldn't have a problem leaving, but Quincy, I wasn't too sure about him. We'd been friends since the second grade, but from a white boy I didn't know what to expect. When I asked him if he was ready to leave his family and everything he had in Los Angeles behind, he made it perfectly clear that wherever Kareem and me go, he go. He's always been like a brotha to me, and no matter what, he comes through for me. Sometimes even more than Kareem. But blood is fasho thicker than water. And whenever Kareem and me have our differences, Quincy stands clear. Never sides with either one of us. He's the only partner I've never had an argument with, never had to fight with, and never had to disrespect. That's why he's my muh-fucking boy. Got more love and respect for him than anybody. He's smart, knows the business, and ain't trying to run shit like everybody else does. What I admire the most, though, is his aggressive ways with the sistas. According to him, he be putting it on 'em. Quincy wouldn't dream of kicking it with a white gal because in his eyes, a sista is definitely the best way to go. I'm sure his green eyes, trimmed goatee, and black spiked hair plays a part in their attraction, but he insists it's the two-carat diamond in his left earlobe along with his charming, deep voice that hooks 'em every time. To me, a piece of ass is simply a piece of ass. Black, white, green, purple, whatever. As long as I'm satisfied, who gives a damn?

Now, the only other brotha who sees it like I do is Donovan. Donovan is the Black Stallion of the crew. Can't even see him with the lights off. But when he cracks a smile, his gold tooth shines like the sun cracking through the clouds. If it wasn't for his thick-cut body and his so-called "bedroom, slanted eyes" (so the women say), he'd be outta there. No matter where we go, he's styling his black wave cap and only takes it off when he wants the women to see his waves. Everybody seems to think we got a lot in common, but something inside me just won't let me trust him as much as I want to. He's sneaky. Always wants to run the show since he's twenty-eight and the oldest in the bunch. Li'l does he know, I'm the head nigga in charge.

Donovan was even trying to run shit when Daddy was around, even when he went to prison. But Daddy cut that shit short and did things his way from the inside. So, when Donovan moved to St. Louis so quickly after Daddy's death, I was actually surprised to hear from him. He bragged about how well things were going for him in the Lou and insisted we needed to be there with him. After his months of coaxing, I couldn't resist. Just maybe, he wasn't that conniving after all.

Either way, we scoped the Lou for months riding down Goodfellow, Natural Bridge, Delmar, and Kingshighway trying to find a nice private place for us to chill on the city's north side. Had to feel like home for me but at the same time I wanted a place with class. So, when Donovan found a huge, three-story brick house off Delmar near the Central West End, we had the entire place gutted out and remodeled to our satisfaction. There was a vacant lot on one side and a boarded-up empty house on the other. Privacy was of key importance. Took less than three months to have the place fixed up, but when it was finished, it looked like it belonged in a magazine. Everything from vaulted ceilings to bay windows surrounds the place. Each one of us has our own bedroom and private bath that take up the entire second floor, led by way of an old cherry wood repolished staircase from the bottom floor. The third level is our playroom. Got pinball machines, a pool table, an entertainment center, and a kitchen to get our grub on.

The most important things in the house are the cameras that view the entire property. There's no way to sneak in or out without somebody seeing you. So, in reality, ain't much for us on the outside but fresh fucking air and pretty-ass women. Not that I'm looking for anyone, because all I need is Jada. She's been my backbone for many years. I used to be out there dirtball bad but she stuck by me. Never gave up on us even when I wanted her to. I'm sure the money I was dishing out helped, but ain't nothing better than a thick, big-breasted, light-skinned sista who got my back no matter what.

As things settled down in the Lou, I sent for her. The fellas weren't too enthused about her moving in with us, especially Kareem, but whatever. Had a fit when he found out about my plans. Wanted me to be a playa forever like he is, but I'm trying to live my life as best as I can. Kareem, though, he be playing with fire. Fucking any- and everything that crosses his path. There's no doubt about it, he's definitely the Pretty Boy and knows it. The ladies fall head over heels for his melting smile, his cocoa chocolate shiny skin, thick lashes, and hazelnut eyes. He's clean cut, can't do without the material bullshit, and preppy as preppy can get.

Me, I don't give a fuck about all that mess. I just like to stay clean, live large, and keep my business on the down low. Truly worried every day, though, that the past is going to come haunt me. And no matter how hard I try to shake these feeling about someday paying for my mistakes, I hold on to what Papa Abrams told me about never going to jail. I'm hoping that people understand I killed for the love of my family, for the sacrifices Papa Abrams made for us; and I have no regrets. If I had to do it all over again, I wouldn't do it any differently. Thing is, I know Papa Abrams probably upset with me for leaving L.A., but some serious shit was about to go down if we didn't jet. Last thing I wanted was to attend the funeral of another one of my partners. Had too many of those, and if the Lou was my way of saving my life, so be it. I was here, and all I wanted going forward was peace.

CHAPTER 1

I could smell the bacon cooking in the kitchen, but when I saw the red flashing lights coming in from the outside through my bedroom window, that's what immediately awakened me. I reached for the remote and clicked on the outside camera only to see the police putting a ticket on Donovan's black Lincoln Navigator. Why would the stupid asshole park backward on the street? Puzzled the hell out of me, because the last thing we needed were the cops showing up. I went to the bathroom, quickly shaved my rough-looking beard, and trimmed down my mustache. My bald head didn't need a shave so I just rubbed some grease in my hands and patted it to give it a shine. After I was finished, I winked in the mirror at the finest mocha chocolate brotha I knew.

I gathered my robe in the front and headed upstairs to the third floor where all the noise was coming from. It was only nine o'clock in the morning, and to see a house full of fellas relaxing around on the leather sofa and chairs upstairs pissed me the fuck off. Didn't these fools have somewhere else to be? And as I stood at the top of the stairs looking in their direction, the expression on my face quickly quieted the room. I guessed Donovan knew I was about to go off so he popped up and asked them to step. I watched as seven brothas, who I didn't know, trotted down the steps one by one. As they passed by me, sons of bitches didn't even have the nerve to speak. To me, there was too much at stake. Everything was kept in this house, including my money, so these many fellas running around could only mean trouble. As Donovan headed down the steps to escort them out, I reached my arm out in front of him.

"Uh, we need to talk," I said.

"I'm sure we do." He smiled at me and tried to move my arm. "Just not right now. Let me walk my boys out and I'll be back up to holler at you in a minute."

"Let them out the back door. The police might still be out front putting a ticket on your car. So, before you come back up, if you wouldn't mind parking your car on the right side of the street, I'd appreciate it."

I moved my arm and Donovan walked down the steps grinning at me. I could tell what he was thinking, but if he wasn't man enough to say it out loud, fuck 'im. I went into the entertainment room and picked up the *St. Louis American* newspaper on the floor then set it down on the table. I turned on the TV and leaned back on the couch. Room was junky as hell. Empty Hpnotiq bottles and Colt 45 cans were all over the place. Thick smoke and hot, musty air stirred in the room.

When Donovan came back upstairs, he took a seat on the other side of the couch and pulled out a joint. He lit it and sat up on the edge of the couch looking at me. "So, what's up?" he asked.

I leaned forward and gripped my hands together. "What's up? You have the nerve to ask me what's up?"

"Yeah, that's 'cause I don't know what's on your mind. You said we needed to talk." He took a hit from the joint and passed it to me.

I shook my head. "What's up is all these unexpected, unknown-ass guests you've been having over here lately. One or two are cool, but must there be a house full of brothas I know nothing about hanging around?"

"I know 'em. Besides, it ain't like they be hanging around every day. But if it's a problem for you, I'll just ask them to stop coming by." He winked. "Okay, Mr. Boss Man?"

"Don't be calling me that, man. You know better than I do that's bad business just waiting to happen. Besides, look at this jacked-up room. It's a mess and I didn't put all our money into this house to let your damn friends come in here and mess shit up for us. So, one or two friends, that's it. If you don't like the rules, you can always find yourself somewhere else to live."

"Look, Kiley," Donovan said, blowing smoke out of his mouth. "I don't want no trouble. I know where you're coming from, but a nigga get bored sometimes. Kareem and Quincy always spending nights with the ladies and you and Jada forever doing shit together, so I kinda like just chilling with my new crew. And don't worry, no hard feelings. I understand where you're coming from."

I reached out for his joint and took a few puffs. Then I handed it back to him. "I hope you understand you're like family to me. My issues are about making sure things around here run smoothly. Too many niggas mean trouble, and from past experience even you know that." I stood up and grabbed his hand then pulled him up. "Now, let's go get some of this good-ass breakfast I've been smelling all morning."

Donovan and me walked down the steps holding each other around the shoulders. When we went into the downstairs kitchen, Jada was putting the finishing touches on breakfast.

"It's about time," she said with her hands on her hips. "I've been down here since seven o'clock and the two of you Negros finally decide to show up."

I went over by the stove where she was standing and kissed her on the cheek, then wrapped my arms around her waist. "Baby, I smelled your good cooking upstairs, but Donovan had some issues that needed my immediate attention."

"He lying, Jada," Donovan said. "Quiet as kept, he told me he was trying to put off coming down here eating your horrible-ass cooking for as long as he could. I was the one who reminded him of how good you cook and changed his mind."

"Well, fuck both of y'all. I made all this food and ain't nobody here to enjoy it. If y'all don't want it, throw it away. I'm taking my ass back to bed." Jada took my hands from around her and started to leave the kitchen.

I grabbed her by the hand. "I know you didn't just believe that bullshit he said."

"I don't know what to believe, Kiley. Y'all play so many games that I truly don't have time for them." She loosened my hand and walked out.

I gave Donovan a hard stare for lying to her; then we rushed the kitchen counter and fixed us a plate. I pushed him out of the way a few times and we laughed trying to pile as many pancakes as we could on our plates. Soon after we sat down at the kitchen table to eat, Quincy and Kareem came rushing through the back door grabbing plates ready to get their grub on as well. Quincy had a black bandana wrapped around his head, and a white long Nike T-shirt that hung down over his baggy jeans. Kareem was dressed in Sean Jeans from head to toe with a pair of leather Timberlands on. By the look of things, it was obvious they'd been somewhere getting their sex on.

"Playas, playas," I said. "Good morning to you brothas too, and can we please go wash our hands or something before bringing all these germs up in here? Kareem, I know your daddy taught you better than that, didn't he?"

"Yeah, yeah, he did." He smiled with a pancake hanging out of his mouth. "But he also taught me don't starve myself either." He and Quincy went over to the sink and washed their hands.

"That's better. But I can't believe these bitches y'all be out with in the wee hours of the morning ain't feeding y'all asses. Damn shame y'all gotta come in here and eat all my woman's good cooking up."

"Aw, we eating," Quincy said, piling his plate up high. "Just not what you might have in mind, my brotha." He laughed as Kareem gave him five.

"Y'all some young nasty-ass niggas," Donovan said. "Kiley and me would never do any shit like that." Donovan looked over at me as I held my head down and kept on eating. "Kiley?"

I looked up and smiled. "What?"

"What, my ass. Don't tell me you go out like that. I remember you said never in a million years would you stoop that low."

"I know what I said, but I'm moving on with the times and so is my woman. If I don't, some-body else will, so—"

"So, my ass. Y'all muh-fuckers crazy." Donovan got up and dumped his plate in the trash. "Just the thought of the shit spoils my damn appetite."

"Just the thought of what, Donovan?" Jada asked, walking back into the kitchen.

"Uh, the thought of, uh . . . sex." Donovan hesitated.

"Sex? What about sex spoils your appetite?" she pushed.

I grabbed her around the waist and sat her down on my lap. "Donovan gay, baby. Having sex with a woman just spoils his appetite."

She looked at me and rolled her eyes. Kareem and Quincy were at the table cracking up.

Donovan grabbed his thang. "Suck on this, Kiley. Jada, if you must know, I was talking about the thought of oral sex. Just can't see myself indulging."

"Oh, that. Well, I knew you wasn't gay, especially since your bedroom is closest to Kiley and mine and I can hear what be going on. But that's your preference. If oral sex doesn't suit you then, hey, don't do it. But, it would be a shame to let all that dark Hershey's chocolate go to waste like that." She looked at me and smiled.

I was slightly bothered that she was giving Donovan some props, but I didn't trip.

"But, Jada," Quincy said, "it helps the relationship, don't it? Don't lie. Tell Donovan how he be missing out."

Jada looked at me and I smiled back at her. She took her hands and rubbed them across my head. "You know, Quincy, some things should just be left well enough alone, especially if you don't know how to perform orally, but at least Kiley tries."

Everybody burst out in laughter.

"What?" I yelled. "What do you mean, I try?"

"I mean you shouldn't be down here talking about our sex life to begin with. So, next time, I'll try not to tell it like it is." She hopped up and ran out of the kitchen.

"Whew. That was deep, big brotha," Kareem said, standing up and patting me on the back. "Kinda disappointed in you. I fasho thought you had it in you, but you can best be sure that if you don't, I do for the both of us."

"I'm sure you do, Kareem. There's no doubt in my mind that you do. Thing is, you shouldn't believe everything you hear, especially if it comes from a woman. "

As we munched down on breakfast, I couldn't help but think about what Jada said and rushed myself so I could go upstairs to check her for dissing me in front of the boys. If she wasn't satisfied, I was sure that some of the other females I used to mess with were. I kept my sex life on the down low with the fellas, 'cause, honestly, it wasn't really none of their business how I performed. I was sure they all wondered how good Jada was in bed but I never shared it with them because that would be disrespecting her. Not only that, if I did tell them how good it was, I didn't want them to try it out for themselves. Then again, she really wasn't any of their type of woman. She had long, thick sandy-brown hair that she always kept tightened up in a ponytail. She was also a bit on the thick side. She reminded me so much of Mama when I met her I couldn't resist wanting her in my life. The fellas were all into small waistlines, firm breasts, and big asses but I was more into a woman's heart. And since Jada's heart was with me, mine was definitely with her. Now, I had my share of small waistlines, firm breasts, and big butts too, but after sex, I was still missing something. Something that none of these brothas seemed to care about: love. Eventually, that's what strengthened me and got me on the right track. At times, just Jada's comforting arms holding me in the middle of the night, when I fear for the worst, means more to me than anything.

After finishing up my pancakes, I excused myself from a conversation of money, sex, women, and lies. I went upstairs to my bedroom, and Jada was resting across the bed sideways looking at a magazine. I opened my robe and laid my body on top of hers. She'd just gotten out of the shower and smelled like a breath of fresh air. She closed the magazine and forced me off her by pushing me back with her ass.

"Don't be trying to butter me up, Kiley."

I stood up. "What's with the attitude, Jada? You've been moody all damn morning."

"No, I haven't. My mood didn't change until you lied to me about Donovan. The question was simple. All you had to say was he didn't like oral sex. If you lie about that, ain't no telling what else you'd lie about."

I went over to the closet and pulled out my powder blue and black sweater and knitted hat to match. Then picked my black Levi's up off the chair. I slid off my robe and started changing clothes.

Jada sat up on the bed. "Where are you going? And I was talking to you, you know?"

"I know. But you wanna argue this morning and I don't feel like it right now. So, conversation over and I'll see you when I get back." I pulled my hat down, took my gun out from underneath my pillow, and slid it down the right side of my jeans. I turned on my cell phone and clipped it to my jeans. I looked at Jada. "If you need me, call me."

She got off the bed and stood in front of the door folding her arms. "I asked you where you were going."

I leaned down and kissed her on the cheek, then moved her over to the side. "And I said, if you need me, call me." I walked out.

I met Donovan on the staircase and he said he was headed upstairs to clean up the entertainment room and then was going to work off breakfast by lifting weights in his room. I told him I'd be back later and thanked him for not making a big deal about our dispute earlier.

When I got downstairs, Quincy and Kareem were still at the kitchen table eating.

"Say, big brother," Kareem said, "where ya headed looking all spiffy and shit?"

"Out. I'll be back later. If anybody needs me, call me. Deuces." I closed the back door and left.

I opened up the garage door and backed out my pearly white Lexus with gold trimmings. Wasn't as flashy as I wanted, but it was nice. I was trying to be as low-key as possible, so Jada and me both drove the Lexus. Kareem and Quincy shared a black BMW but had two Harleys locked up in the basement. Donovan's Lincoln Navigator was always the only car parked in front of the house. The less attention the better. Flashy jewelry, flashy cars, and money fronting wasn't the name of our game.

I was on my way to East St. Louis to see my son. When I moved to St. Louis five years ago, the fellas and me went to this club on the east side, Club Illusion. With Jada taking forever to decide if she wanted to move here with me or not, I met a chick named Ginger Nelson that night. She took me to her place and one thing led to another. I knocked her off a few times after that, but when Jada moved here, I called it quits with Ginger. Next thing I knew, she was blowing my phone up telling me she was pregnant. I was trying to be there for her during the pregnancy as much as I could, but I didn't want Jada finding out about the baby and leaving me. As a matter of fact, nobody knew about Desmon. Not even Kareem. I told Ginger when the time was right, I'd let it be known that I had a son. It's not like we still kicked it anyway, but lately she'd been putting me to the test. It might have had something to do with this knucklehead married fool she was messing with who recently dumped her, but that's what she get for playing a fool. All of a sudden she's so interested in working things out with me. I hadn't been with her sexually since Jada moved here, but I promised Ginger money to take care of my son and time I was able to spend with him, but that's it. She wasn't too happy with it, but ain't much she could do.

I pulled into Ginger's raggedy-ass apartment complex a little after one in the afternoon. You'd think with all the money I was dishing out for Desmon she'd save it and move somewhere decent. I guess I couldn't complain because the inside looked a lot better than it did when I first met her. She at least had sense enough to jazz Desmon's bedroom up like a four-year-old kid's bedroom should look.

I rang the doorbell and waited for her to answer. I could hear Desmon crying, so I banged on the door. She opened it with a cordless phone pushed up to her ear and walked away from the door when I stepped inside. Desmon was trying to stick a DVD in the DVD player and was upset because it wouldn't go in right. I put the DVD in, sat down on the floor next to him, and started to watch *Lilo & Stitch,* his favorite movie we'd seen at least ten times before. Ginger walked into the other room, whispering on the phone, then came back in the living room puffing on a cigarette. She sat down on the couch behind us and started running her mouth.

"I wish you would call sometimes before coming over here." She waited for me to respond but I ignored her. "Kiley?" she yelled. "Did you hear what I said?"

"Yeah, I heard you, Ginger. But call for what, when I got business over here anyway?"

"For what? What if I have company or something? I don't want you just showing up making shit difficult for me."

I turned around and looked at her sitting on the couch. "I don't give a shit about you having company. All I'm here to do is see my son. If one of your immature-ass boyfriends can't understand that, then that's too bad."

"I know you ain't calling nobody immature. Your ass—"

"Hey! Don't disrespect me in front of my son. I'm not in the mood today, Ginger. Why don't you go clean up or something? Place could really stand a good cleaning, instead of you running your mouth on the phone all the time." I turned back around.

Ginger came over by the TV and put her cigarette out in the ashtray on top of it. She blew smoke in my face and stepped over Desmon and me sitting on the floor. I wanted to get up and fuck her up but I had already been there too many times before. She was the kind of woman who liked a beat down. Didn't feel appreciated unless a muh-fucker was busting her upside her head. The last time we got into it, I damn near choked the breath out of her, so now, I did whatever I could to keep the peace. And the best way I knew how was to ignore her.

An hour and a half later, the movie was over. I picked Desmon up off the floor and laid him down on my chest as we rested on the couch. He had fallen asleep and gotten bored with watching the movie; so did I. Ginger tapped me on the shoulder and woke me up asking me to watch Desmon until she came back. I looked at my watch and since it was only five-thirty, I told her I didn't mind.

Wherever she was going, she looked kinda nice. Had her long, curly braids in a clip and they dangled down her back. The hipster jeans she had on gripped her shapely ass nicely. And her aqua blue stretched shirt was showing her caramel brown shoulders and reflected the hardness in her nipples. Ginger was nice looking, but her attitude and outlook on life was definitely another thing that fucked up our relationship. She stood there for a second, I guess wanting me to ask where she was going, but it seriously wasn't any of my business. After she realized I wasn't going to ask, she snatched her purse off the table and left. I picked Desmon up and carried him into his room, then lay back on the couch with my hand behind my head and one foot resting on the floor. I flipped through the channels and tried to find something entertaining. When my phone vibrated, I looked at the number and the call was coming from my house. Knowing that it was Jada by the code she put in, I didn't answer.

I found a college football game on the tube and started to watch it. Awhile later, the front door squeaked open and it was Ginger coming back through the door.

"Did you forget something?" I asked, looking up at her.

She laid her purse on the table and sat down at the end of the couch. "No, I didn't forget anything. I was on my way to Leslie's house to play cards but I needed to ask you something."

"What?" My phone vibrated again and I raised my head to look at it only to see Jada's code again. I ignored it and looked at Ginger. "What did you need to ask me?"

"Why don't you care about me at all? I know we've had our differences, but as much as we do, I still care about you."

I took the pillow from behind my head and sat up straight, laying the pillow across my lap. "I do care about you, Ginger. Maybe not how you want me to, but I do."

"Then why don't you say much to me when you come over here? Why don't you call sometimes just to see how I'm doing? I'm not knocking you for being there for your son, but I could use a little attention too, you know?"

"If attention is what you need, Ginger, I can't give it to you. I can be your friend, but that's it. I'm sure there are plenty of fellas out there who would love to be with you on that level. If you wouldn't have tied up so many years messing with somebody else's man, maybe you would have found the right one by now."

She looked at me and rolled her big, round eyes. "But I don't want just anybody. I kinda enjoyed being with you, until Jada came here. The only reason I started seeing Clyde was because you wasn't available. I just don't understand how easy it was for you to let this go. I mean, you really seemed to enjoy having sex with me."

"I did. But I also told you how important Jada is to me. Not to hurt your feelings or anything but not too many women come like she does these days."

"I guess not," she said, standing up.

She walked back toward the kitchen and when my phone vibrated again, I didn't even look at it. I went into Desmon's room and kissed him on the cheek. I pulled the covers up over him and looked for Ginger to tell her I was getting ready to go. She was sitting on her bed, pulling her shoes off.

"Say, I'll see you next weekend. And don't expect me to call, because I won't."

"Yeah, I know." She tossed her shoes in the corner. "Just don't expect us to be here all the time when you stop by."

"I'll take my chances," I said, winking and turning to leave.

"Kiley?" Ginger said, quickly standing up. "Do you have some money? Desmon need some more tennis shoes."

I reached in my back pocket and pulled out my wallet. I fumbled through several hundred-dollar bills and pulled out three of them. I laid them down on her dresser. "I gave you money last weekend for tennis shoes, remember? Make sure he gets them this time."

She walked over to the dresser to see how much it was. After she saw that it was more than enough, she picked the money up and slid it into her back pocket.

"Now, that takes care of Desmon, but what about me?" She pulled her shirt over her head, then she unzipped her jeans and eased them to the floor.

I stood in the doorway and looked at her eye to eye like I didn't notice her bare well-shaped breasts and lace navy blue panties that only covered a small portion of her coochie. My thang was on the rise but I wasn't trying to go there with Ginger. Knowing that she had a slight bit of my attention, she reached her hand up behind my head, pulling it down toward hers so she could kiss me on the lips. The immediate touch of them, and her bare breasts pressing up against my sweater, weakened me. I removed my hat and laid it down on the dresser; then I pulled the gun out from inside my jeans and put it on the dresser as well. As I raised my shirt over my head, Ginger started to undo my pants. I eased my hand down inside the front side of her panties, and as soon as I started to massage her, my phone vibrated again. I took a deep breath and stepped backward.

"Listen, I gotta go. Something's up, so I'll holler at you next weekend." I put my shirt back on, and picked my gun and hat up off the dresser.

Ginger rolled her eyes and pursed her lips. "Don't make me wait all week for you, Kiley. Call me or something, okay?"

I nodded my head and gazed at her as she walked me to the door in her panties.

As soon as I got in the car, I called Jada to see why she was ringing me like crazy. When she answered, cursing me out for not returning her phone calls, I immediately hung up. When she called back and I didn't answer, she left a message telling me that Kareem and Quincy had gotten into a fight and wanted me to come settle shit down. Pissed, I hurried home.

I drove quickly down State Street, trying to make my way to the highway, when somebody slammed into the back of my car at the stoplight.

When I got ready to get out, I could feel what was about to go down. These two punk young muh-fuckers, looking like they weren't no older than fifteen, were trying to jack me for my shit. One of them came toward me with a gun in his hand as my leg was hanging out of the car, and the other went to the passenger side of my car. I raised my hands in the air and stepped out of the car, pretending to be cooperative.

"Move away from the car, nigga," the first one said, aiming the gun at my chest. Burning up inside, I eased away from the car with my hands in the air. The other one hopped in on the passenger side. The fool with the gun stepped into my side of the car and left his leg hanging out for a second. I kicked the door with my foot and tried to break his damn leg off as I reached for my gun. He fired at me but his aim was completely off. I hopped on top of him in the car, took his gun, and used it to beat his face. As blood gushed from his lips, the other stupid muh-fucker had hopped out and started running. I fired a few shots at him, trying to miss but definitely wanted to scare him. The other nigga sat up and choked on his blood. He begged for his life, but I pulled him out of the car, punched him in the stomach, and shoved him to the ground.

I aimed the gun at his chest. "You pitiful-ass fool!" I yelled. "Get a job and get your own shit, nigga. Today is your lucky day, so take your ass home and thank God for your life." I punted his ass in the side like I was kicking a football, and quickly got back into my car before somebody called the cops.

By the time I pulled in the garage at home, I was fuming. I walked through the back door, and when I passed by the living room to head upstairs, I could see Quincy sitting in the dark on the couch. I turned the lights on and when I looked at him I noticed a cut above his lip and dried blood on a cut above his eyelid.

I sat down in a chair next to the couch, with a twisted face that showed frustrations. "What the hell happened?" I asked.

He shook his head and shamefully gazed down at the ground.

My voice rose. "Go ahead, tell me. Don't be acting like no bitch, man, just tell me what happened."

"Bro, Kareem be trippin. I know he your brother and everythang but that fool got some issues."

"So, that's not telling me nothing I don't already know. What the fuck happened here today between y'all?"

Quincy pulled his bandana off his head and rubbed his hair back with his fingers. I could see that his knuckles were bruised. "Well, last night, I met this gal at a club. Afterward, Kareem and me took her home and boned her and her friend. So, today, I get a phone call, right? It's the friend, wanting to get with me. I told her to come on by and to holla at Kareem when she got here. He got upset with me thinking I wanted the bitch. When she came, he started frontin', acting a fool. Dissing me in front of her like I'm some punk or something, so I popped the muh-fucker in his mouth. We scrapped for a while and then he went into his room with her."

"Let me get this straight: you sons of a bitches fighting over some twat? Is that what you're telling me?"

"Naw, he fighting over some twat. I was fighting 'cause brotha disrespected me."

"Where's Jada?"

"She's upstairs. She tried to break it up but when Kareem called her a fat bitch she tried to call you. After that, she went into y'all room and shut the door."

"Where was Donovan?"

"He stood there and watched."

"He didn't try to break it up?"

"Man, please. You know Donovan like that kind of shit. He wasn't trying to stop nothing."

I stood up and looked at Quincy's lip. "You gon' be all right?"

"Yeah, I'm cool. Just trying to stay downstairs to calm myself."

"Well, why don't you call one of your lady friends up and take her out for a nice dinner and a movie. Things might get a li'l ugly around here. Come back in a few hours after they settle."

"That's cool. But you know by now Kareem and me got to get our clown on at least once or twice a year, don't you? Tomorrow it'll be like the shit never happened."

"I know, but we starting to slip a li'l bit. We used to have each other's backs, and seem to me that's starting to change. With Rufus getting out in a few months, I don't need no fuckups right now. He's always been the one making trouble so I don't need y'all doing it as well."

"You're right, partna." Quincy gave me five. "Sorry this time, but it was hard to hold back."

"I know," I said, heading upstairs. "Holla at you later, man. I hope you got money. And ask that sista who works at the bank to go with you. I kinda like her ass better than those other hoochies you be bringing over here."

"Who, Veronica?"

"Yeah, Veronica, that's the one."

He patted his back pocket. "Yep, I got money, plenty, and plenty mo'. So, deuces, man, I'll holla at ya later."

My intentions were to go see about Jada first, but I was sure she knew I was already in the house by looking at the monitors. Kareem's bedroom door was closed and I knew Donovan was upstairs in the entertainment room because I could hear the floor squeaking. I put my ear against Kareem's door and when I didn't hear much, I lightly tapped on it.

"What!" he yelled.

I turned the knob and opened the door. I didn't turn on the lights because I could see this chick sitting up on top of him, naked. "I need your company to leave."

"Nigga, you crazy. Shut my damn door and holla at me in an hour or so."

The bitch who was on top of him had the nerve to snicker like the shit was funny. I pulled my gun out of my pants, used the nose of it to turn on the lights, and stood with my arms folded. When she turned around and saw the gun underneath my arm, she grabbed for the cover and slid over to the side off Kareem. He sat up on his elbows, looking at me with his jaw dropped. He had no clue what kind of day I was having, but he of all people knew when I wasn't playing.

"Kiley. Can a brotha finish up something he started, please? You're a li'l bold stepping up in here, invading my privacy."

"Bold? Aw, you ain't seen bold. Bold is giving this bitch one minute to put her clothes on and get the fuck out of this house. Bold is snatching your ass from underneath those covers, beating the shit out of you for calling my woman a fat bitch, and bold is allowing a stupid asshole like you to put pussy before partna." I looked at the bitch still lying in bed. "Thirty seconds now, ho, I don't see you moving."

She grabbed her clothes off of the chair and started putting them on. Kareem lay there with stone coldness in his eyes. When the woman walked toward the door, I grabbed her around the neck and whispered in her ear, pressing the gun up against her back, "Don't bring your ass around here again. You ain't welcome in this house. You understand?"

She nodded her head and when I let go, she flew down the steps to exit.

Kareem pulled the covers back and got out of bed. "Now, that shit was totally uncalled for," he said, putting on his clothes. "I can't believe you siding with that white bitch-ass Quincy."

"Kareem, what's your problem? You around here dissing every damn body. Talking to a brotha how you fucking feel like it, then you want respect. Pussy got you all fucked up, don't it?"

"This ain't got nothing to do with a piece of ass and you know it. Quincy put his hands on me so I wasn't going to back down like no punk. Then you come up in here going off on me and shit. Like I'm the one who started the shit. In case you forgot, I'm your fucking brother. Don't go putting this fool before me."

"Listen, I don't give a shit who started it!" I yelled, darting my finger. "When you're wrong, you're wrong. You twenty-five years old and he's twenty-seven. Y'all up in this house carrying on like some damn teenagers. Grown fucking men, acting like kids who need a babysitter when I'm away. Then, to disrespect my lady? Now, you know that's some unacceptable shit! I don't give a fuck who you are, nobody disrespects her but me."

"Shit, she shouldn't have called us no stupid muh-fuckers. I don't give a rat's ass who she is; the way she talk to me is the way I talk to her." Kareem slid his shirt down over his head and grabbed his keys off the top of his bed. "Listen, things got heated and people got their feelings hurt. Sorry. I can't change what I said but I'm not like you, Kiley, especially when it comes to women. All that smart-ass talking and yelling is enough to drive me crazy. I don't understand how you just sit there and take it, but when a brotha step to you like that, you'll break his back. So, question is, does pussy have you fucked up?"

"Maybe, maybe not. But Jada's not the only one who gets away with bullshit in this house. All of you do. And the thing is, ain't neither one of you fools doing a damn thing for me and you still get my respect. On the other hand, at least she's fucking me correctly. So, when you around here talking about you can't help yourself from disrespecting people by saying that they deserved it, think about how many times I've wanted to fuck you up but didn't. Or how many times I've gone out on a limb for you when you messed up. I did what I had to do out of love and respect for you. Don't sit here and tell me you can't do something as simple as respect my woman and respect my partna by only seeing him as a 'white boy.' Remember, that's the same white boy who gave up a lot of shit for you as well. More so, gave up everything for you and me both. All I'm saying is think. Think hard before you let all that bullshit slip out of your mouth."

"Yeah, yeah, yeah, I hear you. I'll apologize tomorrow. I'm getting ready to go play the tables on the Casino Queen."

I pulled my keys out of my pocket and tossed them to Kareem. "Quincy got the car so use mine. And make sure you carry your piece, 'cause these punks tried to jack me today."

"Straight? What happened?"

"I'll tell you about it later. So hurry up and get out of here so I can go comfort my woman from this abuse you niggas been dishing out."

"All right. But tell her I'm sorry."

"You tell her yourself. And before you leave go upstairs and take that fool Donovan with you. He's been whining like a bitch about feeling left out."

"Will do, big brother," Kareem said, heading upstairs. "I love ya, you damn peacemaking, non-lovemaking-ass Negro."

"Don't talk that shit, Kareem. I stood by that door for a few minutes and didn't hear that bitch moan not once. Sounded like you were sleeping on the job to me."

"Ha, don't fool yourself. I had just pulled the tape off her mouth before you knocked."

"Whatever, nigga," I laughed, walking down the hallway to my room.

Jada was sitting up in bed watching *Scary Movie* with the lights out. She didn't even look at me so I figured she was pretty upset. I went over to the closet and started taking my clothes off so I could take a bath. When she noticed I wasn't saying anything to her, I figured it would be a matter of minutes before she started questioning me.

"Why didn't you answer your phone when I called, and who in the fuck do you think you are by hanging up on me?"

I ignored her and pulled the drawer out to get my cotton pajama pants. Before I could, she was all up in my face, yelling and screaming with spit flying.

I slammed the drawer shut and tightened my fists, just in case she was in the mood for a quick beat down. "Jada, get the hell out of my face before you get hurt!" I yelled.

"Hurt me, you damn liar! I'm sick and tired of your shit! You left your ass out of here, didn't tell anybody where you were going, then tell me to call you if I need you. And when I do, your ass ain't available. I'm going back to L.A. Shouldn't have ever moved to this crazy house to begin with."

"Fine, Jada. Go ahead," I said, storming off into the bathroom. "Sick and tired of your threats anyway." I slammed the door.

Jada's mouth was driving me crazy. I put my hands on her one time before for disrespecting me, but the feeling I had afterward was a feeling I never wanted to feel again. She knew how pissed I was at myself for hitting her, and knew I would never do it again. That's why she continued to push me. Said whatever she wanted to me, knowing that I wouldn't do anything to her. Anybody else would be in their grave for smacking me on my face and punching on me like she did. Ginger can be a witness to that. She quickly found out that if you put your hands on me, I will most certainly fuck you up. No doubt, Jada was the exception.

After I finished up in the bathroom, I opened the door and Jada was lying on her side in bed, sniffling like she'd been crying. When I tried to comfort her, she pushed me away. *Fuck it,* I thought, and shrugged my shoulders. I got in bed, turned away from her, and crashed out.

CHAPTER 2

When I turned over in bed and reached for Jada, she wasn't there. I looked at the alarm clock and it was three forty-five in the morning. I pulled the covers back and got out of bed to look for her. Since everybody's bedroom door was open, I knew none of the fellas had made it home yet. As I started upstairs to the entertainment room, I heard a laugh coming from downstairs. When I got down there Quincy was sitting at the kitchen table talking to Jada while she was standing in front of the counter.

"Say, man, what's up? We were just talking about you," Quincy said.

I could immediately tell he was high by the glassy look in his squinted eyes. "I'm sure it's nothing nice if you're in here talking to Jada," I said, gazing at her.

"Quincy," Jada said. "I'll see you when I wake up. I'm going back to bed." She rolled her eyes and left the kitchen.

Jada's attitude was something I had learned to cope with. There were times when I wanted to straight up kick her ass for acting the way she did. But many times I held back, especially since I knew that putting my hands on her would be wrong.

I opened the cabinet to get a glass. Then I poured some water and sat down at the table with Quincy. "So, how was the movie?"

"We didn't go."

"Why not?"

"We stayed at her place."

"Getting high?"

"Naw, she don't go out like that. I fired up some herb on the way home."

"I see." I took a sip of the water. "So, what were you and Jada talking about?"

"Nothing much. When I got here she was sitting on the back porch. We just walked into the house a few minutes before you came down. However, she did call you an asshole."

"That's nothing new. She's a good woman but the shit she say sometimes just makes me want to—"

"I know. And she is a good woman. Washing, cooking, and cleaning after four grown-ass men. But sometimes"—Quincy took his fist and punched it against his hand—"whewww, she be having it coming."

"Yeah but that ain't gonna prove a damn thing. What I don't like is her threats. Every week I gotta hear about how she hates she moved to St. Louis and about how she's moving back to L.A. I'm to the point where I don't even give a damn anymore."

"Maybe she's unhappy. I don't see why or how but with women, you just never know."

"You're right. They sho know how to hide things better than we do." I stood up and put my glass in the sink. "Are you heading up?"

"Naw, I'm heading out. I'll be back by late afternoon."

"Boy, you nigga's know y'all be running the streets. Where in the hell do y'all be all day and all night?"

"In a li'l of this, and in a li'l of that. Over here, over there. Wherever, man. Life didn't end after we left L.A. I know you're trying to keep shit on the down low but you still gotta live. I don't think I've ever seen you this cooped up."

"I know, but I worry every single day that the cops are going to knock on that door and arrest me for murder. It's not a good feeling but, hey, that's why I have everything in this house I need. Ain't much on the outside for me other than . . ." I stopped, thinking about Desmon.

"Other than what? I mean, what's up with your Saturday runs? You never tell anybody where you're going. We're still cool on the money thang, right?"

"Of course, and it has nothing to do with that. It's personal business that can only be attended to on Saturdays."

"It ain't another woman, is it?"

"Naw, ain't that either. And don't keep prying 'cause it's my business, okay?"

Quincy stood his high ass up and reached in his back pocket. Then he looked down and fumbled around the table feeling for his keys. As I moved in closer to him, I could tell he was not only high but drunk as well. I picked his keys up that were right on the table in front of him and put my arm around his shoulder.

"Your bed. That's what you need."

He belched and pointed his finger at me. "I agree," he said loudly, putting his arm around my shoulders.

Quincy and I walked upstairs and by the time we made it, he was hauling ass to the bathroom to throw up. I shook my head and laughed as I headed back to my room to confront Jada.

The room was dark, and when I eased into bed, I could feel her back against mine. I poked my pillow a few times to get it comfortable then laid my head down. There was complete silence. After a few minutes of lying there with my eyes open, I felt Jada's hands as they lightly touched my ass. She turned around and started massaging my chest. Surprised by her sudden forgiveness, I turned around and faced her. My hands searched her naked body, and I spread her legs open, inserting my fingers deep inside her. I rolled them around until she was dripping wet. Then I slid down to the end of the bed, standing to drop my pants. Jada came down to the end of the bed and sat directly in front of me. She put my dick in her hands, skillfully stroking it. When she felt it harden, she got down to business. I closed my eyes as the back of her throat felt warm, then placed my hands on the dresser behind me so I wouldn't lose my balance. As I felt myself wanting to come, I backed out of her mouth. She stood up in front of me and pecked my lips. "I'm sorry for disrespecting you," she said. "I know I get carried away sometimes, but I do love you."

I didn't say anything because I refused to mess up the mood. I sat her on top of the dresser, held her legs apart and looked down as she inserted me. She reached over and turned on the lights as I leaned forward and licked her nipples.

We watched as I pounded her insides with fast thrusts to make her coochie respond so well to me.

Intensely fucking, Jada lifted my sweaty head and kissed me. "Kiley?" she whispered, staring me eye to eye. "Talk to me, baby. I don't like it when you're this quiet."

I sucked her lips into mine and wet them down with my tongue. Then I slid myself out of her and leaned down. I placed my mouth between her legs and rolled my tongue quickly around in circles. She tried to squeeze her legs together but I held them tightly apart with my hands. As I made love to her with my tongue, I felt her body shaking. She scratched my back with her long fingernails and sprayed my lips with cum. I stood up, wiping away her sweet juices.

"Come on, hop on my back," I said, scooting slightly down. She wrapped her arms around my neck and got on my back.

I lifted her off the dresser and carried her to the bathroom. I stood in front of the mirror as both of us looked in it. She smiled, leaned down and kissed me on the cheek while her hands were still wrapped tightly around my neck.

"We make a cute couple," she said, looking back into the mirror.

I shrugged my shoulders a bit.

"What do you mean, you don't know? And why aren't you talking to me?"

I turned around and sat her on the bathroom counter between the sinks. She slid back and folded her arms in front of her.

"Baby, you gotta stop talking to me the way you do. I—"

She couldn't wait to cut me off. "I said I would. Damn! It ain't like you talk calmly to my ass all the time." She started to get down off the counter, but I placed my hand on her midriff so she wouldn't move.

"Listen to you. Do you even hear how you sound?" I shook my head. "You coming off too cold, baby. Too damn cold for me. Now, for the last time, I'm asking you to calm the shit down. Next time, I might not be so nice."

"Next time you can kiss my ass, Kiley. You act like I'm the one who treats you like shit. You leave here whenever you want to, call me when you feel like it, and expect me not to get mad. If you don't want me getting mad then answer your damn phone when I call your ass."

I shook my head again, and picked up a towel from the rack behind me. I wet it with warm water and soap and wiped myself down. She got

down off the counter and brushed up against me
when she walked out of the bathroom. I didn't
know what her problem was. She didn't used to
be this way. Seemed like for the last couple of
years, she'd had a new attitude. Whatever it was
about, I seriously couldn't figure it out.

I reached for another towel and wet it with
warm water too. Then I went into the bedroom
and lay on the bed next to her. She opened her
legs as I washed her down with the towel. When
she rolled over on her stomach, I could tell she
was in the mood to fuck again, but I wasn't up
for this "fuck me, fight me" bullshit tonight.
We'd played that shit too many times before, so I
left well enough alone and continued wiping her
down with the towel.

By five-thirty in the morning, tired, Jada and
me were trying to finish watching a Tyler Perry
movie on DVD. But when we heard a car door
slam and laughter outside, I flipped the TV on
to the outside cameras to see who it was. It was
Donovan coming into the house with his arms
wrapped around this chick's shoulders. She
was looking pretty damn good from what the
monitor viewed, so Jada took the remote from

me and turned it back on the movie. I was wondering where Kareem was at, so when I heard Donovan passing by my room, I yelled his name. He tapped two times on the door, then opened it.

"What's up, playa?" he asked, leaning in the doorway with a pack of beauty on his side hugging him around the waist.

I couldn't help staring. "Where, uh . . ."

"Kareem?" Donovan quickly said, grinning.

I grinned back. "Yeah, I'm trippin'. Where Kareem at?"

"He told me to drop him off at Felicia's house in Ladue."

I shook my head. "Bad news, man. I don't like that broad. You should have brought his ass home."

"Please. You know how Kareem is, especially when it comes to older women."

"I know, but, uh, don't be rude. Aren't you going to introduce me—I mean, us—to your friend?"

"Aw, yeah," Donovan said, looking at his woman. "Candi, this is Kiley and Jada. Y'all, this is Candi."

Jada didn't speak. I waved and said hello, then Candi smiled and said hello back. Before Donovan closed the door, I gave him a thumbs-up and he nodded his head. As soon as he closed the door, Jada turned and slapped me on my face as hard as she could. My cheek burned and I squeezed my eyes to ease the pain from the blow.

"What in the fuck is wrong with you?" I yelled.

"You don't be flirting with that bitch right in front of me!" she yelled. "Don't you have any damn respect for me?" She snatched up her cover and pillow, heading for the door.

"Jada, I'm warning you," I said through gritted teeth. "Your time is just about up, baby. Keep on with the bullshit if you want to—"

"Fuck you! I can't wait to leave this goddamn house," she yelled, then slammed the door.

I turned the TV off and sank myself down in my satin sheets. Jada in bed with me or not, I was taking my ass to sleep. It was obvious the bitch was crazy. One minute she wanted me to fuck her; then she wanted me to fight with her. Either way, I was running out of patience.

Question was, was I really happy? I lay there thinking about how I almost fucked Ginger for the first time in years, then I got excited listening to Donovan work his Miss Pretty Young Thang in the other room. His headboard was banging hard against the wall and I could hear her soft, sexy moans. And when I heard her come, I felt like it was me she was releasing herself on. Out of all the women who came into this house, I'd never looked at any of them in that manner.

With the exception of Quincy's gal, Veronica, from the bank. Now, she was a sight for sore eyes too. Considering the hundreds of females who had been in and out, my attraction to just two of them wasn't bad. Thing was, I wasn't sure if it was my disappointment with Jada's attitude, or if it was really something else.

CHAPTER 3

I chilled in bed until one o'clock Sunday afternoon, doing nothing. Jada came in, showered, changed clothes, and said she'd be back. I didn't even ask where she was going because that's what she wanted me to do. I told her to be careful and pretended to be occupied cleaning my gun.

Feeling a slight bit hungry, I went to the upstairs kitchen to get a bite to eat. There was some leftover pizza from the other night so I warmed it up in the microwave. Quincy came strutting upstairs with no shirt on, blue jeans hanging down so you could see his boxers, and his wet hair was slicked back like he had just gotten out of the shower. When he put his hand on his forehead and plopped down on the couch, I knew it was a hangover day for him.

"This is a bad-ass feeling," he mumbled, turning on the TV.

"Yeah, I know." I walked over to the couch and set my plate of pizza on the table in front of me. "Weed and wine don't mix well."

"So, where's . . ." Quincy took his fist and punched it against his other hand. "Jada?"

"You crazy, fool. She's probably out at Frontenac Plaza buying her ass a new Gucci purse or something. I don't know, didn't ask."

"Did y'all make up?"

"Yeah, we fucked. If you call that making up, then I guess we did."

Quincy eased down a bit on the couch and grabbed his thang. "Man, I'm tired of fucking. My shit wo'e out. Going forward, all I need is a good blow job, that's it."

"That's it? And how long is this idea supposed to last? You brothas get mo' ass than I do and I got a woman living in the crib with me."

"For a while, I anticipate. I had sex about"— Quincy lifted his hands up and started counting on his fingers—"eleven times last week. Nigga don't need that much twat."

"Some muh-fuckers do. I bet Kareem's ass was double that number. He's been out there bad. Every time I look up somebody new running through this damn house with him. And as much as he stay in the streets, I know he getting his mix on out there."

"Yeah, you're right about that shit. Where he at anyway? Did he come in yet?"

"Yeah, he here. That trick Felicia dropped him off not too long ago. His bedroom door closed so I take it he's sleeping."

"Well, I was hoping to talk to him about what went down yesterday."

"Give that fool 'til eight or nine o'clock. If he ain't up by then, wake his ass up and call him on his shit."

"Will do, my brotha. Most certainly will do."

Quincy went over to the kitchen and warmed up a slice of pizza too. As he was coming back over to the couch to sit down, Donovan was coming up the steps holding hands with Candi. Quincy glanced at them, looked at me, then looked at the TV. When Donovan and Candi sat down on the couch, Quincy's eyes stayed focused on the TV.

Noticing Candi constantly staring at me, I kicked up a quick conversation. "Hey, Don, I didn't know y'all was still here."

"Yeah, dog. Crashed the fuck out." Donovan leaned his midnight black ass back on the couch and put his arms around Candi. What she saw in him, I couldn't figure out. Had to be his body, just had to be. I couldn't hate 'cause I had to give credit to a brotha who worked out hard every

day to keep himself buff. Not that my body was
in bad shape, 'cause I still had some ridges left
over from boxing and taking karate for over
twelve years.

"Yeah, I just got up my damn self," I said. "Bed
was so comfortable, I couldn't pull myself away."

"Even comfortable without Jada, huh? She
was hot, wasn't she? I mean, we heard the slap
and all. Didn't we, baby?" Donovan said, looking
at Candi.

"Yes, we did," she answered, smiling at me,
while slowly rubbing Donovan's waves back with
her hand.

My eyes stayed focused on Donovan, since
Candi wouldn't stop staring. "She claimed I was
flirting with your woman. How she ever got that
idea, I don't know. I mean, don't get me wrong,"
I said, observing Candi. "You're a very attractive
young woman but . . ."

"But what?" she said.

"But, he already got a woman he loves more
than life itself," Donovan interrupted.

"True that, my man," I said, pointing my finger
at him. "True that. Most definitely love my
woman."

Candi shrugged and addressed Donovan. "Are
you ready to go?"

"Are you?"

"No, but I think I'd better. Besides, I got a few things I need to take care of today."

"Well, let's go," Donovan said, standing and stretching.

When Candi stood up, Quincy took a quick peek at her curvy well-shaped ass. It was squeezed into some black silk stretch pants that hung down over her thick-heeled black shoes. Her thin, long black hair was parted through the middle and draped down both sides of her shoulders. And the red and black striped half shirt with oversized sleeves set her pretty ass off. Donovan definitely had himself something to work with and probably didn't even know it. She was dark but not as black as him. Her plush, arched eyebrows, buttered brown lips, and round dark brown eyes put her into a category all by herself. Fucking fabulous.

"Bye," she said, waving at Quincy and me.

We waved back, and as soon as they were down the steps, Quincy cocked his head back. "How in the hell did he pull that shit off?"

"Man, that's what I've been asking myself all damn morning."

"She like yo' ass though, man, I'm telling you."

"Nigga, please. What in the fuck gives you that idea?"

"When she came up here, I could tell. Did you see how fast I turned away?"

"Yeah, but what's that got to do with it?"

"I was watching her ass from the corner of my eye. She had this . . . this 'Ooo, I could just tear that brotha up' look."

I laughed. "You are crazy, fool. And even if she did, Donovan my boy. I don't go out like that."

"Shiiit, I would," Quincy said.

We turned our heads as Kareem came up the steps fussing about the noise. He stretched his arms out wide, while standing behind the couch in his Ralph Lauren boxers. "What's up with all the noise? That's why I don't come home anymore. You niggas make too much noise for me."

"I'll tell you what all the noise about," Quincy said, turning the TV to the outside camera. "Check this out." He pointed to Candi walking to the car with Donovan.

Kareem slowly walked around the couch and sat down with bugged eyes. "Damn! Was she up in here and I didn't know nothing about it?"

"Yep," Quincy said. "All damn night. With Donovan."

"Get the fuck out of here. I mean, he ain't bad looking but that's some shit I can pull. Did he fuck her?"

Kareem and Quincy looked at me. "What? Why y'all looking at me?"

"Aw, you know. His damn room right next to yours, nigga, don't play stupid."

I smiled. "I ain't gon' be telling y'all that man's business. If he wants you fellas to know, he'll tell y'all."

"Come on, Kiley," Kareem said. "Tell us, man, did he?"

I hesitated for a moment. "Yeah, he did. And from what I could hear, pretty damn well, too."

"Damn, that's messed up," Kareem said. "Some fools have all the luck."

"I wouldn't exactly call it luck," Quincy said. "Donovan's lucky she didn't creep into Kiley's room this morning and fuck his brains out."

"Whaaaat?" Kareem said. "She digging on you, man?"

"Hell naw," I said quickly. "Quincy been smoking too much herb. Shit got 'em trippin'."

"Bullshit and you know it. Go pull that tape out of that camera on the wall right now, rewind it, and let's watch it. You brothas will see what the fuck I saw."

Kareem hopped up to get the tape.

"You two are crazy," I said, watching Kareem take the tape out of the camera. "Man, don't do that."

Kareem ignored me, put the tape in the VCR, and rewound it. When he pushed play we watched all kinds of shit on the tape. Even a brief moment of Quincy getting down with this chick in this room. Kareem let it play for a minute and then Quincy snatched the remote.

"Don't be trying to learn my tricks of the trade," Quincy said.

"Now why would you do that in this room knowing there's a camera in here?" I asked. "I hope she knew about it because that could mean trouble for yo' ass."

"Come on, Kiley. She knew. I told her and afterward we watched it together. It's not like I gathered y'all up in here with some popcorn and said let's watch it."

"All right, just checking. I thought our bedrooms were for privacy."

"New subject," Quincy said ignoring me, fast-forwarding the tape. When he saw Candi and Donovan coming up the steps on the tape, he stopped it. "Okay, Kareem, check her out."

Kareem and Quincy sat on the edge of the couch looking attentively at the TV, then turning their heads a couple of times and looking at me.

When it was over, Kareem turned his body around and faced me. "Now, that was a bad bitch right there. And if you couldn't tell after watching that tape, she was begging you for a fuck you out of commission. That piece of ass was calling you underneath her breath."

I nodded, knowing what was up. "Okay, so what? That's Donovan's gal. Besides, y'all know how I feel about Jada."

"I know how you feel about Jada," Kareem said, placing his hand on his heart, smiling. "But, if you don't want to have the pleasure of adding those panties to your collection, I will do it for you." He and Quincy slammed their hands together, giving each other five.

"So, Donovan's gal and all, you brothas would step like that?"

"Hell, yeah," Quincy said. "Pussy ain't got no name on it. When I start pulling the panties off and seeing a brothas name engraved across it, then I'll step. Besides, you act like we ain't never got down like that before. Donovan had yo' shit before, my shit, and Kareem shit. Vice versa so why trip now?"

"You got a point," I said. "But I'm not interested in Candi. I got some deep-down funky flava feelings for Veronica."

"Who?" Quincy turned his head, looking around the room. "My Veronica?"

"Yes, Quincy. Your Veronica."

"Veronica who I was with last night?"

"Yes. Veronica who you were with last night."

He shrugged. "All right, cool. Have at it."

"So, you wouldn't care?"

"Kiley, please." He leaned his head back and rested it on the couch. "I ain't in love with nobody. Unless I tell you I'm in love, feel free, she's fair game."

I nodded; then I looked at Quincy again. "Are you sure?"

Quincy stood up and grabbed a piece of paper and pen from on top of the TV. He wrote her number down on the paper and gave it to me. "Here, call her. Invite her to go out. I wouldn't care. I'm telling you the truth."

I took the paper out of his hand and looked at it. Then I put it in the pocket of my robe. "Y'all never cease to amaze me. Don't y'all have love for anybody?"

"Love for you, big brother," Kareem said, placing his hand on his heart again. "That's about it, other than these two other knucklehead niggas I got to bust upside the head every once in a while." He looked at Quincy.

"Yeah, sorry about that shit yesterday," Quincy said. He and Kareem gave each other five again.

"Me too but you know I don't mean no harm with that 'white boy' shit, don't you?"

"Yeah, you do. You prejudice, man. Racist like a muh-fucker. Thing is, I ain't white though. I ain't black either. I'm just fucking colored. So, whenever you refer to me, refer to me as a colored man."

"Okay you colored freak with green eyes and straight black shiny hair," Kareem said.

We all laughed, but when Jada came up the steps with bags of shit from Frontenac Plaza, Kareem and Quincy stopped laughing, looked at me, and smirked.

"Don't stop talking on my account," she said with her sassy-ass voice.

"Say, Jada," Kareem said, clearing his throat. "Sorry about calling you a fat bitch yesterday. That wasn't cool and I just wanted to apologize."

She threw her hand back. "Whatever. Save that shit for one of your bitches. I'm sure your brother had to coax you into apologizing to me so forget it."

Kareem was getting ready to go off, but Quincy interrupted before I did. "Yo, Kareem, let's go outside and hoop for a while. I got this slam dunk I want to put on your ass."

Kareem stood up and yawned. "Please, white men can't jump, fool."

"You're right. They can't, but a colored man can, so let's go."

Before they left, Quincy looked at me, punched his fist in his hand again, and nudged his head toward Jada. I tossed a pillow at him and they left.

Jada was busy pulling all the shit she bought from the Plaza out of the bags. She ran up and down the steps, putting things up, and before she emptied the last bag, she came over to the couch and sat down next to me.

"Here, I bought you something," she said, putting the bag on my lap.

I reached in the bag and pulled out a gray cashmere sweater. "Thanks," I said, looking at it, then put it back into the bag.

"Thanks? Is that all I get, a lousy-ass thanks?"

"Damn, Jada. What in the hell do you want me to do? Strike a fucking match, stamp my feet, and jump for joy over a sweater."

"No, I didn't say that. You could have at least kissed me for thinking about your selfish-ass."

"Selfish? You out here spending my goddamn money and I'm the one who's selfish. You have got to be out of your rabbit mind calling me selfish, and if you think I'm going to get excited about a sweater that my money bought you're crazy!"

I got up to go downstairs to get away from Jada. As I was leaving, she called me a "stupid motherfucker." Not that selfish wasn't bad enough, but stupid? And, the bitch was spending my money? No doubt about it, she had to be taught a lesson.

I backslapped her ass so hard it sent her flying almost to the other side of the couch. She held her face and started to whimper. I warned her several times about her actions, and there had to be repercussions for a woman who didn't know her place. I tightened my robe and walked my ass right downstairs to my bedroom to change clothes. I knew she would come charging, so I hurried, because I didn't want to hit her again. Once I was dressed, I slid my gun down inside my pants and grabbed my keys off the dresser. And as soon as I opened the door, she was on her way down the steps with a knife in her hand. I rushed her and pinned her up against the wall, taking the knife out of her hand.

"So, now you want to kill me, huh?" I said, pressing my body weight against her up against the wall. She didn't say anything, just kept on crying. I smacked her face again, and when I backed away, she fell to the floor. "If you're this unhappy with me, take your ass back to Los Angeles. What I ever did to you but love you, I don't know."

"I hate you!" she yelled, as I headed down the steps.

"Good, Jada. Thanks for being honest. I'm glad somebody in this damn relationship is."

When I walked out the back door, it was chilly. Kareem and Quincy were outside sweating like dogs playing b-ball with their shirts off. They could tell by the twisted look on my face I was mad and they halted the game.

"Everything all right, man?" Kareem asked, panting and putting the ball underneath his arm.

"I'm cool. Listen, I'll be back in a couple of days. If anything urgent comes up, hit me on my phone."

"All right. But are you sure? I mean, you look kind of upset."

"Kareem, not right now!" I yelled. "Just call me if you need me."

"Damn, sorry for asking," he said, as I continued walking.

I went to the garage and backed my car out. When I got down the street, I called Ginger's house to see what Desmon was doing. She answered sounding asleep and it was almost three in the afternoon.

"It's me. Were you asleep?"

"I was, but what's up? I didn't think I'd hear from you this soon."

"Where's Desmon?"

"Lying here taking a nap with me. We've been up since six this morning, helping my grandmother get situated in a nursing home, so we're tired."

"Okay, well go back to sleep. I'll holla at y'all tomorrow."

"Did you want to come over?"

"I did, but that's all right."

"I'm up. Besides, we got some unfinished business to take care of."

"Yeah, that's what I'm afraid of. I'll call you tomorrow, okay?"

"Kiley, don't even be like that. I'll keep my hands to myself, if that's what you want."

"No, it's not what I want but I don't need the temptation right now. Kiss Desmon for me and I'll call you later." I hung up.

I stopped at K's liquor store on Hanley and bought a bottle of Seagram's Gin & Juice, and a bottle of Hennessy cognac. Already feeling down on myself for hitting Jada, I drove to the airport Marriott and got a room until Wednesday afternoon. I figured it was going to take me that long to cool off or maybe even longer. I knew that going to see Ginger wasn't going to solve my problem; sleeping with her would only make matters worse. She didn't deserve to be used by me knowing that I would run right back to Jada once things settled down. And even though Ginger didn't seem to mind, I knew it had to hurt when I dumped her to get back with Jada. So for now, my dick just had to suffer, and so did I for putting my hands on the woman I loved.

CHAPTER 4

The few days I spent at the Marriott were somewhat peaceful. I got so fucked up my first night there, I couldn't tell if I was coming or going. I even got in the car and drove around for hours thinking about how shit with Jada and me was slowly but surely falling apart. Thing was, I didn't really care. I moved to St. Louis for a peace of mind and that's what I intended to get. Just last night, though, I woke up in a sweat dreaming that the cops kicked the door down and came to arrest me. When I resisted, they cuffed me and shot me in the face. My heart was racing, and when I realized it was a dream, I was relieved. A man like me should be dreaming about money or fucking somebody's brains out, but there I was having nightmares about going to prison or dying.

By late Tuesday evening, Kareem and Quincy started calling like crazy leaving unnecessary messages. But when Kareem told me Candi asked about me, I finally called him back.

"Kiley, I'm hurt," Kareem joked. "Why you leave me like this, man?"

"And let me guess, your hand is on your heart right now, ain't it?"

"How'd you know?" He laughed.

"'Cause I know you better than you know yourself, li'l brotha."

"I don't know about all that but when are you coming home?"

"Tomorrow, maybe."

"Maybe?"

"Yeah, maybe."

"Don't you miss us, man?"

"Not really. I needed this time to clear my head."

"Are you alone?"

"Of course. I don't need to be slammed in the middle of some legs in order to clear my head like you do."

"That's 'cause you weak. Ain't nothing wrong with relaxing with a nice woman by your side. That's why I took it upon myself and gave Candi your phone number."

"What? Now, why did you do some shit like that?"

"'Cause I know my big brother better than he know himself. And right about now, I'm sure that thang aching for some booty. So, with that in mind, while we were upstairs shooting some pool earlier, she asked about you. When Donovan went to the bathroom, I slid her your phone number."

"Why y'all hating on Donovan, Kareem?"

"We ain't hating. When Candi left, I asked Donovan if I could get a piece of the action and he said he didn't give a damn. Said as long as I didn't mess with Tricia, he was cool."

"Tricia? Now she definitely ain't no dime."

"I know, but neither is Jada," Kareem said, clearing his throat. "So, uh, do you catch my drift?"

"Your opinion, but where's Jada at anyway?"

"She's been locked up in y'all room since you left. She came out a few times, but hasn't said much to anybody. But, man, whew, that eye. Damn!"

"What do you mean by 'that eye'?"

"That muh-fucker closed and looks like she got beat by a gang of bitches."

"Nigga, quit lying."

"Seriously, ask Quincy. She came in the kitchen when we were in there and when I looked up, she scared the shit out of me."

"Seriously, though, I didn't even hit her that hard," I said, knowing damn well I did. "That's how I know you lying."

"Okay, wait a minute. Since you don't believe me, ask Quincy." Kareem gave Quincy the phone.

"What's up, Bruce Lee?"

"Man, that shit ain't funny," I said, swallowing the lump in my throat. "Is Kareem lying about Jada's eye?"

"Nope. That muh-fucker swoll."

"Bad?"

"Yes, bad."

"All right," I said, feeling awful behind my actions. "Put Kareem back on the phone."

"Yo."

"Listen, I won't be back until Friday. There's no way I can stand to look at Jada like that. In the meantime, please let her be. Don't be laughing and shit, making jokes about it, okay?"

"Kiley, you know me better than that."

"Yeah, I do. And that's what worries me. I mean it, Kareem, no bullshit.

"All right?"

"And take your hand off your heart like you really care."

He laughed. "But . . . but you still never told me where you at."

"I'm not going to tell you. I don't want y'all bugging me. Again, only call me if it's important."

"Candi is important. You should have seen her ass over here today. I promise you, I'm tapping that if you don't."

"Suit yourself. I gotta go. Deuces." I hung up.

Feeling down on myself about not controlling my temper when it came to Jada, I took a hot, steaming shower and lay across the bed with a towel wrapped around me. I rolled up a joint and rested back on the bed blowing the smoke in the air. Hit after hit, I tried not to envision what Jada's eye looked like, but I couldn't get the thought of it off my mind. I promised myself I would never hit her again. My fists were too powerful and I knew it. What a coward I was to hit her like that. All I had to do was leave.

After I was full of herb and tipsy from a few swigs of Hennessy, I picked my cell phone up to call her. Wasn't in my plan but I couldn't resist. When Donovan answered the phone laughing, I asked to speak to Jada.

"Hello to you too, partna," he said.

"Ay, what up? Didn't mean to play you off but I need to talk to Jada."

"Hold on. I'll get her." Donovan put the phone down. I could hear Quincy's and Kareem's mouths in the background.

When Jada answered the phone she sounded sad. "Hello," she said, softly.

"I'm sorry," I said, taking another swig of the Hennessy. Jada didn't say a word. "Jada? Did you hear me?"

"Yes."

"I said I'm sorry."

She hung up. I put the phone down and didn't call her back because I guessed she just wasn't ready to forgive me. Hearing how sad she sounded really tore me apart. I wanted to go home and comfort her, but I knew my presence would only lead to another argument. Instead, I called Ginger's place to check on Desmon. She put him on the phone and after I chatted with him for a while, she took the phone.

"This is quite a surprise hearing from you three times in one week. I'm feeling kind of special."

"Don't. I'm just calling to check Desmon."

"Are you sure your calling here don't have anything to do with the other day? You had a sudden change of heart, didn't you?"

"Nothing about my heart changed, Ginger. My dick just got a little anxious."

"Anxious, huh? Is it anxious now?"

"Very."

"And why's that?"

"Maybe because my woman is upset with me."

"Oh, I see. I knew it was something. But, uh, I've always had the remedy to lift your spirits, should I say?"

"Lift my spirits, no. Rise my thang, yes."

She laughed. "Call it what you'd like but it is what it is."

"Bye, Ginger, I'll see you Saturday."

"So, that's it?"

"Yeah, that's it."

"I'm going to get you yet, Kiley."

"Not before somebody else does," I said, as Candi's name and number flashed on my caller ID. I rushed Ginger off the phone but not fast enough to answer Candi's call. I quickly called the number back like I didn't know who it was.

"Ay, did somebody just call this number?" I asked.

"Is this Kiley?"

"Depends on who's asking."

"This is Candi."

"Yeah, so, what do you want?"

"I want to see you."

"See me for what?"

"To tell you what I've been thinking."

"You don't need to see me to tell me what you've been thinking, do you?"

"Yeah, I kind of do. And I don't feel right telling you over the phone."

"Well, I'll be home by Friday. Stop by then and tell me."

"I can't do that, especially when other people will be around."

"How do you know I'm alone right now?"

"'Cause your brother just called and told me."

I debated telling her where I was, then decided to do it. "Um, I see. Well, I'm at the Marriott near the airport. I'm not going to be good company, so state your business quickly."

"I promise you I will."

I gave Candi my room number and she said that she was on her way.

All I could think about was how bold women had gotten. Sleeping with one friend, just to hit up the next. They were definitely some devious creatures. Seemed like shit the fellas and me were supposed to be doing, but I guessed women were better at this game than we were. Still thinking about Jada, I took a huge swallow of the Hennessy and closed my eyes.

When Candi knocked on the door, I got up and looked in the mirror. My eyes were burning red from the blunts I'd smoked, so I blinked several times to try and clear them. After I tightened the towel around my waist, I peeked out the peephole to make sure it was her.

I opened the door, and when I heard my cell phone ring, I walked away as she came in. The number was coming from the house with Kareem's code behind it, so I turned the phone off and tossed it on the bed. As I took a seat in a chair, Candi took her coat off and laid it on the bed. She wore a plaid short skirt and some knee-high black boots with a black ribbed long-sleeved sweater. Not one piece of her long black hair was out of place, and when she took a seat on the edge of the bed, her dark chocolate legs gave me a serious rise.

"So, tell me. What brings you by?" I asked casually.

"Kareem said you could use some company."

"Well, Kareem was wrong. Maybe he's the one who needs some company."

"No, he made it perfectly clear that it was you."

"Look, Candi, let's stop with the games. I'm here 'cause I needed time to clear my head. I wasn't anticipating any distractions."

"And I'm here because I liked what I saw the other day. If you want to talk about this some other time, we can."

"If that's all you came here to say, actually I would." I stood up and walked over to the door.

Candi picked her coat up off the bed and laid it across her arm. She came toward me. "Can I at least have a kiss for coming all this way?" she asked standing in front of me.

Her lips looked too juicy to ignore. I leaned down and pecked them. She dropped her coat on the floor and placed both of her hands on my face.

Then she stuck her tongue deeply in my mouth. I couldn't resist the sweet taste so I kissed her back. As the kissing got intense, I slid my hands down her back, then underneath her skirt. Bare smooth ass was all I could feel so I massaged her butt cheeks together with my hands. As I went for her front, I felt the silkiness of her panties. I reached up to her hips and slid her red thong down to the floor. Walking back over to the chair to sit down, I started seriously thinking about what I was about to do. Hadn't been with another woman in almost four years. Why was I so willing to do this now when I loved Jada so much?

Candi leaned down and unzipped her boots while standing at the door. Then she slid out of her skirt and pulled her sweater over her head. Strutting herself over to me, she pulled her hair over to the side and sat her dark chocolate naked body down on my lap sideways. I wrapped my arms around her waist and looked at her thick juicy nipples that were staring me in the face. I leaned over, cupped her left breast in my hand, and drew it into my mouth. Not being able to resist the feel of her insides, I slid my hand down and tickled her with my fingers. The deeper they went in, the more she grunted. She closed her eyes and leaned her head back as she rolled her lower body around on top of my lap. I eased myself up out of the chair, grabbed her by her waist, and leaned her hands down on the bed. As I stood behind her, I loosened the towel. It fell to the floor, and when I pressed myself inside, her knees bent. She could barely keep her balance, but I promised to be gentle. We worked slowly together for a few minutes, then I spread her cheeks apart and went deeper inside. It felt so good that I couldn't help but pound harder. She was bouncing her ass against me as fast as she could. And since I didn't want to come before she did, I slid myself out, laid her on the bed, and straddled her across my face. She worked me on the other end and as the taste of her was melting in my mouth, I had to let go. She did too.

Hard banging on the door alarmed me. When I woke up I was lying across the bed drenched in my sweat. My head was pounding and dick was hard as a rock when I realized I'd been dreaming about fucking Candi. I quickly hopped up and opened the door. It was her. I smiled and visualized what I had dreamed about as she came in. Had to be a dream, especially since she was wearing some blue jeans. I looked at my watch.

"I talked to you almost three hours ago. What happened?"

"I got pulled over for speeding. The police searched my car and called for backup like I was some type of criminal or something. Then after all was said and done, he didn't give me a ticket but had the nerve to ask for my phone number. I was pissed."

"I'm sure you were. But what made him search the car anyway?"

"I have no clue. First time that shit ever happened to me. I was kind of scared."

"Um, then maybe you should have gone back home."

"No, I wanted to come here first."

"Why? Why is it so important that we talk?"

Candi took her coat off and sat down in the chair. I sat in the other chair and looked at her from across the table.

She fidgeted with her nails, avoiding eye contact. "Don't think I'm crazy or anything, but I'm kind of feeling you. I know I've been kicking it with Donovan and he's cool but you got a certain . . . assurance about yourself."

"Assurance, huh? You haven't been around me long enough to know how assured I am."

"I don't have to be around a person long. I can look at you and tell. Everybody in that house looks up to you, admires you, maybe even wants to be like you. After getting to know Quincy and

Kareem a little better today, I knew my intuition was correct."

I rubbed my bald head, feeling good, yet uneasy. "I'm flattered, Candi. But, uh, I usually don't go behind my partnas. They mean a lot to me and I'm a li'l disappointed that you dissing my boy behind his back."

"Kiley, Donovan and I are just friends. We've been kicking it for a few months but he sees who he wants to and so do I. So, can we do this or not? If it makes it easier for you, you can come to my place to kick it with me."

"It helps, but it doesn't make it easier. And as much as I would love to take your ass right now and fuck your brains out, I'm not going there. Partially because of your relationship with Donovan, but most of all, because I'm in love with someone."

"Is it that serious between you and Jada? Donovan said it wasn't."

"Donovan can kiss my ass. We're having a difficult time now but hopefully the bullshit will pass like it always does. And if it doesn't, I'll keep what you said in mind."

"See, that's what I like about you. Most brothas would jump at the opportunity right now. You're different, Kiley. I hope Jada knows what kind of man she's got. If she doesn't, there's no doubt in my mind that she's going to lose you."

"Maybe, but, uh, I hope she realizes what she's got, too."

Candi and I sat at the table talking for a while. After I told her about my dream, she told me that's exactly how she'd imagined it and wanted to show me right then and there. I fought hard not to give into her and was relieved when she said she'd better get going.

When I walked her to the door, she laughed.

"What's so funny?" I asked.

"This is where I'm supposed to drop my coat and let you massage my ass."

"No doubt, that would be nice but . . ." I laughed.

She didn't drop her coat but she did grab my neck and stuck her tongue deeply down my throat. I felt the effects of it and backed away. I searched in her mysterious eyes that showed motives. Motives for what, I didn't know. "Maybe some other time, okay?"

"Sure, Kiley." She wiped her lipstick off my lips and opened the door. "Bye," she said, waving and heading down the hallway.

I stood there and watched; it was so hard to let something that fine get away, but I had to.

When she stepped onto the elevator, I closed the door and sat up on the bed thinking about her.

Maybe she was interested in money? Sex? Possibly. By the look of things it was obvious to her that I was the man in control of things. Being with Donovan wasn't going to get her the things she wanted. So, maybe it was time for me to watch my back even more. Women like Candi had a way of working that pussy on a nigga, making him lose focus. I couldn't let that happen to me. But the more I thought about it, the more I knew that I had been living in a shell for the past five years, in fear of everything and everybody around me. Truly afraid to trust anyone. Afraid to explore the Lou like I wanted to. And all with good reason, of course. I really never knew if or when my time was coming. Thing was, I could feel it. Every minute of the day, I couldn't help but think about when all of this would be over.

CHAPTER 5

I pulled into the garage early Friday afternoon. Donovan's car wasn't out front so I knew he was gone, but the BMW was still in the garage. Didn't mean much, 'cause Quincy and Kareem always had other means of transportation. But when I came through the back door, Kareem was there with his head down on the kitchen table, snoring. I smacked him on the back of his head to wake him. He quickly pulled his gun out from down inside his pants and aimed.

"Boy, don't fuck with me like that." He smiled, laying his gun on the table.

"So, I see I'm not the only paranoid fool around here."

"Hey, you the one who taught me don't leave home without it."

"But you at home. You gotta walk around the house with it, too?"

Kareem picked the gun up and kissed it. "This my baby right here. She go wherever I go."

I smiled. "Is Jada here?"

"Naw, man. She went somewhere with Donovan."

"Are you sure?" I asked, as she always spoke ill of Donovan.

"Yeah. They left about an hour or so ago."

"She say where they were going?"

"Nope, and I didn't ask."

I turned and headed down the hallway.

"Ay, Kiley?" Kareem whispered.

I turned around. "What's up?"

"Did you get a chance to see Candi?"

I walked back toward the kitchen and stood in the doorway. "Yeah, I saw her."

"Did you . . . you know? Tap that ass," Kareem said, smiling.

I shook my head. "Nope. Wasn't in the mood."

He frowned. "And a bitch like that couldn't put you in the mood, I guess?"

"Kareem, when you gon' grow up? I said I just wasn't in the mood."

"G'on, man. Get the hell out of my face. You really starting to disappoint me, nigga."

"Sorry to hear that. If my not fucking a lot of women disappoints you, your fucking too many of them disappoints me." I left the kitchen and headed upstairs.

In my room, I sat down in the chair and took off my Timberlands. I pulled my cream sweater over my head and unbuttoned my well-pressed jeans. As I stood there with my shirt off, rummaging through the mail, I heard the front door slam. Then I heard Jada and Donovan talking as they were coming up the steps. When she walked into the room, she looked surprised to see me.

Donovan stood, looking at me while Jada strutted by me with a bag from McDonald's. "Hey, stranger," he said. "Welcome back."

I nodded and continued looking at the mail. "Glad to be back."

"You hungry?" He lifted up a bag from McDonald's. "Got two Quarter Pounders with Cheese in here."

"Naw, knock yourself out. But thanks."

"Anytime." He patted his hand against the wall and left.

Jada sat on the bed, turned the TV on, and pulled her food out of the bag. I reached over to the door, closed it, and sat down in the chair. I stretched my legs up on the bed and crossed my feet.

"So, I guess you're still not talking to me, huh?" I asked, looking at her eye that was still slightly swollen.

She picked up a French fry and put it in her mouth. "Did you have fun with your other woman?"

"Jada, I wasn't with no other woman. I've been at a hotel since Sunday, alone."

"Yeah, right. It don't matter anyway. Whoever she is, she can have your abusive ass."

I reached into my back pocket, pulled the receipt out from the Marriott, and laid it on the bed. "There's proof if you need it. Why? I don't know when I haven't cheated on you with anybody. Maybe you're feeling guilty about something."

"I'm already hip to your reverse psychology game. And I'm not going to sit here and play it with you." She grabbed her bag of food off the bed, getting ready to walk out.

I hopped up, snatched the bag out of her hand, and pushed her down on the bed. Seeing the fear in her eyes, I laid my body on top of her. "Why are you here, Jada? Is it the money? It's the money, ain't it?" I asked, holding her hands down so she wouldn't hit me. Her eyes watered as they searched into mine. The redness in her eye from my punch just ate at me. I shook my head. "I'm not going to hit you. I just need to know why you are here when you seem so unhappy."

"I'm not unhappy," she said softly.

"Well, what's the problem? Is it me? Am I not fucking you correctly? Am I not loving you enough? Tell me, what am I doing wrong?"

She loosened her hands from mine and reached for my pants to pull them down. "Make love to me, Kiley. All I need is for you to make love to me."

I grabbed her hand to stop her. "No, Jada. All I need is some questions answered. I'm tired of the 'fuck me, fight me' bullshit, baby. I can't do this with you anymore."

"Please," she begged. "I promise you things will get better. And once we're finished, I'll answer any questions you have for me."

Knowing how bad I wanted to feel her, I put our conversation off until later and went to work. Sex between us was long overdue. Her insides were dripping wet and needed instant relief from me. Throughout the whole time, she was telling me how much she missed me and never wanted me to leave her again. And feeling the way I did, I never wanted to be away from her another day in my entire life.

After we finished, she rested her head across my lap while I rubbed my hands across the baby hair on her hairline.

She closed her eyes and smiled. "That feels so good, Kiley. And, whew, the sex was the bomb. You must not stay away that long again."

"My sex is always the bomb, ain't it?"

"Of course it is. But that time felt a little different." She sat up and looked at me. "I'm just spoiled, baby. The reason I act the way I do is because you've created a monster, and now you don't know what to do with me."

As she talked to me, I couldn't help but look at the swelling in her eye. I took her face in my hands, placing my lips lightly on her eye. "You're not a monster. Baby, you can have anything you want. All I ask is that you not provoke me and make me hurt you like that anymore. In my eyes, you deserve to be spoiled. Just don't take advantage of me when I'm simply just trying to make you happy."

She leaned forward and kissed me. "I'm happy. Happier than you will ever know."

Jada rested her head against my chest and I felt like a new man. My woman was talking like she had some sense and my dick was finally relieved. After we chilled in our room for a while, we showered and went upstairs to go check out some movies in the entertainment room. Jada sat on my lap and hugged me tightly around the neck while we sat in the dark watching *Halloween*. Shortly after, Quincy joined us; and when Donovan came up the steps with Candi, I damn near died. I was uncomfortable as hell.

"What y'all watching?" Donovan asked, sitting down on the couch. Candi looked over at me then sat down next to Donovan.

"Shh," Jada said, grabbing my neck tighter. "I can't hear."

"Baby, this is the latest *Halloween* movie," Donovan said to Candi.

She nodded and glanced over at me again.

I couldn't concentrate on the movie, so I told Jada I was going downstairs to warm up a TV dinner or something. She rose up off my lap and sat down on the couch. Before I walked out, she yelled for me to warm her one up too.

In the downstairs kitchen, I looked in the freezer and found a chicken nugget and a Salisbury steak dinner. I put them in the microwave for Jada and me; then I heard some heavy heels on the hardwood floors. I knew they were Candi's.

She strolled into the kitchen with an ice bucket in her hand. "Here you go," she said, giving it to me. "Quincy asked me to give this to you so you could put some ice in it."

I took it out of her hand and opened up the freezer. I stood with my pants unzipped, barely hanging onto my naked ass underneath, and I felt Candi looking down at the smooth hairs above my dick. After I gave the ice bucket back to her, I pulled my pants up and zipped them.

"You're too late," she said, smiling. "I already saw what I wanted to see."

I shrugged. "Did you like it?"

"Loved it." She winked and walked out of the kitchen.

I watched her ass, shaking my head. *Damn!* I thought. If only I were a dog.

I put Jada's and my dinners on some plates and carried them up the steps. When I got upstairs I had to walk by Candi and Donovan sitting on the couch. She looked up at me and grinned. Knowing every bit of what was going on, Quincy cleared his throat and smirked as he looked at the TV.

Jada rolled her eyes at him then leaned over next to me. "Thanks, baby." She puckered up for a kiss.

I kissed her and Candi glanced over at us, then turned her head. Quincy looked at me and grinned. All this head-turning shit was making me nervous. The only two who didn't seem to be uncomfortable were Donovan and Jada. They were seriously all into the movie.

I was glad when the movie was finally over. Quincy quickly got up and turned on the lights, and before his mouth started running, I told Jada I was ready to go to bed. She took my hand, said good night to everybody, and we left. I got a last glimpse of Candi, but she didn't see me because she was talking with Donovan.

Since Jada was chilling out with her attitude, I left well enough alone. We never did have our deep conversation she promised, but I had no intentions of spoiling her good mood. I kissed her on the forehead a few times and after a few strokes up and down her back she was out like a light.

When I heard Donovan's footsteps pass by my room, I listened for Candi's heels and heard them, too. Minutes later, the bed started hitting the wall. Hitting it so hard, it woke Jada up. She looked up at me, as I was still wide awake.

"Now, that's a damn shame. Ain't that much fucking in the world," Jada said, as Candi started to moan loudly. "Not only that, dick definitely ain't that good."

I looked at her. "And how do you know?"

"I mean, ain't no man's dick that damn good where it makes you act a fool like that." She laid her head back down on me. "Except for yours." She looked back up at me and smiled.

"That's right. Clean your shit up, baby," I said. Jada laid her head down again and went back to sleep.

I couldn't sleep for nothing in the world, listening to the action going on in Donovan's room and thinking about what Jada said. Was it really a mistake or had she slept with Donovan before? After racking my brain for a few more minutes, I decided to go find out the best way I could, and that was to view every last tape in this house. I was the only person in the house who had a key to the basement door that stayed locked. Primarily, because most of my money was kept down there, in a safe hidden behind a sliding thick wall. If there were anything out of the ordinary going on with Donovan and Jada, I'd soon know by looking at the tapes.

I crept out of bed around four-thirty in the morning. I opened the basement door and locked it behind me. I had to move a gang of spider webs away from the code box, and when I punched in the code, the wall made a loud noise as it slid over. I unlocked the safe first, feeling paranoid about my money, but when I saw nothing had been touched, I locked it again. I brushed the dust off my black leather chair that sat in front of the six thirteen-inch monitors that viewed the house. Soon after, I got busy rewinding and watching the tapes.

I had been in the basement for almost two hours and still nothing out of the ordinary seemed to be going down between Jada and Donovan. There were few sex scenes here and there by the fellas throughout the house but that was it. The only thing I noticed with Jada and Donovan was a few conversations alone in the kitchen. Couldn't tell what they were saying, but she was also in the kitchen talking to Quincy and Kareem so I couldn't make anything of it.

As another hour went by, I started feeling as if my insecurities had gotten the best of me. But when I noticed his hand on her thigh while they were in his car one day, I stopped the tape and rewound it. I zoomed in and played it again. He rubbed her leg up and down three times, and then she turned toward him and laughed. After that, she got out of his car.

I wasn't really sure what to make of it but I picked it apart about five more times in my mind. Still puzzled, I continued to watch more tapes. Nothing else showed up for another hour and a half, except more laughter between the two and her coming out of his room with his laundry in a laundry basket.

When I heard a noise coming from upstairs and looked at the second-floor monitor, I saw our bedroom door open. I hurried and locked everything up in the basement and ran upstairs.

As soon as I shut the basement door and locked it, Jada met me on her way to the kitchen.

"What were you doing in the basement this early in the morning?" she asked.

I took a deep breath. "Nothing, baby. I just needed some money. Was running a li'l low."

"Aw. Are you hungry?"

"A li'l bit," I said, walking behind her into the kitchen. I sat down at the kitchen table.

Jada opened the refrigerator and pulled out three packs of bacon. "I guess I should cook for everybody, huh? Maybe even for that loudmouth bitch in Donovan's room. If I shove some bacon down her throat maybe the tramp will cool out."

"Now, that's not nice, baby. Besides, she left anyway, didn't she?" I said, knowing damn well Candi was still upstairs.

"No, she's still here. Her loud-ass giggling is what woke me up again. Donovan gon' have to take his ass to another room. This shit is getting ridiculous."

"Well, would you rather have Kareem in that room instead, or Quincy? Take your pick."

She looked at me and rolled her eyes. "We'd definitely never get any sleep then."

We both laughed.

After Jada threw down on breakfast, we took our plates upstairs to eat. I grabbed a food tray and sat up in bed. Jada put her plate on the dresser and went into the bathroom.

She pounded her fist against the wall next to Donovan's room and laughed loudly. "Stop, Kiley. Ooo, baby, please stop!" she yelled so they could hear her. When she got more into it saying, "Fuck me. Fuck me good," I whispered for her to stop. We laughed as she picked her plate up and got in bed with me. When my cell phone rang, I looked at it and it was Donovan's cell phone number.

"What up?" I said.

"Y'all think that shit funny, don't you?" he said.

"What shit? I don't know what the hell you're talking about."

"That pounding on the wall bullshit. That's what."

"Nigga, I was making love to my woman, if you don't mind."

"Playa, who do you think you're fooling? You the most silent fucking lovemaking nigga I know. I ain't ever heard all that commotion over there before."

"And you never will because I don't have a raggedy-ass loose headboard banging up against the wall. I got a beautiful white marble wall unit bed, and the best thing about it is the damn thing is stable. Ain't going nowhere no matter how hard I work it."

Jada snatched my phone and turned it off. "That's too much information. He don't need to know how you work it." She tossed the phone in the chair next to the bed.

After Jada fed me breakfast in bed, we made love for about an hour or so and afterward I was snoring like a hog. By the time I rolled over, it was close to five o'clock in the evening. I was supposed to go see Desmon, but I was too tired. Jada woke me up and said she'd be back, so I didn't have a car to go see him even if I wanted to. I reached for my cell phone and called Ginger's house to tell her I was going to stop by tomorrow. When she answered, I could sense her attitude.

"We got something to do tomorrow," she said, smacking on something. "Desmon and me going to see my grandmother."

"Ginger, come on now, quit making excuses. I can tell by the sound of your voice that you're upset with me, but I'm tired. I was up all night taking care of some business."

"Let me guess . . . with Jada, right?"

"No, not with Jada."

"Well, did y'all make up?"

"Of course, don't we always?"

"Yeah, I figured that much. It just bothers me how you keep putting her before your own flesh and blood, though."

"No, I don't. Why do you say that?"

"Because, you ain't even man enough to tell her about your own damn son. If she loves you so much, then she'll learn to accept him. What I don't understand is why he got to be a fucking secret? Kept in the dark like he some out-of-control badass child or something."

"Ginger, don't start talking that shit right now. You know how much I love my son."

"Then if you do, you wouldn't be ashamed of him. So, answer the question, Kiley. Why does the only damn son you got have to be a secret? Are you ashamed of him?"

"No, not at all. I just want to keep things on the down low until I'm ready to break the news."

"Down low, huh? You've been saying that for four years now. He's going to be ten years old and still on the down low. I don't know if having you in his life is a good thing or a bad thing, especially when you come over whenever *you* feel like it. Not when he ask for you in the middle of the night or when he wants you to see his new race car set or for you to read him a simple-ass bedtime story. I hope you're feeling like a proud papa these days."

"Ginger, just be quiet. If you're not going to be there tomorrow then I'll stop by there in a few. And if you're trying to make me feel like such a bad father, I don't. I know I do everything for Desmon that I'm able to do. Not only that, he doesn't want for a damn thing. So, chill, all right?"

"Fuck all this material bullshit over here. He don't need that shit. He needs his fucking daddy. That's what he needs. If shit didn't work out between you and me, cool. So be it. But he doesn't deserve to be without. If anything, you need to be on his time, not him on your time. When he needs you, you be there."

"I said I'll be there!" I yelled, just as Jada walked into the bedroom.

"Okay, fine. Then tell him you're coming. That way if you lie, you lie to him, not me." Ginger gave the phone to Desmon. Jada looked at me like "who in the hell are you yelling at?"

"Hi, Daddy," Desmon said in a low voice.

"Hey, what's up?" I got up off the bed, went into the bathroom, and closed the door. I turned on the water so Jada couldn't hear me. "I'll be over in a li'l bit to see you, okay?"

"Okay."

"Do you want anything?"

"Some chocolate ice cream."

"All right, tell your mama I'm on my way."

Desmon told Ginger I was on my way and hung up the phone.

I turned the water off and walked out of the bathroom with the phone on my ear pretending to still be talking to someone. "All right, man. Yeah, that fool crazy. I'll pick you up in about thirty minutes. Cool. Deuces." I looked at my phone and turned it off.

Jada was sitting in the chair with her feet pressed against the bed polishing her toenails. "Who was that?" she asked.

"My Uncle Vinney. He in St. Louis and want me to come pick him up from one of his partna's crib."

"Can I go with you?"

"Uh, not this time, baby. Him and his friends be drinking, smoking, and cursing all the time. I don't want you being around all that shit."

She looked at me. "Please, I'm around that kind of shit every day. What makes you think that would bother me? So I don't care what you say, I'm going. I don't feel like being cooped up in here on a Saturday night anyway."

Jada had on an old gray jogging suit. Knowing she was going to want to change, I quickly said, "Baby, it's going to take me five minutes to change my clothes. I don't have thirty minutes to wait on you to get dressed when I told him I'd be there in thirty minutes. After I drop him off,

I'll come back and we'll go downtown to hang out, okay?"

"All right, but don't have me waiting all damn night, Kiley. I'm tired of being cooped up in here all the time."

I rushed putting my clothes on before she changed her mind and jetted. I stopped at a Quik Trip and bought Desmon some chocolate ice cream. When I got to Ginger's place, she opened the door up and, as usual, was running her mouth on the phone. I picked Desmon up and took him into the kitchen to give him his ice cream. I put it in a bowl and sat down at the table with him eating.

Ginger came in puffing on a cigarette. "I didn't even think you were going to show." She sat down in the chair next to me and pulled an ashtray up in front of her.

"I told you I was coming. Have I ever lied to you before?"

"Yes, several times. You lied about today. If I hadn't chewed you out, you never would have come. You lied when I met you and said you didn't have a girlfriend. You lied when—"

"Okay, Ginger. So, I'm a liar. I'm the worst damn father Desmon could have and the worst thing that ever happened to you. Are you satisfied?"

"I won't be satisfied until you finally acknowledge your son. When you start taking him around your family, your woman, and your friends, then I'll be satisfied."

"Well, the only family I have in St. Louis is Kareem, my friends couldn't care less about my son, and he's not any of my woman's business."

"That's really sad, Kiley. I'm sorry to hear how much your son doesn't fit into your life. Good parents are proud of their children. Wouldn't dream of keeping them from anyone. You should really be ashamed of yourself. And if you're not, I'm ashamed for you. Let's just pray that Desmon's too young to understand what kind of man you really are."

Ginger put her cigarette out in the ashtray, got up from the table, and went into her bedroom. Feeling bad about the situation, and knowing that she was partially right, I stayed almost the entire night with Desmon. By the time I kissed him good night and closed his bedroom door it was almost one o'clock in the morning.

Ginger had gotten in her bed and gone to sleep. I woke her up and told her to come lock the door. She got up and walked me to the door in her leopard-print bra and panties.

"Good night," she said, opening the door for me to leave.

I guess she was really upset because she didn't even try to shake a brotha down before he left. That was a good thing.

On my way to my car, I remembered what had happened to me the last time I was in East St. Louis and thought about those fools who tried to jack me. Just to be on the safe side, I took my gun out and laid it on the seat next to me. I drove down the street ready for any muh-fucker who dared to trip.

No sooner had I driven two blocks from Ginger's house, Donovan's black Navigator cut me off and pulled in front of me. Jada hopped out the driver's side with a silver metal bat in her hand and started pounding the shit out of the Lexus. I ducked as she smashed the driver's window with it. The glass came flying through the window and a few shards caught me in the side of my face.

I grabbed the gun in my hand and quickly rolled over to the passenger side to get out. When I did, I aimed it at her. "Put the damn bat down, Jada!" I yelled.

She ignored me and kept banging my damn car with it. I ran around the car, and when I tried to grab her, she swung the bat low, cracking me on the leg. When she tried again, I caught it in midair with my hand and felt my wrist crack as she came down hard with it. In pain, I pushed Jada back and tripped her to the ground. Trying not to hurt her ass, I hopped in my car and took off. I wanted to roll right over her but instead, I sped off to the highway.

When I looked in my rearview mirror there was no sign of her, but I did notice blood streaming down the side of my face. With a cracked wrist and a banged-up car, I drove to the emergency room at St. Luke's Hospital and checked in. I lied and told the nurse I slid off the road and hit a tree.

As I paced around in the waiting room, I pulled my cell phone out and called the house. Donovan answered and when I cursed his ass out for letting Jada use his car, he claimed she told him she needed to go to the grocery store. He also told me she left right after I did, so I was sure that she followed me over to Ginger's house. When I yelled at Donovan again, he gave the phone to Kareem.

I took deep breaths, talking to Kareem. I was straight up in a rage. "Man, if that bitch come back there tonight, kick her ass out for me. Go in my room right now and pack up as much shit as you can." I paused, as my wrist was hurting and I could feel pain shooting up my arm. "Can a brotha get some help in this damn place?" I yelled waiting for a nurse to call my name.

"What happened, bro? Are you all right?" Kareem asked with concern in his voice.

"Just do like I told you to. Get Quincy and Donovan to help."

"She didn't shoot at you did she?"

"Hell naw, man. Now stop asking questions and do like I told you to! I'll tell you what happened when I get there."

"Hold on," Kareem said. He laid the phone down and I wanted to jump through it and kick his ass for bullshitting with me. He picked it back up.

"Kareem, don't fuck with me, man! Quit playing games, nigga."

"Stop yelling at me, fool! The cops just pulled up. We looking at them on the monitors right now. What the fuck happened?"

"Listen. Send that nigga Quincy to the door. Tell him to pretend like he don't even know me if they ask for me. Make sure he invites them in but don't let them search shit unless they got a search warrant. You and Donovan, do not be seen. Whatever you do, let them see Quincy and Quincy only."

"All right, man. They knocking so I'll call you back after they leave." Kareem hung up.

I panicked and slammed my fist on the chair. "Can I get some stitches or a bandage up in this son of a bitch so I can get the fuck out of here!" I yelled at the nurse sitting at the desk.

"Mr. Franklin, calm down. Come on back this way and a doctor will be with you shortly."

After I walked into the room, I kicked the door and dropped back in a chair. I gave them my fake ID and told the bitch I was paying cash for the visit 'cause I didn't have insurance. I'm sure that's why they were making me wait, but once they came in and nursed my cracked wrist and put fifteen stitches down the side of my face, they said they'd bill me.

Not hearing anything from Kareem yet, my heart was racing a mile a minute. I didn't want to call home because I didn't know if the cops were still there maybe waiting for me to call. Thing was, I knew Kareem wasn't going to follow my instructions.

When I finally made it to the city and drove down Euclid, it was obvious he didn't. Police were every damn where. I could see Kareem lying on the ground handcuffed and Donovan and Quincy standing close by talking to an officer. Jada was leaning against Donovan's truck with her arms folded. A mean mug covered her face and she kept turning her head from side to side, squinting. I wondered if she was waiting for me to show up. But with too much action going on, I opted to view the scene from afar.

After a while, the police took the cuffs off Kareem and he got off the ground. Most of the other officers got in their cars and left, as Donovan, Kareem, and Quincy went back into the house. Jada stood outside for a while talking to the last officer, then got into the front seat of his car, and they drove away.

Knowing that it wasn't in my best interests to go home yet, and considering the fact I was still riding around with a banged-up Lexus, I went back to the Marriott for the night. Before I did, I called Al, a partna of mine who worked on my car before and asked him if he wouldn't mind taking care of the dents for me. He said he would be happy to; then I asked him to rent a car for me. He had no problem helping a brotha at four o'clock in the morning, especially when I paid him and paid him well for doing so.

I checked into the hotel and couldn't wait to call home. Kareem answered and I could tell he was still wide awake. "All I'm telling you is, I'm killing that bitch, Kiley. I promise you, in love with her or not, that backstabbing ho dies," Kareem spat.

"Why or how did you get seen by the police when I asked you to stay in the house?"

"I did stay in. But when Jada pulled her stupid ass up telling the cops to search the house for you and calling us drug dealers and shit, I went to go shut her up. The police grabbed me and threw me on the ground, before I knocked her ass out."

I took a deep breath. "So, what did they say? I mean, did they say they were coming back with a warrant or anything?"

"Naw, Quincy and Donovan told them she was upset because you broke up with her and put her out of the house earlier today. When they asked to speak with you, Quincy told them you went to Chicago on business after y'all argument today and wouldn't be back until next weekend. The detective left a number for you to call him."

"Call him for what? I told y'all not to mention my name."

"Man, they knew all of us by name. Thanks to Jada. And ain't no telling what else she told them. When they questioned me, I told them we moved to St. Louis after our mother died. For the most part, I think they cool but the sooner you call and clear things up, the better. That way they'll believe fasho we ain't got nothing to hide."

"I'll call the detective tomorrow. In the meantime, I'm going to stay the night at the Marriott. If Jada comes back, let her get her shit and ask her to leave. Don't start no argument with her because that's what she wants you to do. I'll be there before noon tomorrow."

"So, why were you at the hospital? Man, please don't tell me she tried to kill you."

"It's a long story, but I'll tell you when I get there tomorrow. I need to chill right now, so deuces."

I hung up and lay across the bed with my clothes on. I hurt like hell, and Jada had really disappointed me. If she had asked me why I was at Ginger's place, I would have told her. I was planning on telling her anyway since Ginger had been coming down so hard on me about Desmon. I knew I had put him on the back burner to keep Jada happy, but I was starting to think she wasn't worth neglecting my son for. And by the way things were going, I knew it was time for me to spend as much time with him as I could.

CHAPTER 6

I didn't get a lick of sleep that night. All the bullshit that went down was heavy on my mind. Couldn't believe after all these years Jada would snake me like that, especially when she benefited from the money more than anybody did. And the fucked up thing about it was that the fellas warned me. I simply thought they were just hating, but they saw shit about her I didn't see. Sad thing about it was that a part of me still loved her.

Riding around in the rental car, I scoped the streets for a while to make sure the coast was clear before I went home. Everything looked normal, so I pulled into the garage and quickly let the door down after I was in. By the time I got to the back door, Kareem and Quincy were there to greet me. I'm sure they'd seen me coming by looking at the monitors.

Kareem looked at the side of my face and saw my arm in a sling. He shook his head and opened the door for me. "I'm killing her. I swear I am and I don't care what you say," he said. I went inside and sat down at the kitchen table. I hadn't gotten any medication for my cracked wrist and was still in excruciating pain.

I leaned forward with my elbows resting on my knees and looked at Kareem and Quincy. "We gotta start making some other plans. I got a bad feeling this time something's about to go down. Do y'all remember what I said I wanted to do if it comes to this?" I asked.

"Yeah, man," Kareem said. "But I don't want to move again. This is fucking home. If we run now, shit will start to look suspicious. I say we chill. If the cops keep coming back, then we make other arrangements."

"I agree with Kareem," Quincy said. "Let's not jump the gun. Jada's gone. If she tells the police anything else, they gotta find the evidence first. And ain't nothing up in this house to be found. Besides, I think they looked at the situation yesterday as a woman being upset because she was kicked out by her man. Nothing more, nothing less."

I looked down at the floor, thinking. "All right. But please be on guard. If you bring somebody up in this damn house, make sure you know who the fuck they are."

"Cool, cool," Kareem said. "Will most definitely do that, my brotha."

"And, Kareem, all this talk about killing Jada, just let it be. I got plans for her myself, so let me handle my business how I want to, okay?"

"Whatever. But if she comes back here talking that shit, I can't make you any promises. I'm sorry, that's just how it's got to be."

I looked around. "Where's Donovan?"

"He got a phone call and said he'd be back," Quincy said.

"From who?"

"Don't know. He just said he'd holla at you when he gets back."

I stood up and walked over by the kitchen window. I moved the curtain aside and looked out. "I don't trust that nigga. Something about him just bugs the hell out of me." I turned and looked at Kareem and Quincy. "What about y'all? How do y'all feel about him?"

"I mean, he cool," Kareem said. "Ain't too many brothas I trust, but I think more than anything, he's envious of you. Other than that, I really don't have a problem with him."

"What about you, Quincy. How do you feel about him?"

"He all right, I guess. Do I trust him? Can't really say. Never really thought much about it."

I nodded. "Okay. Well, I'm going upstairs to chill for the rest of the day. What's up with y'all?

Quincy and Kareem looked at each other. "I was thinking about bringing some safe, secure, trustworthy booty up in the crib to relax with. If not that, then, maybe Kareem and me gon' go down to the Union Station and chill."

"I like your first idea better," Kareem said. "Brotha need a li'l love and tender care to take all this bullshit off my mind. Should I call someone for you too, big brother?"

I laughed. "Naw, man. Knock yourselves out. Today will be a rest day for me. And since I can't get down like I want to with this fucked up wrist, what the hell."

"Shit, as long as your dick ain't broke, I'm sure you can find a way to work around it."

"I'm sure I could too, but I got other things on my mind."

I went upstairs to my room and stripped naked, then lay across the bed for a while. With my mind full of unanswered questions, I got out of bed, slid on my pajama pants, and went into Donovan's room. I sat on the edge of his bed, pulling out his drawers and looking for some answers. Nothing was there but a bunch of condoms and pictures of naked women, aside from his underwear. I lifted his mattress up and there was about $500 in cash under there.

After that, I checked his closet. He had so many damn clothes and shoes I didn't know where to begin. I fumbled through his things; then I saw a white box that was full of paper and more pictures were underneath it. I pulled the box out of the closet and sat on his bed, again, looking through it. I got excited looking at some of the women in the pictures because some of them definitely had it going on. I laughed when I saw a few pictures of some females I knew in L.A., but when I found a naked picture of Jada, I was numb. My heart fell to the ground as I looked through the box and found more. They weren't recent pictures, but had to been at least six or seven years ago. We had been together since high school, so I knew they had to have been taken while we were together.

And if the pictures weren't enough, the letters I found were definitely enough to eat me alive. She'd written him letters telling him how much she loved him and wanted to end things with me. Her most recent letter was right before she moved to St. Louis. She told him that when he decided to move to St. Louis, it brought her closer to me, and how when she moved here, how difficult it was going to be for her living in the same house with both of us. She made him promise to never tell me and assured him if I ever found out they would both die.

I crumbled the paper in my hand, feeling like a fool. I folded the other letters, put them back into the box, and put the pictures in my pocket. I placed the box back in the closet and left Donovan's room. I went back into my room, and as I rummaged through my closet, I noticed a few things of Jada's missing. Expensive shit, like two fur coats, her Gucci purses, and when I checked the drawer for her Rolex watch I'd given her last Christmas, that was gone too.

Quincy and Kareem were upstairs in the entertainment room, so I went up there to see if somehow Jada came back into the house last night without them knowing it. I had an idea who took her stuff but I just wanted to be sure.

They were in the midst of playing pool, and I leaned against the pool table, taking a puff from Quincy's joint. "I don't mean to interrupt y'all game but by any chance did Jada get into this house last night?"

Kareem took the joint from me, took a hit, and shook his head. "Nope, no way. We ain't even had no sleep. Quincy, Donovan, and me were up all night long talking."

"Did y'all see Donovan leave with anything?"

"Nope," Kareem said.

I looked at Quincy. "Me either. I didn't see him leave with anything but wasn't like I was really paying attention."

"Well, how often did he leave y'all sight?"

"A couple times, if I can recall," Quincy said. "But it wasn't for that long."

"All right, fellas. By the way, where are the ladies at? I thought y'all said some soft legs were coming over."

"On their way right now, playa," Kareem said, ready to shoot the eight ball.

I smiled and went back downstairs.

I leaned back in the chair in my room, waiting for Donovan to come. When I called him on his cell phone he didn't answer, but I was sure he'd be coming home soon since he knew I was looking for him. As I sat there watching the monitors, I pulled Jada's pictures out of my pocket a few times looking at them disgusted as hell. Bitch had straight up been fucking my partna. And had the nerve to tell me how much she loved me and wanted to be with me forever. How in the hell could I not know something was up, especially with the vibes I was getting from the both of them? I asked myself over and over again: did she really love him? Or was it her way of getting back at me for messing around on her in L.A.? Either way, I felt like pussy had caused me to lose focus. Donovan was supposed to be my boy, but I did more for Jada than I did for anybody.

When I saw a car pull up in front of the house, I noticed two women getting out. I figured they must have been the chicks Quincy and Kareem invited over, and I watched as they went to the door and rang the doorbell. As soon as Quincy opened the door, I saw Donovan's black Lincoln Navigator pull up. I hopped out of the chair and ran downstairs to make it to the kitchen before he came in the house. I figured Kareem and Quincy were going to be upstairs in the entertainment room with their company, so the downstairs kitchen was a private place for me and Donovan to talk. As I jetted down the steps, I bumped into Quincy and the ladies on their way up.

"Damn, man," Quincy said. "Slow down. Where are you headed moving like that, and can you at least say hello to the ladies?"

I hurried to speak, anxious to meet up with Donovan.

I went into the kitchen and when I heard Donovan coming through the front door, I slammed a plate on the floor, knowing he would come to the kitchen to see what was up. Of course, he did, and I'm sure he thought a fight or something was going on. As I bent down to pick the broken glass up with my good arm, he stood in the doorway looking at me. Seeing that I was having a difficult time he squatted and helped me get the shards off the floor. We both dropped glass pieces in the trashcan and then took a seat across from each other at the table.

Donovan stretched his arms out, observing his muscles. "Wheww, these damn things are tight. I just came from the gym and seriously think I pulled a muscle."

I looked at his casual attire. "Damn, nigga's dressing like that going to the gym these days?"

"Naw. I changed before I came home. My workout clothes are in the car."

"Hmmm. But, uh, Kareem and Quincy said you had some important business to tend to."

"Yeah, I did. Tricia was bugging me about picking up her new dinette set from the furniture store. I'd been putting it off for so long and she was starting to get a bit upset with me."

"Right, right. I know how it is when a woman gets upset. Shit they do can most definitely be costly."

"Yeah, I see." He nodded, then looked at my arm. "I knew you and Jada got into it but, damn, how did she break your arm?"

I lifted my arm on the table, while staring at Donovan with a hard stare. "My wrist, my brotha. She cracked my wrist. But I'm sure she told you the details, didn't she?"

He stretched his neck from side to side, starting to fidget. "Why would she tell me? I haven't seen her since she left with the police last night."

I cleared my throat. "Naw, that's a lie, muh-fucker, and you know it. You took that bitch some of her things today, didn't you?"

Donovan eyes shot down to the floor, then he rested his hands behind his head and leaned back in the chair. Fidgeting again, he opened and closed his legs, then slid his hand down over his dick. "Listen, I wasn't trying to go behind your back or anything, but she asked me to bring her a few things so she could leave town. I really didn't think you would mind, since you wanted her out of your hair anyway."

"Did you think I would mind if you fucked her?"

"*Fuck* her? Man, please. What in the hell are you talking about? It ain't even like that."

I reached in my pocket and pulled out the naked pictures of Jada. I tossed them across the table so he could see them. Reaching down, I pulled out my gun and laid it on the table in front of me. "Do those jog your memory? Don't lie, you playa-hating, backstabbing son of a bitch. I'm sure after taking a look at those, it'll refresh that fucked-up memory of yours."

Donovan picked up one of the pictures and looked at it. Then he laid it back down on the table. I knew he kept a gun on him as well, so before he could even think about getting to it, I picked mine up and aimed it directly at him from across the table.

"I knew you was a no-good muh-fucker, Donovan. One thing my daddy told me before he died was to watch your black ass. And true enough, pussy is just pussy, but don't no nigga who call themselves a friend of mine snake me like your punk ass did."

Donovan stared down the barrel of my gun, carefully watching as I held my hand steady on the trigger. His beady eyes showed fear. "Okay, Kiley. That shit between Jada and me was a long time ago. I haven't been with her in quite some time, and if you're talking about when I had sex with her last year when y'all had that big argument about her spending too much money. She . . . she came in my room in the middle of the night and teased the fuck out of me. All I was trying to do was get laid."

"Lay on this, muh-fucka!" I pulled the trigger and the bullet went flying straight into Donovan's upper right shoulder. The force of the shot pushed him backward, knocking him out of his chair.

"Damn!" he yelled, holding his shoulder as blood rushed from it. When he kneeled on the floor and tried to reach for his gun, I quickly got up and stood over him. I kicked him in his gut and reached down inside his pants to pull his gun out. I rested the steel against his temple.

"It's a pain being a conniving fool like you. I'm sorry that you felt suicide was your only option, and it's a damn shame you had to use your own gun."

I was getting ready to pull the trigger, when Kareem and Quincy came rushing into the kitchen.

"Kiley!" Kareem yelled and ran up to me. He looked at the chicks standing behind Quincy, who looked scared and ready to find the nearest exit. "Evidence, man! Too many witnesses!" he yelled. "Let it go, brotha! Please let it go!"

Donovan rolled to the ground and lay on his back, while holding the wound to his shoulder. "Help me," he cried out. "Som . . . somebody help me, please!"

Blood was all over the floor, and not giving a fuck, I laid my gun down and removed his from behind him. Not finished with him yet, I smacked him hard across his face with it. "Get the fuck out of here and take all that bitch Jada's shit with you." I looked at Kareem and Quincy.

"Get this muh-fucka to a hospital. If he dies on the way, push his ass in the river and clean up behind him."

As I headed out of the kitchen, my eyes connected with the ladies in the hallway, shaking like they were standing in zero-degree weather. "You didn't see what you just saw, you didn't hear what you just heard, and if you run your mouth to anyone about what happened here today, I will make sure it's the last time you ever talk again."

I went upstairs to change clothes so I could get the fuck out of there. I wasn't sure what Donovan was going to do but I wasn't taking any chances. I didn't think he was going to the police because he was a man on the run just like the rest of us. The farther away all of us stayed from the po-po, the better.

As I was changing clothes, Kareem came upstairs into my bedroom breathing hard. "Okay, he in the car, but what in the hell is going on? Day by day this shit is getting fucked up and I don't know a damn thing."

I stared at him, with fury still in my eyes. "Would you stop asking questions and do like I told you to for one damn time in your life, Kareem?"

His face twisted. "Fuck naw! I need to know what the hell is going on, now! You've been putting me off long enough, ordering me around, and I'm getting tired of the shit."

"Listen, I don't have time to argue with you right now. Just get the hell out of here and I'll call you later to explain."

"So, back to the damn hotel again, huh?" He punched the wall with his fist. "Damn! I'm getting sick and tired of being your puppet! Is it that goddamn hard for you to tell me what's going on!"

I glanced at the hole in the wall and closed my eyes trying to cool down. "Kareem, I told you I would explain this to you later. All I'm trying to do is get the hell out of here in case somebody heard that gunshot. So, for the last time, do like I told you to, okay?" I said, calmly.

Kareem cut his eyes and left the room.

I plopped down in the chair, closed my eyes, and rubbed my face with my hands. I felt like I was truly losing my mind. I straight up almost killed one of my boys over a stupid-ass bitch. The things I said I was never going to do anymore, I was starting to do again. All I wanted to do was live peacefully, but I didn't see that happening. I took a few deep breaths, finished putting my clothes on, and left.

***

Instead of going to a hotel, I drove to Ginger's house. When I saw this low-riding Q45 with silver shining rims and a dropdown TV in the back, I knew what time it was. But company or not, I wasn't leaving. Ginger opened the door, looking shocked to see me. When she saw the stitches on my face and my arm in a sling, she asked me to come in.

Whoever the brotha was, he was sitting on the couch with Desmon on his lap. As soon as Desmon saw me, he hopped down and came over next to me. I couldn't pick him up 'cause my wrist was still in pain. I nudged my head toward the front door and she turned to the brotha sitting on the couch.

"Uh, Theodis, if you don't mind I need to talk to Kiley about something," she said.

"Are you asking me to leave?" he asked.

"Naw, fool. She's asking you to sit right here and listen to our conversation," I snarled.

He slowly stood up, staring me down. Ginger went over to him, whispering something to him.

"Ginger, no need to kiss his ass. Let the man go. I'm not feeling up to it right about now anyway," I said.

"Kiley, look. Let me handle this." She put her hand on Theodis's chest. "Would you just please go? I don't want no trouble. I'll call you later."

He snatched his coat up off the couch and walked slowly by me.

After Ginger closed the door, she rolled her eyes at me and plopped down on the couch. She lit a cigarette. "See, I knew that shit was going to happen. That's why I told you to call before you came over here, Kiley."

I sat down on the couch next to her and put Desmon on my lap. I rubbed his hair back with my hand and kissed him on his fat cheeks. "Why haven't you gotten his hair cut yet?"

"Look, don't start with me. I'm taking him tomorrow, if you really want to know. I can already tell you're upset about something. I hope you didn't come over here to dump on me."

"Naw, I didn't. I just needed to see my son."

"Looks like you need more than that. What happened to you? Were you in a fight or something?"

"Yeah, and you should see the other fool. He really fucked up."

"I hope so 'cause looks like you got your ass beat."

"Actually, he did, but, uh, do me a favor."

"What?"

"Go lay Desmon down. I need to talk to you about something."

Ginger put her cigarette out and took Desmon off my lap. "Lucky for you it's his nap time anyway. Do you want anything while I'm up? I was just about ready to fix me and Theo . . . Never mind."

"Yeah, get me some water and bring me a few aspirin with it. If you were cooking dinner for you and Theodis, call that nigga back over here after I leave."

Ginger smiled, stepped in front of me, and carried Desmon out of the room. Relaxing, I stood up and stripped naked. I took my sling off and rested back on the couch with a hard dick, waiting for Ginger to return.

When she came back into the living room with the aspirin and water in her hand, her jaw dropped. She laid the aspirin down on the table, and without hesitating, she eased her body down on top of mine. "I thought you said you wanted to talk."

"I'm the mastermind when it comes to lying, according to you, so I lied. Talking was the last thing on my mind, and since I suspected you were about to get down with Theodis, I didn't want you being deprived after putting him out for me."

Ginger scooted back a li'l bit and slid out of her oversized T-shirt. She was bare underneath, and when she laid her soft body back on top of mine, I felt like I was in a different world. I was so accustomed to Jada's thick body on top of mine that Ginger's lighter body felt kinda strange. After she pecked me on the lips a few times, she slid down and got on her knees between my legs. I leaned my head back and looked at the ceiling, as she stroked my dick with her hands. I rubbed her hair and watched her give me pleasure with her mouth. The feeling was so good, the touch was so right, and the more I watched the harder it was for me to keep control. I closed my eyes and started thinking about Jada. Although I tried not to think about Donovan fucking her, the thought stayed with me for a while.

Realizing that I couldn't take Ginger's pleasure anymore, I opened my eyes and slowly sat up. Ginger backed up and grabbed a hair clip from the table to put her braids up in a bun. I kneeled down on the floor and sat her on the table in front of the couch, slightly pushing the table back so we could have room. She opened her legs up wide and when I crawled in between them, she wrapped her legs tightly around my neck.

"Kiley? Why are you doing this to me?" she moaned, rubbing the back of my head.

I searched her insides with my tongue, and backed up a few times to peck her thighs.

"Because I need you, Ginger. If just for one damn night, I need you," I said, looking up at her. She pressed my head back down between her legs and I continued my business.

Once I finished loving Ginger's insides, she got on her knees and allowed me to dip into her sopping wet pussy from behind. Trying to release my tension, I banged her so hard, she begged me to stop. When I wouldn't, she fell on her stomach and let me have my way. Getting tired with that position, I turned her over on her back, teased her walls with my goodness, and then placed her legs high on my shoulders.

When I slammed myself deep inside, she screamed and backed up. "Baby, look," she said, looking at me with her big, round, watery eyes. "You have to take it easy with me. I know you're frustrated about something but—"

I kissed her on the lips to shush her, then dropped her legs to the floor. As I slowed things down, she smiled and started moving her body to a slower motion with mine. Getting into the rhythm, I leaned my sweaty face down next to her and whispered in her ear, "Why you tight like this?"

"Beeecaaaause," she strained like I was still hurting her.

"Because why?"

"Because I've been waiting on you to come satisfy me with this amazing dick you got, that's why."

I sped up the pace as I felt her body responding. "How long have you waited for this?"

"Too long," she moaned as a tear fell from her eyes. "So long, I'm embarrassed to tell you."

A few moments later, Ginger screamed and finally came. I still had something left in me, so I rolled her over on top and swayed my hand from one breast to the other. Feeling how hard I was, she tried to ease off me but I wouldn't let her. I held her hips and helped her move to a rhythm I was comfortable with. And after a nice long ride together, we were both exhausted.

Ginger dropped her head down on my chest and let out a sigh. "Kiley, you can't be coming over here getting down with me like this and expect me not to have any feelings for you. This is crazy and you know it."

"I know. And I appreciate you taking care of my needs, but I have some other things I need to work out right now. I'm only being honest with you when I tell you that I don't have time for a serious relationship."

"So, what do you want from me? Do you want me to just be here for you when you need somebody to screw?"

"No, I'm not saying that. All I'm saying is I can't give you what you want. I'm too confused. If anything, I don't want you in the middle of this mess between Jada and me. Last time, you were the one who got hurt and I don't want to do that to you again."

Ginger let out a deep sigh. "Well, I guess I need to decide if I want more from you than just sex. But sexually, you're extremely good. Question is, is it 'good' enough for me to forget about all the other qualities I want in a man?"

Ginger lay silent for a while, then rose up off me. She went into the bathroom and closed the door. I moved over to the couch, lit a joint, and used my cell phone to call home. When no one answered, I called Kareem on his cell phone.

"Yeah," he said, answering with an attitude.

"What's up?"

"Nothing. Nothing at all. Just feeling like a million dollars after dumping a nigga's body in the river."

My heart dropped. "Did he . . . ?"

He laughed. "Naw, fool. He's at the hospital though. They said he lost a lot of blood so they kept him."

"Why do you play so much, Kareem? You need to stop that shit, especially at a time like this."

"Fuck you, man! I'm trying to put some humor to all this bullshit that's been going on with you. You my damn blood and you keeping too much shit from me. I don't like it one damn bit!"

"I know and understand how you feel. So, calm down. I'll be home tonight and we can talk then. Is everything else cool?"

"Yeah, so far. Quincy and me been kind of wondering what's going with you."

"Well, I'll be there tonight. And I got a surprise for you brothas."

"What? I hope it's some twat. Since you scared our booty away earlier, ain't no telling when them bitches coming back this way again."

"Naw, it's better than twat."

"Only thing better than twat is money. And I'm not overly thrilled by something I already got."

"Oh, trust me, you will be thrilled. I'll see ya later. Peace."

"Deuces." Kareem hung up.

When Ginger got out of the shower, I asked her if I could take Desmon home with me. She fussed about it for a while, saying that she was worried about my sudden change; but when I reminded her how much she'd been coming down on me for not spending time with him, she agreed to let him go with me.

At eight o'clock, I woke Desmon up and put on his brown suede jacket and pants Ginger bought him at the flea market. She put on his tan boppy hat and boots, and when I tilted his hat to the side, she smacked my hand and put it on his head straight. "He ain't no thug, Kiley."

I turned his hat back to the side. "I didn't say he was. He just looks more like me when it's that way, so leave it alone."

Ginger kissed Desmon at the door and hugged him like she was never going to see him again. Her eyes even watered as we walked to the car waving at her. I buckled him up tight in the back seat, and after four years, my brothas were about to see what had really been keeping me on the right track more than anything.

CHAPTER 7

I stopped by the grocery store on Gravois and bought Desmon some chocolate ice cream before we headed home. For a four-year-old he was awfully quiet, and when I tried to make conversation with him, he didn't say much. I couldn't complain because I was quiet my damn self as a kid. Just kind of observed things a lot and was a fast learner.

When we pulled into the garage and got out of the car, Quincy opened the back door for us. He was trying to fry some chicken in some fishy-smelling leftover grease on the stove while Veronica sat at the kitchen table and watched. When Quincy saw Desmon, he moved the skillet off the fire and looked down at him. Desmon took his hat off and held it in his hand as I stood behind him with my hand on his shoulder.

"What's up, playa?" Quincy said, holding his hand out for Desmon to give him five. Desmon smiled and slapped Quincy's hand. "What's your name?"

"Desmon Jermaine Abrams," he said softly.

Quincy looked puzzled and scratched his head. "Aw, that's a cool name."

I massaged Desmon on his shoulders then looked at Quincy. "Where's Kareem?"

"He upstairs taking a nap. He told me to wake him up when you got here. But, uh, you babysitting for one of your ladies or something?"

"Naw, nothing like that." I looked at Veronica and put my hand out to shake hers. "Hey, sorry. I don't want to be rude but how you doing?"

"I'm fine, Kiley, and how about yourself?"

"Cool. Couldn't be better."

"That's good. And your son looks just like you. He is really adorable."

Quincy cocked his head back, then frowned at Veronica. "Woman, that ain't his son." He took a double look at Desmon then gazed at me. "Is he?"

"Meet me upstairs in about five minutes; I got something I need to holla at you about." I turned to Veronica again. "Nice seeing you, Veronica, take care and do yourself a favor: don't eat that shit he's cooking. Smells horrible, wouldn't you say?"

She laughed, and Desmon and me headed upstairs to Kareem's room. When I knocked on his door, I yelled for him to meet me upstairs in five minutes.

Desmon ran straight to the pinball machines as I sat down on the couch and flipped on the TV. I called Ginger to let her know we'd made it home so she wouldn't worry. As I hung up, Kareem and Quincy were coming up the steps.

Kareem glanced at Desmon playing the pinball machines then plopped down on the couch. "What, you babysitting for women now?" he asked. Desmon turned his head and looked at Kareem as he talked. Kareem stared at him with confusion on his face. "Man, don't tell me. That . . . that kid looks like you. More so, like me."

"Okay, if you don't want me to tell you then I won't, but, yes, that's my son."

"Get the fuck out of here," Kareem said with his mouth wide open. "When did this shit take place?"

"I know, man, please help my ass understand. Is he from L.A.?" Quincy asked.

"Nope. Born and raised in East St. Louis. Right when we moved here I met this chick named Ginger. Hit that a few times, and bam!" I pointed to Desmon. "That's what came of it. So, my Saturday runs have been all about going to see him. When Jada followed me the other day, she thought I was kicking it with another female, when in reality I was with Desmon."

"So, you kept *my* nephew a secret all this time because you didn't want that bitch Jada to know?" Kareem yelled.

"Man, take your hand off your chest and chill. I was just trying to keep peace in my relationship. Eventually I was going to tell everybody, but the timing was never right, so I waited."

"Waited for what? He ain't no baby or nothing, Kiley. As much as Daddy taught us about the importance of family, I'm quite disappointed in you, big brother."

"Yeah, man," Quincy said. "No matter what, you should have told us."

"You niggas starting to sound like Ginger. I don't feel good about keeping him a secret, but my biggest concern was just being there for him." I called for Desmon to come over by us, as he seemed to be occupied playing with the pinball machine. He stood in front of me, looking shy with his finger in his mouth. I turned him around facing Quincy and Kareem. "Desmon, these are your uncles, Kareem and Quincy. If you need anything, and I mean anything, these are the fellas you need to see if I'm not around, all right?"

Desmon nodded.

"And as long as you stick with me," Kareem said, moving over next to him, "I'll teach you everything you need to know about—"

"Man, don't start, all right? Too early for him to be learning the game," I interrupted.

"Too early? I was talking about teaching him how to play video games."

"Bullshit, man." Quincy laughed. "But, Desmon, if you really want to be a genius, I'm the man who can teach you, all right? Kareem can teach you how to be a playa, that's it."

Desmon smiled at both of them and went back over to the pinball machine.

Kareem put a pillow under his head and lay back on the couch, looking up at the ceiling. "I apologize for what I said, Kiley, but I thought I would be the first one to have a kid." He lifted his head up. "Let me clear that up—a son. Not a daughter, but a son." He laid his head back down on the pillow, then folded his hands together. "I'm proud of you, though, just hope you never put pussy before parenting again."

I leaned back on the couch and spread my arms out over the top. "Never. It was stupid of me to do it to begin with but now that it's out in the open, I feel so much better. Ginger is going to have a fit, but I would like for him to live here with us."

Quincy took his bandana off and scratched his head. "Do you really think that's a good idea? I mean, right now, things kinda shaky. Wouldn't you agree?"

"Yeah, but you can't have better protection than what you have in this room right now. Ain't nothing going to happen to him as long as I'm around."

Kareem turned on his side and looked down at the floor. "Don't let him move in with us just yet, Kiley. Wait until some of this bullshit clears the air. More than anything, I'd hate to have him around if something bad goes down like it did between you and Donovan. Anyway, why did you shoot that fool? I knew there was a bunch of animosity stirring between y'all, but damn, was it necessary?"

"Muh-fucker slept with Jada behind my back. Then had the nerve to remove shit from this house and take it to her. Honestly, if she was here when I found out, I would have killed her ass, no doubt about it."

Quincy started shaking his head. "Now that's some foul shit. I would have shot his ass too. He deserved to die, knowing how tight you and Jada were."

"Don't go putting all the blame on Donovan," Kareem said, sitting up. "Now, by all means, that nigga was wrong. But that dick sucking ho was at fault just as much as he was. I wish you would have shot that . . . All I can say is I hate that bitch, Kiley. More than anybody on this fucking earth.

If you ever get back with her ass I'm disowning you."

"Don't worry, I won't. A part of me hates her too, especially after everything I did for her." I put my hands on my face and massaged my beard. "Listen, what hospital did y'all take Donovan to?"

"Barnes Hospital on Kingshighway. Why?" Kareem asked.

"'Cause I guess I'd better go make sure he's okay, huh?"

"Man, fuck that nigga," Quincy said. "He deserved what he got."

"I agree, but he still my boy. And because I refuse to let pussy overtake partna, I think I'd better go."

"Suit yourself," Kareem said. "I'm staying my black ass right here."

"Me too. If you wanna go, you go alone. Besides, I got Veronica waiting downstairs for me to finish up this scrumptious dinner I'm cooking."

"I thought you wasn't interested in Veronica," I said.

"I never told you I wasn't interested. I told you if you wanted to holler, then go ahead and do so. Since you didn't make a move, I invited her over because I was bored. So, tell me now. Are you interested or not?"

I shook my head. "Naw. Knock yourself out.
All this going behind each other bullshit is going
to get somebody seriously hurt. Being a snake
doesn't fit well into my vocabulary."

"Okay, don't say I didn't offer. And as far as I'm
concerned, snake or not, if you see something
you like, have at it. The only reason Donovan
fucked up is because he knew the severity of yo'
relationship with Jada. Me, there would be no
love lost."

I stood up, and when I called for Desmon to
come with me, Kareem told me to leave him
there with him and Quincy. Said he wasn't too
cool about his nephew going to see a traitor. I
hugged Desmon and told the fellas I'd be back as
soon as possible.

When I got to the hospital, the nurse told me
Donovan had just gotten out of surgery. Since
she said it would be a short while before they set
him up in a room, I went to go take a seat in the
waiting room. As I opened the door, I saw Tricia
sitting in a chair with her arms folded, while
looking up at the TV on the wall. Curious to find
out how much she knew about the incident, I
eased over in the chair next to her. She quickly
turned around.

"Hey, Kiley," she said, hugging me. "I was wondering when y'all were going to show up."

"Yeah, uh, Kareem and Quincy were the ones who brought him here. They had to leave to go take care of something for me. I came as fast as I could."

"Well, I'm sure he'll be glad to know you're here."

"So, have you had a chance to see him yet?"

"Yes, after Kareem called and told me what happened, I got here just in time for his surgery. He was kind of out of it but he was glad to see me."

"I see," I said, rubbing my head. "So Kareem was the one who called and told you what happened?"

"Yes. He called me when him and Quincy were leaving the hospital. Told me Donovan accidentally shot himself in the shoulder."

I sighed with relief. "I yelled at Don all the time for playing around with his gun. I knew some shit like this was going to happen."

"I know. He takes that damn thing everywhere he goes. Scares the hell out of me. But in the shoulder, that's a difficult spot to shoot yourself, don't you think?"

"Kinda. But who knows how it happened? I'm sure Donovan will tell us all about it."

Tricia and me continued talking as we waited for Donovan to get set up in a room. I paced the floors for a while, thinking about how I had to see him first before anybody started asking questions. Kareem seemed to be ahead of the game more than me, so I decided on sticking with the same damn story. Hopefully, upset or not, Donovan would agree to it and this mess between us would be over.

As I stood at the vending machine getting Tricia and me a soda, I saw Candi walking up to the nurse's station. I was sure she was looking for Donovan, so I rushed through the doors to talk to her before Tricia saw her.

"What's up, Candi," I said, walking toward her.

"Hi, Kiley. Kareem said you'd be here. How's Donovan?"

"He cool," I said, moving in another direction. "So, you talked to Kareem?"

"Yeah, I did. I called for Donovan and Kareem told me what happened. He also told me I could find you here so I came as fast as I could." She smiled, turned around, and started toward the waiting room. When she walked in, Tricia turned around in her chair and checked Candi out from head to toe. I gave Tricia her soda, and when I sat down next to her, Candi sat in the chair next to me.

I leaned back in my chair and introduced them so they could speak to one another. Tricia held her hand out for Candi to shake it. "Hi, Candi. I'm Donovan's girlfriend."

Candi shook her hand. "Hello, Tricia. I'm a good friend of Donovan's."

Tricia eased her hand away from Candi's and looked at me. I stared up at the TV and didn't say a word.

A few minutes later, Candi stood up and went over to the vending machine to get a soda. Tricia whispered to me asking what kind of friend Candi was to Donovan. I shrugged and said she was just a friend. Feeling uncomfortable, I got up and went to the restroom to call Kareem and curse him out for trying to cause trouble. When he answered the phone he was laughing, because I'm sure he was waiting on my call.

"Why you playing games, Kareem?"

"What? Nigga, I have no idea what you're talking about."

"Yes, you do. You were hoping these two would be up in here scrappin', weren't you?"

"Man, look. Candi called looking for Donovan and I told her where she could find him. I just didn't want you being at the hospital all alone, that's all."

"Whatever. Where's Desmon?"

"He's in my room with me listening to some music. I'm teaching him how to dance."

"Nigga, you can't dance. Don't be teaching him to make a damn spectacle of himself."

"Naw, actually, he's teaching me how to dance. He don't talk too much but he sure know how to dance. Doesn't surprise me, since he's family and all."

"You just don't get enough, do you? Where's Quincy? Is Veronica still there?"

"Naw, she gone. After we all choked on that greasy nasty-ass chicken he fried, she left."

"You didn't feed any of that shit to Desmon, did you?"

"Nope, he had sense. After one look at it, he turned it down."

"That's my boy. Definitely knows when something ain't right. Well, I'll be back in an hour or so. They taking forever to put Donovan in a room, so we're just sitting around waiting."

"So Tricia and Candi didn't even slap each other around?"

"Nope. None of that bullshit is going down, so that's what you get for trying to cause trouble."

"Damn, but I'm sure when Jada get there all hell is going to break loose." He laughed.

"What do you mean by when Jada gets here?"

"I mean, she called asking if she could come get her things and when I told her that her delivery boy shot himself, she asked me where he was. I told her, so don't be alarmed if you see her. And it would really hurt me to my heart if you would just fuck her up one last time for me."

"Kareem, you need to think before you do shit. Are you trying to get my ass locked up?"

"No, I just want you to be a man for once in your life and give that bitch what she deserves."

Before I said something to Kareem that I was going to regret, I just said, "Holla. I'll see ya later."

"Deuces, and don't do nothing I wouldn't do." Kareem hung up.

To no surprise at all, when I came out of the restroom, Jada was standing in the waiting area talking to Tricia. The sight of her weakened me, but I couldn't forget about all she'd done to me. I took a deep breath and went into the waiting area. She looked over at me, then continued her conversation with Tricia. I wanted to grab her ass and fuck her up for what she'd done but I couldn't. Now wasn't the time or the place, so I chilled.

I sat in a chair across the room from them, and Candi stood up and came over by me. She put her purse on the floor and sat down in the chair next to me. "You don't mind if I sit here, do you?" she asked.

"No, not at all. You can sit wherever you'd like."

"Good. And I guess you wouldn't mind me telling you that I didn't come here to see Donovan. I came here to see you."

I massaged my beard and rubbed my bald head. Wrong place, wrong time. "Candi, stop by the house later to talk to me. I came here to make sure everything is cool with Donovan, not to be sitting here talking about you and me."

"I don't mind coming by the house later, but I'm sure you'll find a reason not to talk to me then. Question is, when are you going to stop putting me off like you do? I can tell how much you like me. Doesn't make sense for you to keep trippin', especially when things didn't work out with you and Jada."

"And how do you know things didn't work out with Jada and me? Never mind, let me guess; Kareem, right?"

"Kareem told me, but Donovan told me, too. So, what's holding you back now?"

When I looked up, Jada was staring Candi and me down like a bloodhound. I could see the fire burning in her eyes, not knowing what Candi and I were talking about. Candi leaned forward, staring at me with her hand pressed against her face, waiting for an answer.

"Ain't nothing holding me back, Candi. I just need more time. Why don't you leave and come by the house later. We'll talk about it then."

"I don't believe you, Kiley. Furthermore, I don't think you're going to be there if I stop by. I get the feeling you're trying to avoid me." Candi lifted her hand and rubbed it against the side of my face where my stitches were. "Come walk me to my car. I'll leave, but you better be available for me tonight." Catching me off guard, she leaned forward and pecked me on the lips. Shocked, I backed away.

Just then I saw Jada coming our way.

"Excuse me, I see this bitch didn't waste any time digging her claws into you. All I want to know is when can I come pick my shit up? Every time I call your stupid-ass brother be playing games with me, and I'm getting sick and tired of it."

Candi gave Jada a fake smile, then wiped her lipstick off my lips. I grabbed her hand away from my lips and laid it down on my lap. "Jada, feel free to stop by and get your shit any time. Actually, the sooner the better. I got plans tonight, so if you'd like to stop by in the morning, cool. I'll have as much of your stuff packed as I can so you don't have to stay long."

I stood up, and Candi did as well, picking her purse up off the floor. As we started to walk away, Jada grabbed me by my injured arm. A sharp pain quickly rushed through it and I bit down on my lip. "Jada, don't grab my arm like that again. Don't think I won't fuck you up in this hospital, because I will."

She put her hand on her hip and started rolling her neck around. "And don't think I'm going to sit here and let you disrespect me like this either. Haven't you had enough of cheating on me? That's why your face all fucked up and your arm is in that damn sling now, because you couldn't keep your dick in your damn pants."

Candi pulled me away because she knew I was about to get myself in some serious trouble. "Kiley, come on. She ain't even worth it, baby. Let's go," she said calmly.

Jada took a few steps, standing face to face with Candi. "Stay out of this, bitch! This has nothing to do with you, so take your trifling ass home, would you?"

Everybody in the waiting area was staring us down, and as soon as Jada started talking some more shit, Candi smacked her hard on her face. Before Jada could hit her back, I quickly intervened and pushed her back in a chair behind her.

"Look, why don't you quit trippin'? I said come get your things tomorrow. Now chill."

"Naw, move, Kiley. This ho crazy if she thinks I'm going to let her put her damn hands on me." Jada tried to push me back so she could get at Candi, but when I looked at Candi and told her to leave, she didn't hesitate. Tricia came over and asked Jada to calm down. People sitting in the waiting area were shaking their heads like we were some ghetto, out-of-control niggas. Embarrassed, I went outside to look for Candi, but she was already gone.

As I walked back into the hospital, Tricia was on her way out.

"Tricia, where are you going? I thought you were going to stay to see Donovan."

"I'm going home, Kiley. Tell Donovan I don't have time to be up in here with his whores. Y'all need to stop the games and appreciate a good woman when you got one." She walked away.

I stood there, knowing Jada must have fed Tricia some bullshit about Candi. Sick and tired of her mess, I rushed back into the hospital to set the record straight with her. I saw her sitting in a chair, and grabbed her out of it. "Come on, we need to talk," I said, pulling her outside by the arm.

"We don't have a damn thing to talk about," she fussed, trying to tug away from me. "You fucked up and you know it. Don't try to talk to me now about the bullshit."

I shoved her against a wall outside the hospital. Luckily no one was around, so I quickly tore into her. "Listen, I'm not trying to get back with you, Jada. I saw the pictures and the letters you gave to Donovan, so what we had is over. When you followed me the other day, I was visiting my son. I had a son four years ago when you were in L.A. trying to figure out if you wanted to come live with me since you'd been fucking around with Donovan." Jada's eyes bugged and she was speechless. "Yeah, baby, that's right. I recently found out you were fucking around with him. So I would never want your ass back. After you come get your stuff, I never want to see you again and I mean that shit!"

Jada pursed her lips. "So, the best lie you can come up with is to say that you were visiting your son? What kind of fool do you take me for, Kiley? If you were cheating on me that's all you have to say. You got busted, so fuck it."

"I really don't care what you believe. I was faithful to your ass whether you believe it or not. You fucked this shit up. Not me, you did. A search for another brotha like me is going to be tough, so good luck. And like I said before, the faster you come get your shit, the better." I gave her a hard stare and headed back into the hospital.

"Kiley!" Jada yelled. "What happened between Donovan and me was a long time ago. He was there for me when you kept seeing other bitches while we were in L.A. How dare you treat me like I'm the one who fucked this up!"

I didn't even respond, just kept on walking. I stopped by the nurses' station to ask what was taking so long, and after standing there for fifteen more minutes, they told me Donovan's room was ready.

I opened the door and he was sitting up in bed, staring at the TV that wasn't even turned on. His shoulder was wrapped and IVs were running through his hands. When he saw me coming into the room, he turned his head and gave me a look as if he wanted to jump out of bed and kick my ass. Before he could say anything, I sat down in a chair next to him and apologized for what I'd done. He raised his bed up higher so he could sit up and talk to me.

"No need to apologize, especially when you have no regrets," he said, looking back up at the TV.

"You're right. I don't regret it, but the thought of me putting pussy before partner is what bothers me."

"Well, if you're here for me to make you feel better about what you did, I suggest you go elsewhere for comfort. I admit sleeping with Jada was wrong, but shooting me was taking shit to the extreme. What if I had died? Would you be standing over my casket apologizing right now knowing that I wouldn't be able to hear you? Or would you be at home thinking about how you should have handled this situation a li'l better?"

I shrugged. "Man, I handled the situation as best as I could. I was in major shock when I saw her pictures and read those letters she wrote to you. So since my pride got hurt, somebody else deserved to get hurt too. Just sorry it had to be you."

"Whatever, man. You took this shit too far and you know it. Aside of what went down between Jada and me, you never liked my ass anyway. I could always tell you were closer to Rufus and Quincy; that's why I moved to St. Louis. But when I realized I couldn't make it without you niggas around, that's when I asked y'all to move here. A part of me wished I would have just moved on, but I'm tired of running, honestly thought I was here to stay for good. Now, after what happened between you and me, I'm out again. Everybody feeling betrayed by me, when I was just trying to be there for a sista who longed for some attention."

"Man, I know you probably thought you were 'being there' for Jada, but in reality all you was trying to do was get laid. Remember, that's what you told me when I confronted you about it. Bottom line is Jada played us against each other. Sad to say, we fell for it." I stood up, looked out of the window, and then slid my hand into my pocket. "I didn't come here to talk about Jada. What's done is done. I just came here to apologize for something at the time I felt like I had to do."

Donovan snickered. "Well, if shooting me was your only alternative, that's too bad. I almost lost my life over some bullshit, and frankly, I'm not too damn happy about it. I'm sure Kareem and Quincy have sided with you, and the last thing I want to do is live in a place where I'm not welcome."

"Suit yourself. You don't have to move out, but if you think it's best, then I can't stop you. In the meantime, you might wanna know that Jada came up here trippin'. When she saw Candi and Tricia in the waiting room, she managed to let the cat out of the bag about you and Candi. Tricia left here pretty damn upset."

"Well, you know how that is. The truth always comes to the light. But, no trip. I'll call Tricia and work things out with her later. If you and the fellas wouldn't mind gathering up my shit for me I'd appreciate it. I'd like to move out when I leave the hospital in a couple of days."

"Only if you'll be willing to do me a favor. And remember, I'm working with one hand now so I'll do what I can about packing."

"Thanks to you I'll be working with one arm too. So, what's the favor?"

"I'd like to keep this incident on the down low as much as possible. Everybody kinda thinks you shot yourself in the shoulder. They have no idea what really happened between us."

"Hey, who am I going to tell, the police? Tell you what; as long as you pack my things up for me, maybe this shit is squashed. For now, the only worry I have is calling my woman and buttering her up so she'll let me move in with her."

I reached out for Donovan's hand and he took it. "I hope we can squash this, but I know you too well, man. You get a pleasure out of retaliation."

He released my hand. "Maybe I do, or maybe I don't. That's just a chance you're going to have to take."

"Don't get yourself involved in something you can't handle. My past history proves I never lose. I'd hate to see us go out like that, but if you want to hold a grudge that's all on you. Good luck to you, my brotha. And if things don't work out for you, you'll always have a place to come back to." I headed for the door.

"Kiley?"

"What's up?"

"I'm sure after I work things out with Tricia I'm going to have to put Candi on the back burner. Would you mind keeping her occupied for me until things cool down?"

I looked at him and winked. "If I keep her occupied, she'll never come back. If you're willing to give her up, it better be for good."

"Well, do your thang, my brotha." He grinned. "You seem to be the head nigga in charge, so do whatever works best for you."

I turned and walked out the door.

It was way after midnight by the time I got home. When I knocked on Kareem's bedroom door, Desmon and him were in his bed sound asleep. I'd already stopped by Quincy's bedroom, and since the door was closed and I heard laughter, I didn't interrupt. I picked Desmon up and carried him into my room. Kareem was so out of it he didn't even hear me come in. After I laid Desmon in my bed, he went right back to sleep.

And before I got in bed myself, I called Ginger to let her know everything was cool and Desmon was staying the night with me. She was a li'l cold to the idea, but when I promised to bring him back tomorrow, she thanked me for being there for him, and hung up the phone.

Knowing that Jada would probably be over as early as possible to get her things, I stayed up until three in the morning packing them up for her. It was painful, but I knew ending it with her was in my best interest.

From what I could see, Candi had called several times throughout the night, but I didn't have the desire to call her back. She was right about me not being available for her, but I just wasn't in the mood to deal with her just yet.

CHAPTER 8

I rolled over in bed and looked at the monitor, only to see Quincy open the back door for Jada. I told him and Kareem she would probably be coming through this morning to pick up her shit, and asked them to keep things cool with her. With her being here at seven o'clock in the morning, I guess she couldn't wait to get on my bad side and ruin the rest of my day. I pulled the covers over my head and pretended like I was sleep when she came in the bedroom. The door was closed and she didn't even have the decency to knock. She turned on the lights as if the light that was shining through the window wasn't bright enough. Then she pulled the cover off Desmon and me.

"Uh, so, who is this, Kiley?" she asked, standing beside the bed with her hands on her hips.

I sat up on the bed, stretching my arms. "Who did I tell you he was?" Desmon opened his eyes and sat up on the bed. I turned around and looked at him. "Desmon, go wake your Uncle Kareem up. Tell him to go downstairs and fix you a bowl of cereal." I reached over and gave him a kiss. He hopped down off the bed and headed to Kareem's room. Jada watched him as he walked by her.

"You kept him a secret from me all this time? He's about five or six ain't he?"

"Four, but that ain't none of your business anymore. You came to get your things, so hurry up and get them so you can go." I made my way to the bathroom to avoid her.

"I can't believe you, Kiley. You've been messing around with some other woman all this time and treat me like I hurt you so damn bad. I did what I had to do based on what I saw. If you would have just—"

"Jada!" I yelled. "Please. I'm not going to explain myself to you anymore. No fucking need to, you understand? Okay, so I was wrong for not telling you. Now what? My not being honest with you about my son doesn't compare to you sleeping with my damn friend. And stop making it like it was such a long time ago when you crept into his room and fucked him less than a year ago."

Jada's eyes widened and she shook her head. "No, it wasn't even like that. He came to me at a vulnerable moment when I was upset with you.

He knew I always loved you, Kiley. I never loved him. I only slept with him to get back at you. I gave him those pictures and wrote those letters hoping you would find them. I was hoping that just maybe your jealousy would kick in and you'd realize what you were missing. I didn't expect Donovan to keep that stuff all this time."

"Yeah, yeah, whatever, Jada. You act like I was fucking everything in sight back in L.A. I was young and didn't realize what I had, but after I did, you kept it going with Donovan, so don't sit here and make up shit to justify your own damn mistakes. Just admit it."

Kareem and Desmon came into the room. Kareem looked at Jada and rolled his eyes, then looked at me. "Hey, my man here wants some cereal. Ain't no cereal. I ate the last of it a few days ago."

"Well, find him something else to eat. I need to finish talking to Jada for a minute."

"Better yet, hand me his clothes over there. We'll go to the grocery store and get us some for-real-ass breakfast food," Kareem said.

I picked Desmon's clothes up off the chair and gave them to Kareem.

"Thank you, sir. And don't be up in here busting nobody's head while I'm gone. If you do, make sure the white meat shows, and wait until I get back so I can watch." He laughed.

Jada gave Kareem a fake smile. "Ha, ha, funny, Kareem. You're a stupid motherfu—"

He pointed at her. "Watch your mouth, bitch. I was talking to my brother. I wasn't talking to you."

Jada started toward Kareem. I stood in between them to keep them apart.

"I ain't gon' be too many of your bitches, Kareem," Jada spat.

I sighed. "Kareem, let it go. Just go to the store and hurry back."

"I will, but make sure this bitch out of here when I get back."

"Fuck you, you silly-ass—"

I turned and snapped at Jada. "Shut up and get your things and go. I didn't ask you to come over here and disrespect my family. At least have some respect for my son." I turned to Kareem again. "Go. Desmon don't need to be around all this mess."

Kareem left, mumbling something underneath his breath. I walked around the room, gathering my things to take a shower.

"Do you think you can help me take some of this stuff to my car?" Jada asked with an attitude.

"No, I don't think I can. I packed most of it with one hand, so helping you take it to your car is out of the question."

I went to the doorway and yelled for Quincy. He opened his bedroom door and looked down the hallway at me. "Would you come help Jada take her things to her car?"

"I guess," he said, walking down the hallway. When he picked up a few bags off the floor, I went into the bathroom and closed the door.

I stayed in the shower for as long as I could. Then I shaved, put on my Gucci jogging suit, and patted my face with some aftershave. When it sounded like the coast was clear, I came out of the bathroom. Jada was sitting in the chair reading a magazine with her feet propped up on the bed.

She lowered the magazine so she could see me. "Where are you getting ready to go?"

I took my gun from underneath my pillow and slid it down inside my pants. Then I reached for my sling and put it on my arm since it was still bothering me. "Are you ready to go? Because I'm getting ready to leave."

"I asked where you were going, Kiley."

I ignored her and put my cell phone in my pocket. "Let's go."

"Where are we going?"

"You're leaving. And I got some business to take care of."

Jada laid the magazine on the floor, closed the door, and came over close to me. "Look, I'm sorry, okay? I was wrong for sleeping with your friend, but you left me no choice."

I lightly pushed her over to the side and opened the door. "Apology accepted. Now, let's go."

She plopped down on the bed and rubbed her hair back with her hands. "Kiley, I don't want to leave like this. But if you tell me there's somebody else, I guess I have no choice."

I let out a sigh. "Jada, there's no one else. This has nothing to do with anyone else; it's about you and me. You played me, baby. I loved you more than anything in the world, did everything for you, and you played me like a damn fool."

"Okay, so we both messed up. But is this worth losing our twelve-year relationship over? Can we at least be friends?"

"With friends like you, who needs enemies? Let's just walk away from this with what li'l respect we have left for each other. Now, I got a run to make, so you gotta jet." I held the door open but she still didn't budge.

I left out of the room and Jada followed. I stood in the doorway to Quincy's room and looked at him leaning back in a leather chair listening to some music with a headset on. His eyes were closed and the music was so loud he couldn't hear me. I reached for the volume knob and turned it up. He quickly opened his eyes and took the headset off his ears. "Damn, brotha, what you trying to do? Bust my damn eardrum or something?"

"Naw, playa. Just making sure it was loud enough for you. Say, I'm going to go see about my car. Tell Kareem and Desmon I'll be back as soon as I can."

"Will do. I got a few runs to make myself, but if I leave before they get back I'll leave them a note."

Jada poked her head in Quincy's door. "Thanks for helping me with my things, Quincy."

"Aw, no problem, Jada. Glad to be of assistance." Quincy winked.

"Tell Kareem if he needs me to hit me on my phone," I said.

Quincy put the headset back on and continued listening to music.

Jada followed me down the stairs. I opened the back door, turned the lock, and closed it behind her as she walked out. Whoever's car she was driving was parked outside the gate in back of the house. How quickly she had gotten a car kinda puzzled me, but I wasn't prying. She could have sold or pawned the expensive things

that Donovan took to her the other day to buy
a car. Really not giving a fuck, I opened the
garage door so I could leave. She was damn near
walking on the back of my shoes trying to work
my nerves. When I tried to open the car door,
she slammed it back and stood in front of it with
her arms folded.

"When are you going to listen to anything that
I've said to you?"

"I have listened. There's nothing else to talk
about, so move."

She reached up and placed her hand on my
face. "Baby, please don't do this to us. We've
come such a long way together and I don't know
what I would do without you in my life." A tear
rolled down her face.

"You'll soon find out, Jada. Go back to L.A.
According to you, you hate living in St. Louis.
Go back to your whack-ass family and your
jealous, conniving-ass friends. You'll fit right
back in." I tried to push her over to the side but
she still wouldn't move. "Come on now, Jada.
Quit playing games so I can go."

"Damn it! This ain't no game. I love you,"
she cried. "I don't want you with anybody else.
Would you please forgive me? I promise you
things will get better. No more lies, and now that
everything's out in the open, nothing can come
between us."

Jada leaned against me and kissed me on the lips. Feeling a li'l sympathy for her, foolishly, I wrapped my arm around her waist and sucked her lips into mine. As I felt our connection, I eased my hand down over her plump ass and squeezed it with my hand. And after my dick hardened from the thought of fucking her, I pushed her back against the garage wall, pressing my hardness against her. I dropped my head, kissing her on the neck, feeling guilty about wanting her so much.

She lifted my face up and stared me in the eyes. "I'm at the Radisson on Lindbergh. Come there tonight. I'll make it up to you."

I closed my eyes, trying to fight back my feelings for her. "We'll see." I backed away from her. "Maybe, all right?"

She placed her lips on mine again, then backed away. "I need a definite answer. I know more than anybody how you say you'll do one thing but you do another. Will you please come so we can talk sensibly about this?"

"Yeah, Jada. I'll be there by seven o'clock tonight. I need to go see about my car right now, though, okay?"

She smiled and wiped another tear from her face. "I'll let you get going, but again, I'm sorry for hurting you. I never intended for things to go this far."

"Me either." I opened the car door and got in. I watched Jada through my rearview mirror as she got in her car and drove off.

I could barely concentrate on the drive to Al's place. Fucking Jada was heavy on my mind, and how stupid I was for telling her I would see her tonight. I knew it would be a big mistake, but I just wasn't strong enough to kick her to the curb like I thought I could. She was definitely, without a doubt, my weakness. And she knew it. She knew no matter what she did to me, I would always run back to her. Why? I couldn't even figure it out my damn self. This wasn't love; it was stupid love. And the worst of it was this love was going to interfere with Kareem's and my brothaship. He'd probably disown me if I ever got back with Jada. He would somehow feel I chose her over him, and if I even thought about explaining it to him how I really felt, he wouldn't understand.

By the time I left Al's place with my new, shiny, fixed-up Lexus, it was almost two in the afternoon. Ginger had been calling me like crazy, asking me to bring Desmon home, and I told her that after we came from the movies, I would drop him off. I stopped by Macy's and picked him up a new outfit, and then called Kareem to tell him I was on my way home. He said he'd given Desmon a bath and bragged about how delicious the breakfast he cooked was. When I told him I was taking Desmon to the movies, he said since Quincy was gone he'd tag along to go holla at the ladies.

Keeping close tabs on the time, I found myself rushing so I could get to Jada by seven. When I pulled up in the garage, I grabbed the Macy's bag and ran up the steps to the back door. Kareem was standing in the living room on the phone, smiling.

"Hold on, Candi, here he is."

I shook my head and whispered, "Tell her I'm not here."

"Yeah, hold on." He laughed and gave the phone to me.

I handed him the bag and pushed his shoulder. Then I took the phone. "What's up?"

"I knew you were going to play me last night. What does a sista have to do to get a little of your time?"

"Be patient, that's all."

"Patient? I've been patient long enough. I know you're going to the movies with Kareem, can I tag along?"

"Naw, I got my son with me today. Listen, I'll call you when I get back, all right?"

"Kiley, look, if you want me to back off, then I will. Just say the word. Don't lead me on telling me you'll call me and you'll see me soon when you have no intentions on doing so."

"I said I'll call you later, Candi."

"Sure. But if you don't—"

"If I don't, I just don't," I said, frowning.

Candi took a deep breath and hung up.

I put the phone down and went upstairs to change Desmon's clothes. He was jumping up and down on Kareem's bed with his new dark blue and white velvet sweat suit on. Kareem had already changed his clothes for me. Since he didn't have his shoes on, I grabbed them off Kareem's dresser and sat down on the bed. Kareem was in the bathroom brushing his teeth.

"Come on, Desmon," I said, pulling him down next to me. "Let me put your shoes on."

He stopped jumping and sat on the bed next to me. Kareem came out of the bathroom with a toothbrush hanging out of his mouth mumbling something.

"What? I can't understand you with that thing in your mouth."

He went back into the bathroom and rinsed his mouth. He came back out wiping his hands with a towel. "I said I'm trying to make sure my breath is fresh for the ladies." He came over by the bed and blew his breath on me. "Am I cool?"

I leaned back and so did Desmon. "Is he cool, Desmon? Did you smell anything?"

Desmon nodded. "Yes." He smiled.

"Did it smell nasty?" Kareem asked.

"No, it smell like toothpaste."

Kareem held his hand out and Desmon gave him five. Then they did a hand jive Kareem must have taught him to do. "There you go, playa. Keep your breath fresh like your uncle and you'll have all the women."

Desmon grinned and I continued putting on his tennis shoes. Kareem had on his suede black pants with an off-white ribbed sweater, and his black hip-length suede black jacket with white fur around the collar. He covered his eyes with his round, lightly tinted glasses and checked himself out in the mirror.

"Damn I look good." He turned around and looked at me. "Don't I?"

"Nigga, you look a'ight but we just going to the movies. You dressed like we going to the club or something."

"Man, to show you how outdated your ass is, it's more women at the mall than there is at the club. And the best thing about it is that you get a chance to mingle with a diversity of women at the mall. Not just one certain kind."

"Whatever, man, let's just go."

I picked Desmon up off the bed and put him on the floor. Kareem sprayed on some cologne and gave the mirror one last look before we left.

The movie we wanted to see didn't start for another hour so we walked around the mall checking out the latest fashions and the women. Kareem was on cloud nine with the ladies staring at us and was winking at everything that walked by. When he finally saw this shapely brown-skinned sista with fresh-looking twisties and hazelnut eyes like his, he couldn't resist. We stood there talking to her and her girlfriend for about ten minutes. I was trying to keep my eyes on Desmon, so it was hard for Erica to keep me interested. And after Alexis declined Kareem's offer to watch the movie with us and gave him her phone number, we jetted.

By the time we made it back to the movie theatre, Kareem racked up numerous phone numbers. I laughed as we stood in line waiting to get Desmon some popcorn, soda, and candy.

Kareem placed his lips on the papers with the phone numbers, folded them in half, and put them in his pocket. "One of these ladies is going to have an adventurous night tonight."

"With who, you?"

"Yeah, with me, fool. I just have to decide which one."

"Damn, how lucky she must be." I smiled.

"Don't hate, playa. You could be preparing yourself for a night of adventure as well if you'd stop acting all stuck-up like you too good for a sista. They checking you out and you walking by like you gay or something."

"I came to the mall to watch a movie with my son. I had no intentions on picking up women."

"And you think I did."

"Hell, yeah, you did. Dressing like that, spraying on expensive cologne, and pimping through this muh-fucker like you're God's gift to women, you damn right you did."

"Listen, I can't help it if a nigga looking this good. The ladies just can't control themselves when they see me. So what's wrong with me offering them my services?"

"Services, huh?"

"Yeah, services. Just like I'm getting ready to serve that young lady behind you who keep leaning over to the side, trying to check me out."

I turned around and when I looked at her, she smiled. I shook my head as she started coming our way.

"Excuse me. Hi. My name is Toni," she said, shaking Kareem's hand. "My girlfriend over there"—she pointed to her friend who waved at us when we looked—"we were wondering if you fellas wouldn't mind showing us where we might find a good restaurant at around here. See, we're not from here. We're from Atlanta and I was hoping that after the movies we could go somewhere and get a bite to eat."

"We'd love to show you ladies around. Ain't that right, Kiley?" He nudged me.

"Toni, I really don't have time. Maybe Kareem . . ."

Kareem looked at me and rolled his eyes. "My brother is entertaining his son for the day so why don't . . ." He put his arm around Toni's neck and walked off running his game.

After I got Desmon's snacks, we headed to the theatre. Kareem and the two ladies followed closely behind us. When we sat down in the theatre, he sat in between them and Desmon sat next to me. There was an empty seat between one of the chicks and me so I placed our coats there.

Kareem kept the ladies giggling throughout the entire movie. When we left, I agreed to meet them at their hotel later on in the week, and Kareem exchanged phone numbers. As we headed back to the car, I looked at my watch and noticed it was almost seven o'clock. Still anticipating on going to see Jada, I started to rush. And as soon as I drove off the parking lot, Jada was ringing my cell phone. I had to answer. I at least wanted to let her know I was still coming.

"Hello," I said, intending to keep our conversation short so Kareem wouldn't know it was her.

"I really thought you would be here by now. What's taking you so long?"

"I'm just now leaving the movies with Desmon. I'm getting ready to drop him off then I'll be there."

"How long do you think that'll be? I mean, I hope you don't stay long at his house."

"It shouldn't be that long. Maybe another hour or so."

"Kiley, you said seven o'clock. I've been—"

I quickly hung up because Kareem was listening in on every bit of my conversation. "Shit! This phone ain't worth a damn."

"I know, mine be doing the same thing, especially when I'm trying to hook up some booty or something. Seems like the son of a bitch be knowing the plan and cut my ass off right when I'm waiting for an answer." We both laughed. "So," he said, looking at me. "Have you had any Candi lately?"

"I don't eat candy. Bad for your teeth."

"Nigga, don't play. Was that her you were talking to?"

"Naw, that was uh, this . . . this chick I met at Al's shop today."

"Straight. What's her name?"

"Denise."

"Denise? Well, that's cool. Real proud of you for finally moving on and leaving that devil in a fat dress behind."

"Man, don't even be like that. You act like Jada some oversized, unattractive, hateful woman and she's really not."

"Oversized and unattractive? No. Hateful? You damn right she is. Any time she sleeps with your partner, fucks your car up, cuts your face, fractures your wrist, and disrespects your family, she's definitely hateful. Not only that, she's a backstabbing bitch. Just thinking about her just gives my ass the chills."

I just kept my mouth shut.

Kareem looked over at me while I was in deep thought, "Yo, Buckwheat? What's on your mind?"

"Nothing. And who in the hell are you calling Buckwheat?"

"You, nigga, that's who."

"What in the hell does Buckwheat and me have in common?"

"Nothing. I just felt like saying it. Just like I feel like calling you a wuss. Ladies throwing all kinds of pussy at you and you don't even want to catch it. Speaking straight from my heart." Kareem placed his hand on his chest. "I'd say being tied up with Jada so long, you forgot how to lay it on a sista the right way."

I snickered. "And I'd say you're for damn sure wrong. It doesn't take sleeping with several women to learn how to stroke them better. Practicing and experiencing with one woman can teach you everything you need to know, especially if she let you have your way with her."

"I disagree. But you always think big brother knows best, so whatever. And I truly hope you don't mess up the Abrams reputation for laying 'em and laying 'em well." He reached over and backhanded me on my chest.

Kareem and me joked around in the car all the way to Ginger's house. When we pulled up in front of her apartment, he looked at me like I was crazy pulling up to what looked to be the projects from the outside. Desmon had fallen asleep, so I picked him up to carry him inside. I had to beg Kareem to come inside to meet Ginger. He hopped out of the car, complaining about the hood his nephew was living in. When I told him not to judge a book by its cover, as usual, he disagreed.

Ginger opened the door with a hot-pink silk short robe on, and from the clear sight of her breasts showing, I was sure she was wearing nothing underneath. When she saw Kareem leaning against the door next to me, she grabbed her belt and tightened it.

She opened the door wider so we could come in. "Oh, I'm sorry. I thought you were coming by yourself, Kiley."

I stood with Desmon hugging me around my neck, still sleeping, and introduced Ginger to Kareem. After they spoke, I told Kareem to follow me to Desmon's room so he could see how laid out it was. I put Desmon down in his bed and Kareem looked around the room with his hands in his pockets checking it out.

"Now, this is nice. A sports car for a bed. I wish I had some shit like this when I was four. All I remember was cracked walls, spider webs, the smell of your funky dirty socks, and roaches."

"You're silly. And those were your dirty-ass socks and you know it. Funny, though, how kids these days just don't know how good they got it."

As I pulled the cover over Desmon and kissed him, Kareem tapped me on the shoulder, whispering, "Say, what's up with Ginger? She pretty tight."

"She cool."

"Cool, huh? That's all you see is coolness?"

"Evidentially I see more than that if we have a child together."

"Right, right. But you act like her bootifulness don't even faze you. And there's no way you're going to expect me to believe you've been over here almost every weekend for the past several years and never tapped into that while you were with Jada."

I leaned down, kissed Desmon again, and turned his nightlight on. I turned the light switch off as Kareem stood waiting for a response. "Come on, let's go. I'm running late as it is."

He headed toward me and bumped me on the way out of the door. "You ain't right. I think you've been keeping some serious secrets from my ass."

I smiled and smacked him on the back of his head.

When we went back into the living room, Ginger was sitting on the couch reading with an unlit cigarette in her hand. Kareem eased his way into a chair, so I sat down on the couch next to her for a brief moment.

"So, how was Desmon?" she asked, lighting the cigarette, setting the book down on the table.

"That's a dumb question. He was perfect. Just like his daddy. Would you expect me to say anything different?"

"Well, he ain't perfect when he's with me. He just hasn't gotten used to being with you yet. Trust me; the more time you spend with him, things are definitely going to change."

"Thanks for letting me keep him. I'll be back next weekend to pick him up, if you don't mind."

"You know he spends the first weekend of the month with my mother. The weekend after that will be cool."

"I forgot." I stood up and so did Kareem. "We getting ready to jet. I'll call you later in the week, okay?"

Ginger's face fell flat and she looked disappointed. "That's fine. I was hoping you would stay the night, though."

I glanced at Kareem and he smiled. I looked back at Ginger. "Sorry, but, uh, I made some other plans. I'll call you later, I promise."

"Kiley, don't go making promises you ain't prepared to keep. That's how I got myself in this fucked-up situation with you to begin with," she said, bending down, and putting her cigarette out in an ashtray.

I sighed. "Ginger, not right now."

"Then when, Kiley?" She looked over at Kareem. "You know your brother is something else. Why is he so difficult, Kareem? Maybe you can help me figure him out because I sure in the hell can't."

"Hey, I've known him all my life and still can't figure him out myself. I was hoping you could shed some light on the brotha so I can learn something I don't know."

I looked at both of them. "Just let me be me. Come on, man, let's go. Ginger, I said I'll holla." I went to the door and opened it.

After Kareem said good-bye to Ginger and walked out, I closed the door behind him. "I'm sorry I can't stay. You should have told me earlier when I talked to you that you made plans for us," I said, knowing that the smell of food was in the air and the kitchen table was set for two with a bottle of wine.

"I guess you figured I cooked dinner for you?"

"Yeah, I looked in the kitchen." I leaned down and kissed her. "Just be patient with me, I'll make it up to you later."

Ginger moved in closer and backed me up against the door. As we kissed, she untied her robe and opened it. I rubbed my hand up and down her silky, smooth body and just for the hell of it, got a quick taste of her breasts. As she felt my dick harden, she begged me to stay. Wanting to, I just couldn't. I stopped as we were in motion and reminded her Kareem was in the car waiting for me.

As she continued to coax me into staying, I hesitated, and finally said, "Baby, let me go take care of something and I'll come back tonight. It'll be late but I'll be back." I opened the door.

"I hope not too late. I'll wait for you, and please call when you're on your way." I nodded and she closed the door behind me.

As I walked toward the car, I could see Kareem grinning ear to ear. When I got in I looked over at him while shutting the door. "What?" I smiled.

"What, huh? You're a good lying muh-fucker, that's what."

I started the car. "Nigga, what are you talking about? I ain't lied about nothing."

"So, you and Ginger weren't just in there exercising y'all lips, huh?"

"No, as a matter of fact, we weren't. She asked me for some money for Desmon and I gave it to her."

"Really?" he said, reaching over and wiping my lips. "Well, she must have asked you to try on some lipstick because it seems to be all over your lips."

I smacked Kareem's hand off my lips and looked in the rearview mirror. When I saw her lipstick, I wiped the rest of it off. "I told you she be coming on to me sometimes, damn. She be trippin' when I don't want to stay."

"Kiley, when you gon' stop lying to me about shit? What type of fool do you really think I am? She ain't cooking for you, trying to wine and dine you, and you ain't fucking her. That don't make sense and you know it. Thing is, you know everything about me. I tell you all kinds of personal shit. But when it comes to you, you be treating me like I'm some poot-butt nigga off the streets who you don't want up in your business. I seriously thought we had a better relationship than that."

"And we do. I'm . . . just real private, always been that way. Even more since what went down in L.A. For one, my privacy keeps me from being judged and allows me not to get bad advice from people. So, with that being said, I'll be honest with you this time and tell you that I just recently had sex with Ginger after Jada and me broke up. Before that, I haven't fucked Ginger since she told me she was pregnant with Desmon."

Kareem cocked his head back and pursed his lips. "Now, you really expect me to believe that? You've been coming over here, weekend after weekend, looking at that . . . that plump, juicy brown-skinned ass and those succulent tits and haven't wanted to dive into it?"

"No, I haven't. But remember, it's all in the mind, Kareem. That's all you see when you look at her. That's what I saw when I first met her and wanted to fuck her. Now, since I've gotten to know her better, I see many things I don't like about her. So that sexy-ass body doesn't faze me like it used to. Truthfully, the only time I pay attention to that is when my dick is hard and I'm in the mood to fuck. Since Jada was taking care of me before, there was no need for me to come over here thinking about laying her. Lately, though, things have changed. I'm starting to see a change in Ginger so who knows what the future holds."

"Well, I sure in the hell be glad when somebody put it on me like Jada put it on you. That ass must be worth more than fifty pots of gold. If it got you turning down shit like Candi, Ginger, and who knows what else, I can't wait until I'm smacked in the face with that kind of feeling."

"It's not the feeling of sex, my brotha; it's the feeling of love. Now, the sex is what kept me, but love is the ultimate thing that kept me focused."

"Okay, conversation over; love is out for me. I love myself too damn much, I don't even have room in my heart to love anybody else."

I punched him in his chest. "Not even me, playa?"

He punched me back. "Just a li'l sliver in the corner of it. That's it. And you should be lucky to have that." We laughed.

By the time I dropped Kareem off, it was almost eight-thirty. He said he was going in the house to invite one of the ladies he met today over and he'd see me when I got back. I hated to lie to Kareem about my whereabouts, but it would hurt him like hell if I told him about my plans with Jada.

CHAPTER 9

After scrambling for a parking spot at the hotel, I sat in the car for a few minutes thinking. If pussy was what I wanted, I could easily call Ginger or Candi up tonight for that. If reconciliation was what I wanted, I had no business reconciling with Jada and I knew it. And if peace of mind was what I went there for, I knew there wasn't a chance in hell I was going to get it. But something inside of me just wouldn't let me leave.

I hopped out of the car and went to her room. When I knocked on the door, she opened it and walked away. I locked it and leaned against the dresser looking at her sitting on the bed with attitude. It was after nine o'clock, so I tried to understand why she was upset.

"I apologize for being late. The movie took a li'l bit longer than I expected."

"And I guess you're going to apologize for hanging up on me, too. I could tell that bitch was in the car with you by the way you were talking."

"Jada, the only other person besides Desmon who was in the car with me was Kareem."

"Yeah, right. If you've moved on with your life then fine, go right ahead. I just want you to know how much hurt you've caused me," she said, starting to tear up. "I thought we were going to be together forever. I never knew it would come to you choosing someone else over me."

"Why do you feel as if I'm choosing somebody else over you? This has nothing to do with anybody else. When are you going to come to your senses and see that?"

"When you stop fighting with me and allow us to be together again. If there is no one else, then what's holding you back? We've had many ups and downs, especially while we were in L.A., but we always managed to get through it. We had each other after your parents died, when my father died, when you wanted to drop out of school, when I wanted to; we've always had each other to lean on. Why does that all have to change?"

"Because, Jada, it does." I went over to the bed and sat down next to her. I held her face with my hand and rubbed her soft cheek. "Do you even know how much you hurt me by sleeping with Donovan? I feel less of a man right now, because you stripped me of my pride. Made me feel like

I wasn't good enough. Now, I came clean to you a long time ago about my wrongdoings in L.A. but you never told me about you and Donovan. When I kept asking you what was wrong, you knew your attitude at the house reflected your feelings for him. You can't tell me listening to him fuck other women didn't the least bit bother you."

"It didn't, Kiley. I swear to you my sleeping with him was all about making you jealous."

"I will never believe that. I truly feel at some point you cared about him. Maybe not as much as you cared about me, but your feelings for him almost stopped you from moving here to begin with."

"You're wrong, baby. I lied in those letters I wrote to Donovan. I just knew he was going to show them to you to make you jealous, right along with those pictures."

"Well, he didn't. I found out by searching through his things, so whatever, Jada." I got up off the bed as a felt myself getting upset thinking about the shit. "Look, I'm done with talking about the shit. You don't believe me, I don't believe you, so forget it."

"If you wanted to forget it, why did you come here? Why would you waste your time coming all this way to tell me to forget about us?"

I paused for a moment and swallowed before saying anything. "Because you . . . you know I still love you. I'm not going to pretend that I don't, but I can't forget about what you've done to me. I guess I'm here to find out what you expect from me."

Jada came over to me standing by the window and looked me in the eyes. When I turned my head to look away, she grabbed my face and turned it so I could look back at her. "I expect for you to finish what you started today. I want more than anything for you to put the past behind us, and if possible, I want the bedroom I shared with you back. I'm getting kind of lonely in this hotel room all by myself."

She leaned in and placed her lips on mine. I closed my eyes trying to fight back the feelings I had for her but couldn't. As she reached her hand inside my pants, she massaged my dick like she'd always done so well before. And as I realized there was no turning back for me, I raised her nightgown over her head and removed her ponytail clip so her hair could fall. After I removed the rest of my clothes, she took my hand and led me to the bathroom. I wrapped my arms around her waist, and we stood naked, looking at ourselves in the mirror. She reached up and wrapped her arms around my neck, while rubbing the back of my head. I touched her soft, thick breasts, then lowered my hand and combed through her hairs with my fingers. She smiled and looked at me in the mirror.

"I love you so much. The thought of losing you just tore me apart," she moaned, as I separated her slit with my thick fingers.

Exciting the hell out of her, I went in deeper with my fingers. She moved back, pressing her ass against me, while holding on to the counter. And just when I finally heard her insides starting to talk, I pulled my fingers out and teased her from behind with the thickness of my head.

Moaning, she tried to force me inside her with her hands but I wouldn't let her. I moved back away from her and went over to the tub. I lay in it and rested one leg over the top. She came over and reached for the faucet. I stopped her.

"I had no intention of getting wet by the water. I thought you might be able to take care of me without it."

"No shower, huh," she said, getting in the tub on her knees.

"Not yet."

As she slurped me up, I pulled her hair with my hand. Feeling as if I was about to explode, I grabbed tighter. She rose up just in time.

"Damn, pull my hair out, would you?" She laughed.

"I'm sorry, just couldn't help myself."

"Well, help yourself to this," she said, standing over me and resting one leg on top of the tub. I rose up and leaned my face right into it. As her legs weakened, I held them in place with my hand. And when she couldn't take any more, she bent over and placed both her hands on the floor outside the tub. I got behind Jada and had the pleasure of listening to her beg for forgiveness as I pounded her insides. And when she hiked up on the tip of her toes so I could go in deeper, it was all over with. She warned me and told me she was about to lose her balance, and when she did, we both fell forward onto the floor. She rolled over on her back and I eased in between her legs.

"I'm sure this floor is not clean enough for me to have my bare body on it. Can we finish this up in bed, please?" she asked politely.

"Who cares about the floor? That's the last thing on my mind right now."

"Easy for you to say when you're not the one lying on it."

I pulled down a few white towels from the towel rail beside us and when Jada lifted up I slid them underneath her. "Is that better?" I asked, easing myself back inside her.

"You didn't hear me complaining, did you?"

I winked. "Naw, I didn't. Just making sure, though."

I kissed her and got down to business. I made sure this night was a night Jada would remember forever. I gave it to her good all over the hotel room, and by the time we were finished she was out like a light.

I sat up on the edge of the bed, rolled up a joint, and watched TV. Feeling a bit disappointed in myself for loving Jada so much, and for playing the shit out of Ginger, I knew the weed would put me in a mellow mood. I rolled up another joint when I started feeling guilty about lying to Kareem. Curious to see what he was into tonight, I went into the bathroom and called him on my cell phone. Quincy answered.

"We got some hoes in this house," he said, singing. "Freaky hoes in this house."

"Man, quit playing. What y'all playas up to?"

"Nothing. Just sitting upstairs getting fucking fucked up!"

"Yeah, me too. But, uh, who else over there?"

"Nobody. Just Kareem and me."

"I thought you said y'all had some hoes in the house."

"Fool, I was talking about Kareem and me. Do you honestly think I would be dissing some females like that if they were sitting right here?"

"Naw, you're right. I'm trippin'."

"Yeah, you are. Where are you? We thought you would be back by now."

"I was coming back but something came up. I'll be there in a li'l bit though. Did anybody call me?"

"Hold on, I think so. Kareem was the one who answered so wait a minute." Quincy put the phone down and Kareem picked it up.

"Nigga, what do you mean did anybody call you? I ain't yo damn secretary, fool," he slurred.

"Y'all must really be taking it to the limit tonight. Both of y'all sounding like some fifty-year-old drunks. And what happened to all this booty you were supposed to be getting into?"

"Whew, that's a long story. See, I came in the house, poured myself a drink, fired up a few blunts, and when I reached into my pocket for the numbers, they weren't there. You didn't jack me for my phone numbers, did you?"

"Yeah, I'm in a hotel room right now getting my dick swallowed by all six of them, including the two you sat in the theatre with."

"Straaaight? Sounds kinda painful to me. Don't let 'em bite you, okay?" He laughed.

"Serious, though, did anybody call?"

"Let's see . . . Yeah. Plenty muh-fuckers called."

"I mean, for me."

"Aw, right. Uh, Ginger called twice, Candi called two or three times, Al called to tell you something about your car, and Belynda called."

"Belynda? Who in the hell is Belynda?"

"Aw, that was for me."

"Kareem, sober yo' ass up. I'll be home in a li'l bit."

"Cool, and I'll be waiting. Waiting on the love of my fucking life to come home and rescue me from all this . . . this weed and drink in my system."

"Good-bye, fool. And please take your hand off your chest 'cause it ain't that damn serious." We laughed and hung up.

I crept out of the bathroom so Jada wouldn't hear me and started to put my clothes on. When I bent down to tie up my tennis shoes, my keys fell out on the floor and awakened her.

"Where are you going?" she asked, rolling over groggy.

"Home."

"I thought you were going to stay the night with me."

"I was but something came up. I'll be back later."

"Well, what about what we talked about?"

"You lost me. We've talked about so much I'm not sure what you mean."

"I mean, about me moving back into the house."

"Aw, that." I sat down on the bed next to her.

"Wait a minute," she said, reaching over to turn on the lamp. "Are you high?"

Wasn't no sense in me lying 'cause I'm sure my eyes were probably burning red. "A slight bit. I had a few joints while you were sleeping."

"So what about me moving back in?"

"That might not happen, Jada."

"And why not?"

"You know why. You and Kareem are going to kill each other. I want a peaceful house, baby. If you move back in now, Kareem and you are going to stay at it and you know it."

"Kiley, you know damn well that as long as you tell Kareem to chill, he will. After a few days of me being there he'll adjust."

"Naw, and I'm not going to ask him to. Just because I might have forgiven you, Kareem and Quincy doesn't have to forgive you for calling the police on them. Frankly, it would be wrong of me to ask them to."

"So I'm just supposed to spend hundreds of dollars living in this hotel room until your brother is willing to forgive me?"

"No, I didn't say that. All I'm saying is now ain't the time for you to move back in. Maybe in a few more weeks or another month. I don't know, let me think about it."

"Well, while you're taking your time thinking, I'm stuck without a place to go. You know I don't want to move back to L.A. My family barely talks to me since I moved to St. Louis, and my friends, you know all of them got issues."

"Baby, I'm sorry. I'll give you the money to stay here until I decide what to do, but for now, there's no way I can let you back into the house."

"Fine," she said, pulling the covers back and getting out of bed. "Suit yourself. If you want to let Kareem control your life, do it. I guess that's probably the reason you're so anxious to leave now so you can go babysit his ass."

"Jada, watch it. Don't go fucking this up right now by running off at the mouth. Things were going cool between us and I'd hate for—"

"Just go, Kiley," she said, raising her voice. "Please go before I get upset with you again. You got what the fuck you came here for anyway."

"So, now you think I just came here to have sex with you, right?"

"You damn right, you did. Fucked me well and all you wanted was to hear me beg for your ass."

"That ain't the reason I came here and you know it. Honestly, I had plenty of pussy waiting for me . . ." I shut up, realizing I'd put my foot in my mouth.

"Really? Say you did, huh? Pussy all over the place just waiting for Mr. Kiley Jacoby Abrams. Well, you're a bad sucker, aren't you? But the next time you got that much pussy out there waiting for you, by all means, jump on it. This one here," she said, pointing to her pussy, "don't want your dick, no mo'. And I mean that shit. Now, go! And I don't want your goddamn money to pay for this room 'cause I'm outtie!"

I didn't even feel like defending myself. I picked up my keys, grabbed my coat, and left. I knew the "fuck me, fight me" game would be the end result, so I could only blame myself for coming to see her.

When I got in the car and turned my phone back on, Ginger's number flashed across the caller ID. I didn't want to hear her mouth after hearing Jada's, but it only made sense to get it over with as fast as I could.

"Yes," I said, dryly.

"So, that's how I get played? It's three-fifteen in the morning, Kiley. All you had to do was call and tell me you wasn't coming."

"I was, but my phone was trippin', Ginger. Believe it or not, I was just getting ready to call you right before you called me."

"That's a lame excuse and you know it. I just don't understand why I keep letting you do this shit to me. I've been trying to be nice to you, trying to let you spend time with Desmon, cooking dinner for you, trying to be there for you when you need me, and this is how I get treated."

"Ginger, look, I'm sorry. I'll make it up to you later this week. Something just came up and I had to take care of it."

"Your word ain't worth a damn and you know it. And if you tell me you're sorry one more time, I'm gonna scream so loud in hopes of busting your damn eardrum out for lying."

"Are you finished?" I said, getting really tired of the female bullshit.

"You're damn right I'm finished. And if you think I got this shit out of my system tonight, I'll be sure to call you for the rest of the week as I'm drumming up more shit to curse you out about."

"Fine," I said, calmly. "I'll just wait on your call."

I listened to the dial tone after Ginger hung up.

Women. Just couldn't please them no matter how hard I tried. Give 'em some good loving and they go crazy trying to control your ass. And when shit don't go according to their plan, all hell breaks loose. It wasn't that I didn't care about Ginger, but I thought I made it perfectly clear I wasn't up for no relationship with anyone.

So it wasn't my fault she made plans for us tonight without telling me and I cancelled. If I had something to do, damn, I just had something to do. This is the silly-ass shit I try to stay away from.

Quincy and Kareem were passed out in the entertainment room on the couch. The aroma of marijuana was in the air and empty bottles of cognac were on the table. I thought about putting some pepper in both of their mouths since they were wide open; but instead I went to my room and lay in my bed, staring at the ceiling thinking about what tomorrow was going to bring. For some reason, I smelled trouble.

CHAPTER 10

The phone was ringing off the hook. Nobody answered so I rolled over and picked it up myself. It was Donovan. He asked me if I ever got a chance to gather up his things for him, and being so damn occupied for the last few days, I forgot I had told him I would get right to it. After I told him I hadn't, I asked him if he needed a ride from the hospital. He said a friend of his, Marcus, was picking him up in a few and they'd be by the house to pick up his things.

I hung up the phone, then looked at my watch, realizing it was already two in the afternoon. I must have been in a deep sleep because I had no intention of sleeping this late in the afternoon. Knowing I hadn't slept like a baby in a long time, I couldn't complain. I put my robe on and went upstairs to see if Quincy and Kareem would help me get some of Donovan's things together.

When I got upstairs, they were still lying in the same positions as when I came in last night. Two lazy, drunk-ass fools who didn't have nothing to do but sit around and sleep the day away. I picked up the remote to the stereo and blasted it as loud as I could. They both hopped up, and just that fast, Kareem had his gun in his hand, aiming it in front of him. When he saw me standing there, he aimed it at me.

"You dead, playa. Don't be interrupting my dreams when I'm about to lay into Halle Berry."

"Naw, you dead. It took you five minutes to find me."

Quincy fell back on the couch, holding his stomach. He rested one hand on his forehead and massaged his dick with the other. "That cognac don't be bullshitting. Whew, I feel like I'm about to . . ." He quickly stood up and jetted to the bathroom.

"'Run, run!'" Kareem shouted. Quincy didn't make it on time and threw up on the floor. "That nigga can't handle his shit. He need to stop trying to hang with the big boys and settle for some milk."

"Aw, you've had your moments too, so don't be trying to talk about him." I looked over at Quincy. "You gon' be all right, man?"

He nodded and held on to the staircase rail. "I'm cool," he said, holding his stomach and bending down. "I just need some fresh air, that's all."

"Well, let me go open some windows to clear out that smell," Kareem said, getting off the couch. "Then I'll fix you a tonic that will have you feeling better in no time."

After Kareem opened up some windows and I helped Quincy to the bathroom, I stooped to an all-time low and cleaned up his vomit. Kareem sat on the couch watching football, refusing to offer his help. He laughed at me a few times as I gagged and frowned while cleaning it up. It was hard to do with one hand but I somehow managed.

When I finished, I rolled up a blunt and sat on the couch smoking it with Kareem. Quincy came upstairs with no clothes on, massaging a towel through his hair, trying to dry it. He looked down where he had vomited and saw that it had been cleaned up.

"Aw, y'all some really nice fellas. I'm touched. I was on my way up here to clean it up myself." He came over and sat down on the couch, still drying his hair with the towel. When he finished, he folded the towel in half and wrapped it around his neck. He leaned back on the couch and rested his hands on top of his dick. "What y'all watching?"

Kareem and me just looked at each other. I passed the last of the joint back to him and blew the smoke out. "What's your problem?" I asked, looking at Quincy.

"What do you mean, what's my problem?"

"I mean, we ain't interested in sitting here talking with you and you ain't got no clothes on."

"Whatever, man, I'm comfortable. Just don't look at me."

"Shit, we can't help but notice your white bare ass sitting there with your dick slanging."

"Aw, so that's what this about. Y'all upset 'cause you brothas thought a colored man couldn't have it going on like this." He stood up while holding his pipe in his hand.

Kareem and me laughed. "Naw, fool," Kareem said, standing up and pulling his boxers down. "That's a white man's dick. This is a black man's treasure, right here." He grabbed his stuff.

"Please, Kareem," Quincy said. "If you're going to stand up for the black man, you need to come more correct than that. This is top of the line right here."

"Both of you muh-fuckers really need to be ashamed of yourselves," I said, standing up. "Put your dicks up and come help me pack Donovan's shit for him."

"Hold on, big brother. For the record, would you tell this fool why the women love us so damn much," Kareem said. Him and Quincy stood there waiting for a response from me.

I tied my robe tighter, and before I headed downstairs I looked at both of them, shaking my head. "Honestly, I really don't see what the ladies got to look forward to when it comes to either one of you. Y'all both should have played with yourselves a li'l bit more when y'all were kids; and, Kareem, let's just say you'd better start respecting Quincy as a colored man. Through my eyes, he definitely earned my respect to be called one, and more than you, I might say."

"Daaamn," Quincy said, wrapping the towel around his waist and looking at Kareem. "I guess that should clear up any misunderstanding you might have, bro."

"Man, Kiley don't know what the fuck he talking about." Kareem looked at me. "I didn't see you pulling yo' wee-wee out, bragging on yo' shit."

"And you won't. Might scare you. If you want to know, all you gotta do is ask the ladies in my life. They'll be more than happy to share it with you."

I headed downstairs to Donovan's room and they followed.

After Kareem's constant complaining about getting Donovan's things together for him, I told him to forget it and he changed clothes and left. Quincy said the only reason he helped was because he didn't want me doing it by myself.

It was times like this one that Quincy always seemed to come through for me. Just like yesterday when I asked him to help Jada with her things, he didn't even trip. Kareem never would have helped. Even if I begged him to. He was stubborn as stubborn could get, but I definitely understood how he felt about Donovan and Jada both so I really didn't trip.

Quincy and me put some clothes on and started packing Donovan's things. As we were finishing up, the doorbell rang, and when I looked at the monitor, it was Donovan and one of his boys standing on the back porch. Quincy went downstairs to open the door, and since I didn't want his friend scoping the place, I started pulling Donovan's things out in the hallway so he could get them faster and go. They were coming up the steps as I pulled more bags from his room. I looked at Donovan, when he called my name and introduced me to Marcus.

"Hey, man," I said, looking at him. "What's up?"

"Nuttin' much. You and the fellas got y'all selves a nice-ass crib." Marcus looked around, dangling a toothpick from his mouth.

"Donovan, I think we got everything. You can check to see if we missed anything if you want to."

"Cool. I appreciate you getting this stuff together for me." He stepped over the bags and went into his room.

I followed behind him to pull the last two bags out as Marcus and Quincy started taking Donovan's things to the car.

"I'm going to miss this place." Donovan stood with his gray leather pants on, and his jacket covering up his wrapped shoulder, looking around the room. "I've had some good memories in this room. Memories I will definitely be taking with me to my new place."

"So, I guess Tricia still trippin', huh?"

"Yeah, she is." He leaned against his dresser and crossed his feet. "Told me it was over until I learn how to keep my dick in my pants."

"I must have heard that a million times before. She'll get over it, trust me. They always do."

"Yeah, I'm sure she will, but in the meantime, I'm moving on."

"With who, Candi?"

"Naw, not with Candi. Tricia told me Candi was in the hospital, trying to get at you. Told me Candi and Jada got into it and said after you walked Candi to her car, Jada told her the gory details about our relationship."

"Damn, that's fucked up; but you know ain't nothing going on between Candi and me, don't you?"

Donovan put his hand in his pocket and smiled. "Naw, I really don't know what's up. I can only assume, though, that it was the perfect opportunity for you to get me back for sleeping with Jada."

"Donovan, I don't play games like that. By all means, she bad, but she too damn bad for me. That kind of woman can only mean trouble, so trust me when I say fucking her ain't an option for me."

"Well, if you do, ain't no biggie. She's history in my book so ain't no trip." He rose up off the dresser. "So, did you and Jada ever work things out?"

"We've talked, that's it. If it's meant to be, I'm sure I'll see her again."

"That's the same way I feel about Tricia."

I stood there talking to Donovan for a while. Hinting around, he kept mentioning what happened between us and still sounded kind of bitter. To keep the peace, deep down I was really glad he was moving out.

When Donovan started looking for some private things in his room, I left and went into mine. As I looked at the monitor, things outside didn't seem to be going well with Quincy and Marcus. Their mouths were moving and they were standing face to face. Not knowing who this nigga was or what he was about, I took my Glock from underneath my pillow and put it in my pocket. I called Donovan so he could go downstairs with me and see what was up. By the time we got down the steps, Marcus and Quincy were coming through the back door talking shit to one another. Donovan quickly intervened.

"Marcus, why you trippin', man? What happened?"

"Nuttin'," he said, smiling with a mouth full of gold teeth. "White boy can't take a joke, that's all."

Quincy punched Marcus in the face so hard it sent him flying through the back door onto the porch. "You don't know me, nigga! Don't know a damn thing about me to be calling me a white boy."

Marcus got up and tried to rush him, but before he could Donovan stepped in front of him and grabbed his shirt. "Chill out, fool. Why you coming over here trippin'?"

Marcus pushed Donovan back, trying to get at Quincy. "Move, Dee. Ain't no white boy gon' put his hands on me and get away with it."

Quincy turned and started at him again. I tried holding him back as best as I could with one hand. "Let it go, Q. Whatever he said to you just let it go!" I looked at Donovan. "Man, get your animal out of here before he gets hurt. Call me and we'll make arrangements to have the rest of your things sent to you."

"All right, that's cool," Donovan said, standing in the doorway, holding Marcus back as he started cursing at Quincy and me.

"See, I ain't got time for no bullshit like this." Quincy reached into my pocket and pulled out my gun. He aimed it at Marcus in the doorway, who was still trying to push Donovan out of the way to get back in. "Back up, fool!" Quincy yelled. "You have no idea who you fucking with!" He pulled the trigger.

Remembering that I forgot to put the bullets back into the gun after I cleaned it yesterday, I was relieved. Donovan couldn't hold Marcus back any longer, knowing that he was fighting for his life; we all went at it. Quincy and me rushed him. Stomped his ass right at the back door, delivering bone-crushing blows. I cracked him upside the head a few times with my cast, and I kicked his ass down the steps. For the first time in his life Donovan was trying to break us up. As long as he didn't side with Marcus, I left his ass out of it.

Marcus lay on his back, swaying from side to side with a mouthful of blood and promising Quincy and me we were going to die. Quincy ran down the steps, kicking Marcus in his side again to silence him. He then looked at Donovan, madder than I had ever seen him before. "This all the fuck you wanted, ain't it? You knew better bringing a stupid-ass muh-fucker like him over here."

"Fuck you, Quincy," Donovan spat. "Y'all was wrong for this shit. Give or take, I don't know what happened, but this ain't a good situation."

"Are you threatening me, you playa-hating-ass nigga?" Quincy shot back with gritted teeth, getting up in Donovan's face.

"Quincy!" I yelled. "Chill!"

He looked at me, rolled his eyes, then looked back at Donovan. "Cocksucker!" he said loudly. "Answer me, fool. Was that a fucking threat I heard?"

Donovan gave Quincy a devilish smirk. "Never, Quincy. You trippin', dog. All I'm saying is there was a better way to handle this." He looked down at Marcus. "Come on, man. Get up." He walked over to Marcus and helped him off the ground. Marcus held his side and him and Donovan walked off.

Quincy stood there with his white wife beater on and cargo shorts hanging down low. He stared at them until they drove off from behind the house. When he came to the back door, he pushed it and walked past me, not saying a word.

I drummed up a li'l something for me to eat and tried to give Quincy time to cool off. I was thinking how glad I was Kareem wasn't around because shit would have really gotten out of hand. Not sure by how much, but I was sure it wouldn't have been pretty.

Feeling a bit sore from fighting, I ran some bath water and sank myself deep down inside the tub. As I started to drift off, the phone rang. I knew Quincy wasn't going to answer it, so I got out of the tub to get it, since whoever it was kept hanging up and calling right back. When I looked at the caller ID, it showed a telephone number I didn't recognize. Normally, I wouldn't answer but since they kept on calling back I did.

"Yeah," I said, disguising my voice. There was silence. "Hello?" Whoever it was hung up.

I got back into the tub, but this time I took the cordless phone with me. And sure enough, the phone rang again. This time I picked it up and didn't say anything.

"Kiley," Donovan said.

"What's up?"

"That was me who just called. I couldn't hear you so I hung up and called back."

"Uh-hm. Ain't no trip. I just thought you were someone else."

"Naw, listen, I wanted to apologize for today. I never would have brought Marcus over there if I thought he was going to be trippin' like that. After he told me how shit got heated with him and Quincy, I made it clear to him that he was in the wrong."

"That's cool. Just next time you come, come alone. I don't trust those niggas you be hanging out with. And if they trippin' like that, you should be a li'l leery your damn self."

"You know me. I'll definitely watch my back. Do me a favor though and tell Quincy I apologize if he felt like I dissed him. I was just trying to keep the peace."

"Will do. And call me later in the week so we can make arrangements for the rest of your things, especially your furniture. You might need to get a truck to pick that up."

"I'll call you by the weekend, all right?"

"Cool. Deuces, man."

After relaxing in the tub for about an hour I got out, put some clothes on, and went upstairs to talk to Quincy. I could hear him laughing, and by the time I got there, he was rolling around on the floor cracking up at Cedric the Entertainer.

"Is it that funny you got to be on the floor trying to catch your breath?"

"Yeah, man. He fucked me up talking about the chicken wings at Church's Chicken."

"Is this your first time watching that?"

"Yeah. Kareem told me to watch it before but I never got around to it." Quincy got up off the floor and sat back down on the couch.

"Where Kareem at anyway? Did he mention to you where he was going?"

"Nope. It is getting late though. You might want to hit him on his cell phone."

I picked up the phone and dialed his number. He didn't answer, so I called him back a few more times just in case his phone was trippin' like mine always does. Just when I was about to hang up, this chick answered his phone.

"Who is this?" I asked.

"This is Felicia. And who is this?"

"It's Kiley. Is Kareem there?"

"Yeah, but he asleep."

"Wake him up for me."

"He told me not to."

"If he knows it's me he'll wake up. So, take the phone to him and stop wasting my time."

"Hold on," she said with an attitude. After a few minutes Kareem answered the phone.

"What's up?" he asked, sounding irritated. "Hold on, Kiley. I told you don't be answering my damn phone to begin with. That's your problem now, you just don't know how to listen to me when I tell you something!" he yelled. "All right, I'm back."

"Is everything cool?"

"Hell, naw. Felicia be trippin'. She always trying to find out something. Sneaking into the other room, answering my phone. Shit be pissing me off."

"Damn, I was just calling to check on you and tell you about the fight you missed today."

"Fight? What fight?"

"Between Quincy, me, and one of Donovan's boys."

"Whaaat! I'm on my way home. I can't wait to hear about this shit."

"Bye, fool," I said, hanging up the phone.

For some reason Quincy seemed like he was still a bit bothered by what happened earlier. I started watching the comedy show with him, but quickly kicked up a conversation so he would talk about it.

"Say, Donovan called a bit ago. Told me to tell you he was sorry for the way shit went down."

Quincy cut his eyes. "Uh-hm, I'm sure he is." He turned his head back toward the TV.

"What happened between you and Marcus anyway? You never told me what really went down."

"He just disrespected me, man, that's all."

"Disrespected you how?"

"You know, the usual white boy jokes. I get sick and tired of hearing that shit. Why must shit always have to be about black and white? Why muh-fuckers can't just let you be who the fuck you wanna be? I hate that shit. I wish God just made everybody the same damn color. That way most of this racism shit wouldn't even exist. Maybe then we would all be one big happy fucking family."

"If we were all the same color, people would have something else to judge you by. You can't let that kind of shit keep upsetting you. How do you think I feel being out there in the real world? Black man like myself don't stand a chance. Now, people will tell you all that fake bullshit about living right and doing the right things, but I watched my father struggle for a long time before he got off into the game. Before that, he didn't get a fucking thing in return but a stab in the back from my mother and a layoff by the white man. When he started doing shit for himself, that's when good fortune happened for us. Sorry, but it just had to be that way. I have no regrets living how I'm living and if anybody don't like it, fuck 'em."

"I understand what you're saying, but this is something totally different. True enough, I'm white. I know it, and I'm not trying to hide it. It's harder for me because people be acting like it's a crime for a white boy to listen to rap music, or to wear his pants hanging, or wear a bandana on his head. To me, if I like the flavor of rap, if I like wearing baggy clothes, then I should be able to do it without anyone trippin' with me like that. It doesn't mean I'm trying to be black; I'm just trying to be me. So anybody who step to me with that 'how does it feel wanting to be black' bullshit and don't know shit about me, I'm gonna fuck 'em up, no doubt about it."

Knowing somewhat how Quincy was feeling, I went over to the bar and poured him and me a glass of cognac. I continued our conversation from across the room. "Q, you can't fight with everybody who steps to you that way. There are a lot of people who feel like that. You just got to let that shit roll off your back and move on. You know damn well what you stand for. When you start fighting over it all the time, that's when you start losing yourself. Maybe feeling like you're the one out of place, when in reality they're the ones who need to regroup and recognize."

"I guess you're right. I thought about that shit after the fact, but it was too late then."

"I thought about it too," I said, walking over handing him a glass. "Thought about how we kicked that son of a bitch's ass. I forgot you had it in you like that. Since we left L.A., you really haven't had to get down like that, have you?"

Quincy gulped down his cognac and put the glass on the table. "No, I haven't. But you weren't short-stopping either. That karate kicking bullshit you do can break a brotha's back, can't it?

"No doubt. Actually, if I kick 'em in the right spot it could end a nigga's life."

"Whew, I have no doubt. Did Donovan say he took that fool to the hospital? After that ass kicking, I'm sure he needed one."

"He didn't say, but I'm sure he needed one too."

Quincy and me laughed; then we heard the back door close. I knew it was Kareem 'cause I could hear him singing while coming up the steps.

"Whazzz up?" he said, slow dancing with himself singing a rap song by Nelly. He stopped singing when he got to the couch, plopped down, and immediately pulled a joint out of his pocket. He looked at Quincy and me before he lit it and frowned. "I don't see no bruises, so it couldn't have been a good fight."

"Aw, it was a good one," I confirmed. "Would you like for me to tell you how good it was?"

"Yes, my brotha, how good was it?" Kareem said.

"So good that Quincy called the playa a nigga."

"No fucking way!" Kareem yelled. He looked at Quincy. "You actually were that upset that you used the 'N' word?"

Quincy smiled. "Yeah, man. I was that upset. I didn't mean to disrespect nobody 'cause I know how sensitive y'all get by that shit, but he pushed me to the edge."

"Whew, I'm glad I wasn't that fool. Did an ambulance have to come get 'em like the last time he used the 'N' word?"

"Nope," I said. "Not this time, but trust me, he needed one."

"Um, um, um, sholl hate I missed out on that one. Even Felicia's good blow job couldn't top that shit."

"No, I'm afraid not. Not even Jada's."

We all laughed and continued talking. Afterward, I remembered that I'd forgotten to put the bullets back into my gun, and before I did anything else, I went to go load it.

I thought about going to see Ginger, then quickly changed my mind. Instead, the fellas and me kicked up a card game and stayed up all night playing and smoking blunts.

CHAPTER 11

I hadn't heard from Jada or Ginger since earlier in the week. I knew Ginger was probably expecting to hear from me on the weekend, but I remembered she said Desmon was going to her mother's house so there was no need for me to call. Jada, I wasn't sure if she was still in town or not. The last time we spoke she said she was outtie and a part of me really hoped she was. And as for Candi, even she had backed off a little. After I lied and told her I was trying to work things out with Jada, she was kinda upset with me. Told me I didn't know what I was missing. Maybe I was missing out. Then again, maybe I wasn't. Either way, she wasn't getting in my circle anytime soon. Fucked me up, too, 'cause I was getting extremely horny not having any pussy around. Kareem and Quincy had been in and out all week with females, but all I had were memories. Memories of how Jada and me used to get down. Thinking about how easily she could make my dick rise just by looking at her read a book or by standing in the kitchen in her silky nightgown cooking breakfast. I missed the shit out of her; but I sure in the hell didn't miss her loud, sassy-ass voice.

Trying to get my mind off her, I picked the phone up and called Ginger to see if she would be willing to cut a brotha some slack. When she answered with an attitude, I figured I was just wasting my time.

"What's Desmon been up to?"

"Nothing."

"Ginger, you know he's been up to something. You said yourself he's quite a monster."

"I said nothing."

"Did I catch you at a bad time?"

"No, not at all. Just sitting here all by myself, thinking about how stupid I am for loving somebody who don't give a damn about me."

"Damn, he should be ashamed of himself for not loving a woman like you."

"Yeah, you should be. And you should also be ashamed of yourself calling here pretending like everything's cool between us."

"It is cool, Ginger. Why hold grudges, baby? I don't."

"Well, if you don't then why haven't you come over here to see me? And, why are you just now calling?"

"Because I wanted to give you time to cool off."

"Okay, now what? I've cooled off, so come see me tonight."

"Nope, can't do that."

"And why not?"

"Because you want me to come fuck you. If I fuck you and leave, your feelings are going to be hurt. Then I'll have to listen to what I'm listening to now over and over again. Sorry, but I don't want to keep setting myself up like that."

"Setting yourself up for what? And what makes you think I want you to come fuck me?"

"Because."

"Because what?"

"Be quiet and listen." I paused. "Did you hear that?"

"Hear what?"

"Your pussy calling my name."

"No, I didn't."

"Yes, you did. And you wanna know how I know it is?"

"How?"

"Because my dick don't get hard unless it can hear it. And right about now, I'm hearing it."

She laughed. "You are so crazy. If that's the case, why don't you just come over?"

"Cause I just told you I couldn't."

"Why?"

"Because, I told you. You want me to fuck you and I can't."

Ginger and me laughed, going back in forth about why I didn't want to have sex with her. Bottom line: I told her the fellas and me were going out tonight and I'd catch up with her some other time. She thought I was lying, especially when I told her I hadn't been clubbing since I met her. Truthfully, I hadn't. Somehow Kareem and Quincy coaxed me into going out with them, and when I tried to back out they dissed the hell out of me.

By midnight we were getting dressed for a "night of adventure," Kareem continuously stressed. He was like a kid in a candy store, excited about me finally going out with Quincy and him. When I asked what club we were going to, they insisted we kick it on the east side since the clubs in St. Louis closed up too early. And when Quincy mentioned Club Illusion, I only hoped that I wouldn't see Ginger.

Not wanting to look like a fool, I cut through the cast on my arm with a hunting knife and took it off. I wrapped it with a bandage and called it a day. We were spiffed up and ready to leave by one-thirty in the morning. Since it was pretty cold outside, Kareem wore jeans and a cashmere sweater, I wore all black, and Quincy stuck to jeans and Timberlands. All in all, we had it going on.

As I got off at the Fourth Street exit to East St. Louis, the cars and the Metrolink passed by backed-up traffic. We crawled our way through the crowded streets, trying to find a parking spot. Young niggas were hanging out up and down the strip, trying to rush through traffic faster than everybody else. I was trying not to trip, but the Lexus was inches away from being hit several times.

I was relieved when we finally found a parking spot. After taking a few puffs from a joint, we popped some gum in our mouths and got ready for some action. No sooner had we hit the door, Kareem and Quincy was already macking. They'd already gotten to know plenty of ladies, so it wasn't hard for them to keep occupied. The club was crammed like sardines. Instead of standing around looking at the two of them in action, I went to the bar and ordered a shot of cognac. As I waited for the bartender to pour my drink, I scoped the room checking out the ladies. Surprisingly, most of them looked decent. I'd peeped out a couple of them I wouldn't mind going home with.

But before I could pay the waiter for my drink, I looked up and saw Candi walking through the door. She was looking drop-dead delicious.

Had on a silky gold strapless short dress that clung to the curves on her body. It showed the thickness in her dark brown shiny thighs, and her nipples clearly poked through. Her six-inch gold silk shoes were strapped up to her ankles, and as she sauntered through the crowd the fellas were going crazy. I turned my head when she strolled by and got a quick glimpse of her beautifully curved heart-shaped ass. All I could do was think what a fool I was for not hitting that. Brotha would die to have a woman like that blowing his phone up begging for a fuck.

As I stood sipping on my drink, I was playing off any- and everything that stepped my way. Most of the women were cool, but I was trying to check out the set before I made my move. One chick had the nerve to roll her eyes at me when I told her I didn't feel like dancing. And when she walked off, I saw her ask her girlfriend to come ask me to see if I had changed my mind. After I said no to her, I think they got the picture. I just wasn't up for no games, but when the DJ kicked up the music, I couldn't resist going to the dance floor with another chick.

I danced next to Quincy and this other chick. I couldn't help but notice Candi staring at me from across the room. When she saw me looking her way, she waved at me and I nodded my head.

I danced through a few more songs, and after my clothes had me sweating like a dog, I called it quits. I took my jacket off and went back to the bar to order another drink since mine somehow disappeared from the table I sat it down on. The chick who I was dancing with followed me.

"Whew, I am burning hot," she said, fanning herself with her hand.

"Yeah, me too. Would you like something to drink?"

"Sure, if you don't mind. A Long Island Iced Tea would be perfect."

I turned to the bartender and ordered our drinks. As I reached in my pocket for my money, this skinny light-skinned chick came over to stand close to me.

"Hi," she said, reaching into my pocket. I quickly grabbed her hand, thinking she was reaching for my money. "It's my phone number," she whispered. "Why don't you call me later?"

I let her hand go, smiled, and told her I would. Then I paid the bartender and gave the Long Island Iced Tea to the chick I was dancing with. She wasn't that fine but the thickness in her hips and plump ass reminded me of Jada.

"Here you go," I said. "But, uh, I didn't catch your name."

"Oh, I'm sorry. It's Gloria."

"Gloria. I'm Kiley."

"Glad to meet you, Kiley. Are you here by yourself tonight or did you come with some friends?"

"I'm here with my two brothers. How about yourself?"

"I came with one of my girlfriends. Ain't no telling where she's at, though."

"I know. I don't think I've seen my brotha since we stepped through the door, but one of my partnas was dancing next to us on the floor. As a matter of fact, he's still up there," I said, pointing to Quincy.

"That's your brother? He looks kind of mixed with something."

"He is. We actually stepbrothers," I lied.

"Oh, I see. So, do you come over here often?"

"No, he doesn't," a voice said from behind. When I turned around it was Ginger.

"What's up?" I said, giving her a hug. "Ginger, this is Gloria. Gloria, this is Ginger, my son's mother," I said, knowing how much Ginger hated to be introduced as my "baby's mama."

"Hello," Gloria said. When Ginger rolled her eyes and looked back at me, Gloria told me she'd catch up with me later.

"So why you up in here buying these hoes drinks, Kiley?"

I took a sip. "'Cause it's my money and I do what I want to do with my money."

She smiled. "I saw you up there on the floor dancing all nasty and shit. I started to come up there and push that bitch out of the way when you danced on the back of her ass like that, but I thought I'd let you enjoy yourself for one night."

"I wasn't dancing on back of nobody."

"Trust me, you were. You were all like this." Ginger moved up on me like she claimed I was dancing on Gloria. "That's why she couldn't walk away after y'all finished."

"You crazy, Ginger," I said, laughing.

"Yeah, crazy about you."

I bought Ginger a drink so she would cut me some slack for buying Gloria one. When Quincy finally made his way off the floor, I introduced him to Ginger since he'd never met her before.

"Hello, Quincy," Ginger said, shaking his hand.

"So you're Desmon's mother."

"Yep, that would be me."

"Well, you and Kiley got y'all selves a fine young man. He is quite a character, and maaan, he can dance."

"I know. I have no idea where he gets it from," Ginger said.

"He gets it from me. Didn't you see how well I just threw down on the floor?" I said.

"Yeah, you threw down all right. I'm afraid if nobody else was around you'd have really been throwing down."

Quincy laughed and said he was going to the restroom and would be right back. The place was packed, but since it wasn't that big I thought by now I would have seen Kareem. Getting a li'l worried, I told Ginger I'd be back and went to the bathroom to find Quincy. When I walked in he was looking in the mirror combing his hair back.

"Say, have you seen Kareem?"

"He outside."

"Outside? For what?"

Quincy just stared. "Duh, in a car."

"Aw. Damn, he don't waste no time, do he?"

"I think he with this chick he met the last time we were here."

"Uhm, must be nice."

"So are you having a cool time?" Quincy asked.

"Yeah, I am. Sistas looking pretty damn good these days."

"I know. It's so damn hard to decide which ones you want to holla at. But I guess you ain't having that problem with, uh, Ginger hanging around. I had no idea she was that fine."

"Now, you didn't think I pulled Desmon off all by myself, did you?"

"Naw, but I just didn't expect her to look like that. You know, with you trippin' all the time with Jada, Ginger's looks just caught me completely off guard."

"Love, man, I was in love," I said, patting Quincy on the back as we walked out the door. And as soon as we made a right coming out of the bathroom, Candi was standing there talking to this dude with a drink in her hand. Quincy looked at me and shook his head. "Why must you have all the luck?" He smiled, and then he leaned over and whispered something in this chick's ear who was standing in front of us. She laughed and they went to the dance floor.

There was no way for me to avoid Candi. I pushed through the crowd looking straight ahead, but before I could pass by her she grabbed my hand.

"Say," she said, then turned to the other dude. "I'll get at you later, okay?" He nodded and she pulled me in close to her. "You're afraid of me, aren't you?" she said, whispering in my ear.

"No, not at all. I just don't like to be pressured."

"And I don't like to be rejected."

"Well, when you stop pressuring me, I'll stop rejecting you. How about that?" I said, looking down at her nipples that were giving me some attention.

"How about you stop looking at my breasts and dance with me." She took my hand and walked me to the dance floor as a slow song was playing.

After getting a whiff of Candi's sweet-smelling perfume and rubbing up and down the back of her silky dress, I was hooked. Our rhythm was perfect, and I closed my eyes thinking about how I was going to have the pleasure of taking this dress off her tonight. When I opened my eyes, I finally saw Kareem standing in line waiting to get some chicken wings. But when I spotted Ginger on the other side of the dance floor, letting this dude rub all on her ass, I was starting to get pissed. Candi must have noticed my sudden change because she leaned back and asked me what was wrong.

"Nothing, my feet are starting to get tired."

"Would you like to sit down for a minute?"

"Yeah, just for a minute, okay?"

She backed away from me and held my hand as we walked off the floor. Most of the brothas had the look of envy in their eyes as I walked over to a table with Candi and sat down. I turned the chair slightly around so I could keep my eyes on Ginger, who seemed to be having herself a good time. Trying to stay focused on Candi before somebody snatched her up, I offered to buy her a drink. She said she'd already had enough to drink already.

"Are you sure?" I asked.

"I'm sure. What I'd really like is for you and me to get out of here and go somewhere private."

"We will. Just not right now. Give me a few more minutes," I said, looking at Ginger every chance I got.

"Kiley, are you here with another woman? You seem to be really preoccupied."

"Naw, I was just looking for Kareem or Quincy to tell them I'm getting ready to get out of here."

"I can see both of them from where I'm sitting." She placed her hand on top of mine. "Listen, if you don't want to do this with me, tell me. I'm kind of getting mixed signals from you. I felt our connection on the dance floor. Don't play me off tonight, okay?"

I looked into Candi's dark brown round eyes and couldn't turn her down. "Come on, let's go." We stood up and I went over to Kareem to tell him I was leaving. I tried to give him the keys to the Lexus, but he said him and Quincy already made plans to leave with these other chicks. I told him to be careful, and before I left with Candi, I looked around for Ginger. She was gone.

Surprisingly, I was burning up inside, but wasn't shit I could do. As soon as Candi and me stepped out the door, I saw Ginger standing in front of the building shivering with her arms folded.

"Yeah, that's what I thought," she said, looking at me.

I grabbed Candi's hand and we started walking to my car.

Ginger followed us. "Kiley, don't even play me like this."

"Ginger, you played yourself letting that muh-fucker rub all on your ass like that. Stop trippin' now and go on home," I said, continuing to walk to my car with Candi.

"I didn't play you. If you watched, you would have noticed me moving his hands off me several times."

I reached into my pocket for my keys and started to unlock the passenger's side door for Candi to get in. Ginger quickly snatched the keys out of my hand and stood there holding them.

"You're not going to do this to me, Kiley," she said, starting to tear up. "I will not let you disrespect me like this by leaving with her tonight."

"Ginger, give me my keys," I said, holding my hand out.

"No!" she yelled. "Not until she leaves."

"Well, she's not leaving. I invited her to my place so give me my damn keys before we fucking freeze out here." I looked at Candi standing there shivering with her arms folded. She had a coat on but I'm sure she was still feeling the cold as the gusty wind was blowing it open.

Ginger continued to hold my keys in her hand. Instead of fighting with her, I told Candi I was going back inside to get my second set of keys from Kareem, who didn't even have them.

When Ginger heard me, she threw my keys down on the ground. "Here, take your damn keys! Go ahead, take her home and fuck her brains out if you want to! My feelings aren't going to be hurt. I'm not fucking human. Just put me on the back burner for the rest of your damn life. As usual, I'll be there for you to step on when she don't treat you right."

I opened the door and told Candi to get in. When I backed the car up, and pulled off, I saw Ginger in my rearview mirror, walking up the street. When I got near the highway, I pulled the car over to the side and parked it.

I looked at Candi. "Where did you park?"

"Why?" she said, knowing where our conversation was headed.

"Because I'm going to have to take a rain check."

She took a deep breath. "Come on, Kiley. Quit trippin', all right? She'll be okay, trust me. Happens to the best of us sometimes."

"I know, but, where are you parked?"

Candi directed me to her car, and when she got out, she didn't even say good-bye. I didn't mean to play her, but seeing the mother of my child crying like that just did something to me. I drove around for a while looking for Ginger's car. I didn't see it, but since her apartment was only a few minutes away from the club, I drove to it.

Her car was parked outside and she was still sitting inside leaning her head down on the steering wheel. When she saw my lights shining into her car, she lifted her head up and wiped her tears. I went over to the passenger's side of her car to get in.

"Why you out here crying like this?" I asked.

"I'm just thinking about some things."

"Some things like what?"

"Like why I can't seem to get you out of my system no matter how hard I try. Especially when you've told me you don't want to be with me."

"Ginger, it's not just you. I don't want to be with anybody. I'm a hurt man and I got too much on my mind right now. Besides, I thought you were in love with that married fool you were fucking."

"No, I wasn't. I just used him to keep my mind off you. Thing is, you say the same thing year after year. Is there ever going to be a time when you don't have too much on your plate?"

"No, there won't. Ginger, you know so little about me. I've never shared with you my reason for moving to St. Louis and how I pretty much make my living. I know that the less you know about me, the better. When Desmon gets older, and just maybe if I'm not around, I want you to tell him the good things about me, not the bad things. Things you can share with him that you're proud of. Not the fact that I'm a murderer or I made my living as a drug dealer."

"Kiley, I knew that you sold drugs. I'm not that stupid."

"Naw, you don't know. You think I'm your average standing on the corner drug dealer, but I'm not. The game I'm running is large. Larger than you will ever know. So large that I don't even have to deal anymore unless I want to."

"So, aside from that, do you really kill people?"

"I did what I had to do when my father was killed. And if anybody ever does anything to hurt the ones I love, there's no doubt I will most certainly kill again."

Ginger looked surprised to hear me say that. She started biting her nails as if she was nervous. "Well, I guess that's how we all feel. I can't blame you for protecting your family."

"Good. And remember, what I just told you stays between you and me. I never want to hear you repeat any of this to Desmon."

"I won't. You have my word."

"So are you cool now? Is it okay for me to go home?"

"Only if you take me with you."

"Naw, can't do that."

"Why? Why does where you live have to be such a secret? Besides, I already know anyway."

"Really? And how's that?"

She looked at me and smiled. "Because I've followed you home several times after you left my house to see where you lived."

"Say, you did, huh?"

"Yep. I was curious to see how this chick you dumped me for, Jada, looked."

"So, did you get a chance to see her?"

"Yeah, I saw you and her fat ass leaving from your house several times." She laughed. "Me and my girl, Leslie, parked in front of your house many nights, keeping our eyes on things."

"Straight? Now, what if I tell you I wasn't the only one being watched? What if I tell you what kind of car y'all were in, each time you came, and when you left?"

"I'd say you're a liar. There's no way you knew I was there because I can be sneaky when I want to be."

"Ginger, trust me, I saw you. Next time don't wear dark glasses to hide your identity, it makes you look too suspicious. And next time tell your girlfriend to park her Mazda a li'l bit farther down the street."

Ginger's eyes widened. "But how did you see us?"

"Cameras, baby. I saw you on the monitors every single time you came."

"Well didn't your woman suspect anything?"

"Naw, she thought y'all were scoping out Quincy, Donovan, or Kareem. She never knew you were there checking me out."

"Why did you keep letting me make a fool of myself then? You could have told me."

"I thought it was kind of funny. I enjoyed watching the two of you trying to be slick. Especially the time you hid behind her and y'all crept up to the living room window and looked in. Now, that was funny."

"Kiley, I'm so embarrassed." Ginger opened her car door. "I'm gone. I can't even look at you."

I grabbed her hand and kissed it. "Don't be ashamed. We all have some things to be embarrassed about. I'm just glad you opened up to me like I opened up to you. I don't do that often, so consider yourself lucky."

She leaned in closer to me. "So are you coming inside or what?"

"No."

"Why not?"

"Because you want me to fuck you."

"Yes, I do. I want you to give it to me like you never gave it to anybody."

"Whew, that could get pretty painful for you."

"I'm a big girl. Trust me, I can handle it."

Ginger and me wasted no time going inside giving each other a workout. And even though she was a "big girl," as she claimed, she couldn't handle it. One minute she was begging me to fuck her, and when I did, she was begging me to stop. One thing, though, her good-ass loving kept me going for the entire night. I couldn't stop no matter how much she complained about being tired. And when it was finally all said and done, we lay naked in the middle of the living room floor cuddled in each other's arms.

I was knocked out on the living room floor when I heard my phone ringing in my pants pocket. I grabbed my pants from the floor and looked at my phone. It was a number I didn't recognize, so I didn't bother to answer. Instead, I went into the kitchen where Ginger was cooking us some breakfast.

She turned around, looked at me, and rolled her eyes. "Why are you up already? I was trying to surprise you by cooking breakfast."

I wrapped my arms around her waist and kissed her on the neck. "Breakfast don't excite me. However, a good morning slurpee like the ones you gave me last night would."

"Oooo, you so nasty. I never knew you could be so blunt."

"Okay, then a nice, slow, wet, up and down, round and round, feel of your lips would be the best surprise you could give me this morning."

Ginger turned around, placed her hands behind my neck, pulling my lips to hers. She slowly licked her tongue around my lips and then went deep inside, rolling her tongue around in my mouth. "There," she said, wiping my wet lips. "How was that for a morning surprise?"

"It was good," I said, reaching for the knob on the stove to turn off the bacon she was frying. "But somehow, I feel cheated."

I picked her up and she straddled the front of me, holding tightly on to my neck as we kissed our way into her bedroom. As I sat down on the bed and leaned back, she slid down my body, got on her knees, and gave me the surprise I'd asked for.

By the time I left Ginger's house, I was on cloud nine. Couldn't think about nothing but how well she was getting accustomed to doing things my way. She promised me she wouldn't pressure me about getting together and agreed to take our relationship one day at a time. I was glad to hear that, 'cause time was really all I needed. I needed closure with Jada, and maybe after one good fuck with Candi, I'd be ready to give Ginger exactly what she deserved.

CHAPTER 12

My wrist was finally starting to feel better. Maybe because I was using my strength running back and forth to Ginger's place laying into her every chance I got. She'd become a real security blanket for me. Helped me keep my mind off Jada, and spending more time with her and Desmon made me realize how much I'd been missing.

I hadn't heard from Jada for almost a month, and Candi was still getting kicked to the curb. She'd shown up uninvited a few times trying to seduce me with her short dresses and tight-ass jeans, but since Ginger was milking a brotha dry, I really wasn't interested. One night, though, Kareem begged me to meet one of his female companions' friends, Stephanie. We got so fucked up that one thing led to another. When I woke up, she was in bed next to me. How? I really can't remember, but I do remember her titties bouncing up and down as she rode me so well.

So, the next day was a chill day for me. I wasn't going over Ginger's house until later to pick up Desmon, so I figured I could catch up on some rest I'd missed out on from staying up in the wee hours of the morning.

Donovan had finally stopped by last week to get the rest of his things and gave me his new address and phone number. We talked about putting our differences aside, but something still didn't sit right with me. Maybe it was my knowing that he fucked my woman, but I truly thought I'd gotten over that. Either way, I felt a sense of relief since he was gone.

Rufus was calling all week trying to catch up with us. Every time he did, no one was around to answer his call. Trying to find out what was on his mind, I stayed around waiting for him to call.

By late afternoon, Quincy and Kareem came busting through my door, asking me if I wanted to roll with them to pick up some tickets for a play we were going to see at the Fox Theatre next weekend. I really wasn't up for the ride, but I gave them some money to get two tickets for me. When Kareem's cheap-ass whined about the cost of the tickets, I paid for his tickets as well. I wasn't really sure who I was going to ask because Ginger and Desmon had already made plans to go to Chicago with her mother next weekend. I for damn sure didn't know much about Stephanie to ask her to go, and Candi, I didn't want her getting excited about us being together. But when I realized I had no other choice, I called her anyway.

Surprised to hear my voice, she laughed. "I am going to have to make sure I write this down. You called me? What could you possibly want with a woman like me?"

"I wanted to know what you were doing next weekend."

"Um, nothing really. But I was hoping you were calling to discuss what we could do this weekend."

"I got plans this weekend."

"Okay, then I got plans next weekend."

"Cool," I said, getting ready to hang up. "Sorry I asked."

"I'm talking about plans with you so, what do you have in mind?"

"Going to dinner then to a play."

"What's the name of it?"

"*Two's Enough, Three's A Crowd.*"

"Sounds interesting. Sure, I'd love to go. But are you sure you wouldn't want any company tonight?"

"Yeah, I'm sure," I said, looking at the caller ID as a call interrupted. It was from an unknown caller, so I suspected it was Rufus. "Say, let me hit you back later. I need to take this call."

"All right," she said, hanging up.

"Hello," I said quickly. The operator came on, then Rufus spoke up and said his name. When she hung up, he clicked in.

"Whazz up, my nigga?" he shouted.

I smiled at the sound of his voice. "Nothing much, killer. Why you just now calling us, man?"

"Been kind of busy. Place like this keeps a brotha slaving. Besides, when I call you niggas, y'all ain't never there no damn way."

"I'm always here. Ninety percent of my time is spent right here in this house. You done just forgot about our asses, that's all."

"No, I haven't. Truthfully, I just don't want to be a burden to you brothas on the outside. The money you send me every month is truly good enough for me."

"I'm glad it helps. So, when you getting out? I thought you'd be out by now."

"I thought so too, but it could be awhile."

"Why? What happened?"

"I caught another case while up in this muh-fucker."

"How in the hell did you manage to do that?"

"Fucking around with drugs and shit. Trying to slip some shit through the cracks. Not only that, I got myself another case fighting with one of the guards."

"Man, that's fucked up. Why would you fight with them, and why in the hell would you be trying to front drugs when I send you enough money to get by every damn month?"

"'Cause I'm greedy. Thinking I can get away with any goddamn thing I want."

"So how much more time do you anticipate?"

"At least another two or three years."

"Damn, that's fucked up. But you don't even sound like you trippin'."

"What can I do about it? Ain't no need for me to gripe about it. I messed my own damn self up. Besides, brotha like me don't stand a chance in the real world anyway. Couldn't make it on the streets if I tried."

"I beg to differ, but we were looking forward to seeing you, killer."

"Same here; but how the fellas doing? Everybody still hoin'?"

"Did you have to ask? You know some things never change. But we did have to let somebody go."

"Let me guess, Donovan, right?'

"Yep. Did you know that fool was sleeping with Jada?"

"Who? Yo' gal Jada?"

"Yeah. All kinds of shit been going down." I hipped Rufus to what had been going on.

"Now you know that doesn't surprise me at all. Donovan always had it out for you. And even I could tell something was going on between him and Jada back in L.A."

"I kinda felt it too. Thing is, I didn't quite know how to put my finger on it."

"You should have shot his ass fo', five times and killed him. Especially since some fellas from L.A. I still been keeping in contact with recently told me he was the mastermind behind yo' daddy's death."

"What?" I said, sitting up in bed. "Who told you that shit?"

"Ricky and his partnas. The only reason I didn't tell you is 'cause them niggas like to keep up mega shit. They'd say anything to shut y'all down. So, not really knowing the truth, I didn't want to stir the pot when there was no need to stir it. Now that you told me what's been going down with y'all it all kind of makes sense."

"Rufus, if I find out Donovan was behind that shit, I'm gonna kill him."

"Don't go jumping the gun, Kiley. Let me find out some mo' shit first. And please don't tell Kareem, 'cause he got a hot head and will do something crazy. Just play it cool until I get back with you."

"Get back with me fast, killer. I'm not going to be able to sit on this for long."

"I know, but chill. I don't need you up in this muh-fucker with me. Trust me, it is no fucking picnic."

"Cool. I appreciate anything you can find out. I'll put some money in the mail for you tomorrow so you should get it by the end of next week."

"Thanks a million, bro. Love ya. Deuces." Rufus hung up.

I couldn't rest for nothing, thinking about what Rufus said. Would Donovan stoop that low and have my pops killed after everything he'd done for him? Ricky and them had to be trippin'. I wanted to call Ricky up myself to ask him, but him and his boys always had it out for me. He'd fasho lie to me, so I'd get myself in more trouble trying to take Donovan out. The only person I felt like could clear shit up for me was Donovan. If I mentioned it to him, maybe by the way he reacted I could tell if he was involved.

I searched around the room for the piece of paper I wrote his address and phone number on.

After I found it, I dialed the number and asked to speak to him. There was a bunch of noise: fools cursing and laughing in the background, and when he answered, he was calling somebody a stupid-ass nigga.

"Yo," he said.

"It's me. Kiley."

"What's going on, playa? Did I forget something?"

"Naw, naw, nothing like that. I just got a quick question for you."

"What's up?"

"You remember what happened in L.A., right?"

"Depends on what you're talking about. So much shit happened I really can't pinpoint one particular thing."

"I mean, after my father was killed. Tell me this, why did you jet to St. Louis so fast?"

"Come on, man. You know why. Too many muh-fuckers were talking and I wasn't trying to go to jail for nobody. Why you asking?"

"'Cause rumor has it that you conspired the whole damn ordeal."

"What ordeal? You mean with your father?"

"Yeah, that's what I mean."

"Now, come on, Kiley. Do you think I would stoop that low after what Papa Abrams did for me? He treated all of us like his sons. He was the only person I ever looked up to and respected. I can't believe you calling me with this bullshit."

"Hey, I'm just asking. My sources called me today and said they'd be calling me back with more info. I hope like hell you ain't lying to me."

"Your sources can kiss my black ass. And I hope they ain't from L.A. All them damn niggas were hating on us from the get-go and you know it."

"Yeah, I know. But I also know if anything I find out holds its ground, I'm gonna have to shake, rattle, and roll."

"Whatever, Kiley. I understand that you got to do your li'l investigation and everythang, but just make sure you get the facts before you step to me like that. And the fact is, I had much love for Papa Abrams. I would have never stabbed him in the back like that. I just hope this don't have nothing to do with what happened between Jada and me. You really need to let that shit go if it does."

"Aw, I've let it go. It's in the past where it's going to stay. But please know, if you're the one responsible for removing the man who provided for me, loved me, and made a way for me to live the life I'm living today, it won't be pretty."

"Pretty or not, I'm not your man. You did away with the fools who were, so let it be."

CHAPTER 13

Saturday night was there before I knew it. I picked Candi up at her place, and since I was early she invited me in for a drink. I was quite surprised to see how nice her place was. She lived in a two-family flat on the south side of St. Louis, and it looked as if it had been reconditioned in the inside, just like our house. She had some badass Chinese black-and-white marble tables in her living room and two white silk couches, covered with plastic, were on each side of the coffee table. Her china cabinet was embroidered with Chinese emblems, and a collection of china plates were inside. Only thing I wasn't too pleased with was the scents she had lit that gave off a funky spicy-ass smell.

When I asked Candi what she did for a living, she told me she worked part time at Macy's and had a few modeling gigs on the side. But it was obvious that her salary wasn't enough to have a crib like hers. She was either lying about her work, or she had somebody else providing for her, and doing it well.

After Candi and me talked and shared a few drinks, we left to go meet Kareem and Quincy along with their dates at the Steak House on Grand before the play started. As soon as we walked in, we saw everybody sitting down in the back and Kareem motioned for us to come on back. Before we did, we stood in line ordering our food, and when it came time to pay, Candi insisted that she pay. Said since I bought the tickets, it was only fair she paid for dinner. That was a new one on me, and even though I was so used to paying all the time, it was kinda nice that somebody else didn't mind picking up the slack. In reality, kinda made me feel special.

As it neared show time, we rushed our food and headed to the Fox Theatre. We had pretty good seats in the mezzanine, and when the lights dimmed, Candi took her hand and placed it on my leg. Throughout the play, she rubbed her hand up and down my leg, occasionally touching my package, trying to give me a rise. If I was bold like the brotha in the play, I would have put her on my lap right then and there and fucked her brains out.

At intermission, Candi told me she was going to the restroom and would be right back. Kareem, his date, and Quincy went to go mingle, and Veronica moved down in the chair next to me to holla until they came back.

"Are you enjoying the show?" she asked.

"Yeah, it's wild, ain't it?"

"It really is. Jaylin Rogers is quite a character, isn't he?"

"Sure is. Kind of remind me of Kareem. I can see how much he's enjoying it."

She laughed. "I hope not. Kareem don't seem all that bad."

"Naw, he's not. I'm just kidding." I paused. "So, uh, how are things going between you and Quincy? I can't believe you're still around after all his horrible-ass cooking."

"It is pretty bad." She laughed. "But we're doing okay. He doesn't want a relationship, and that's cool with me since I just ended one not too long ago. Besides, he knows I'm not really looking for no one to settle down with right now."

"Me either. Being alone gives you peace of mind. Something I've needed for a very long time."

"So, what's up with you and Candi? I mean, you all seem to mesh pretty well together."

"We cool. She's just a friend. I don't know about us meshing, but a friend like her is all I need right now."

Veronica and me continued talking for a while, until Candi came back and asked for her seat back. By the tone of her voice, Veronica hesitated to move, but grinned and got up anyway. The last thing I needed was a woman with a sassy-ass voice, so hearing Candi speak with that tone kind of turned me off.

During the play, I observed her. I watched her laugh, watched her cry, and admired the attention that she gave me by touching my hands and putting her arm around my chair. I also noticed how she gave me her undivided attention throughout the night and treated everyone else as if they didn't exist.

On the drive to my place, she insisted we go to hers to be alone so Quincy and Kareem wouldn't interrupt. Since I knew they probably would, I agreed.

The phone was ringing as we stepped into the dark living room. Candi ran to answer it, and by the time she did, the caller had hung up. She turned on the lights and reached for my coat to hang it up. When she suggested making us a drink, I sat down on the couch and asked her if she didn't mind if I rolled up a joint. She was a li'l hesitant but said it would be okay.

Watching her going back and forth to the kitchen to refill our drinks, I felt myself getting horny. When she handed me my drink, I took it out of her hand, laid it on the table, and pulled her down on top of me.

"Whoa, wait a minute, Kiley. Why are you rushing me?" she asked.

"Rushing you?" I said, pecking her. "How am I rushing you when you know you want this just as much as I do?"

She eased backward and stood up in front of me with one hand on her forehead and the other hand on her hip. "Listen, there's no way we can get down tonight."

"Why not?" I said, sitting up.

"You know, it's that time of the month. That's why I wanted to see you last weekend."

I was disappointed. "Damn," I said, shaking my head. "This is never going to happen between us, is it?" I laughed.

She sat down next to me. "I know. Every time the opportunity presents itself, something always comes up."

"Maybe it's just not meant to be," I said.

Candi moved over, straddled her legs across mine, and put her arms around my neck. "There's no doubt in my mind that this is meant to be. And as soon as Mother Nature is finished with me, I'm coming straight for you, no matter what." She leaned forward and gave me a juicy, long, wet kiss. I gripped her ass as she sat on top of me, enjoying it.

"In the meantime," I suggested, "there's some other things we can do that Mother Nature won't even interfere with."

"I'm sure there is. But the first time you and I get together, I want it to be right. Foreplay, this time, will not suffice."

Since Candi and me were unable to get down like we wanted to, she pulled out *The Game of Life* and we lay in middle of the living room floor playing it. As we were playing, I started asking her questions.

"I don't mean to be nosy or anything, but how are you able to afford all this stuff and only work part time?"

"Because all this stuff you see was given to me. What I mean is after my mother died, I took her furniture. She had a beautiful home in Ladue with my stepfather, and after she died, he wanted to get rid of it. He's a wealthy white man, and even though I never really liked him that much, he always comes through for me when I need something. So, what about you? Donovan mentioned to me that y'all sold drugs but I never see anything going down like that when I'm around."

"And you won't. Not only that, Donovan had no business running his mouth telling you shit like that."

"Don't go getting all defensive. He really didn't tell me much. And really, it isn't any of my business."

"No, it's not, but we don't deal like that anymore. That's a thing of the past."

"Well, if it's not asking too much, how do y'all make a living when nobody in the house works?"

"We just do."

Candi raised her brows. "Okay, I see how we're going to play this. I open up to you and you tell me nothing about you, right? Besides, I see you getting all uptight so—"

"I'm not getting uptight. I just don't know you, Candi. I have no idea how you and Donovan met and there ain't too many people I trust."

"Donovan and me met at Taco Bell on Delmar. I was standing in line fussing at a man in front of me who was taking all day ordering and Donovan intervened. Actually, took up for me when the man called me a stupid bitch."

"So, why aren't you with Donovan now? I know I didn't have that much of an impact on you."

She laughed. "Really, you did. It was just something about you, Kiley; I just couldn't figure out what it was. The first night I saw you in bed with Jada, you remember that night?"

"Yeah, the night she smacked me for looking at you."

"Yes, that night. I was immediately attracted to you."

"So, what was it? My looks, or the fact you could tell I was naked underneath the covers?" I laughed.

"That was part of it, but it was by the way you spoke. You spoke with confidence, with pride. Instantly turned me on."

"Turned you on so well you went right in the other room and fucked Donovan's brains out, huh?"

Candi rolled over on her back and looked up at the ceiling. "I was faking. Dick wasn't really that good. I was hoping that you would hear me and eventually come rescue me from his non-lovemaking ass."

"You didn't really expect me to bust in the room and take over, did you?"

"Nope. But I was seriously hoping that you would."

"That's funny because I was in my room wishing I was Donovan after I heard you moaning and groaning. If you were faking, you need to be starring in movies."

"Well, sign me up. My moans were as fake as a three dollar bill. Donovan got it going on body wise, but he is most certainly a disappointment for a sista who was definitely looking forward to him setting her out."

"Damn, that's not the first time I heard that. I'm just glad I don't have a reputation like that."

"I don't know if you do or don't, but I like how you're in control of yourself. Not only that, I love a man who seems to be in control of his surroundings."

"I'm glad it appears that way," I said, getting up off the floor with the drink in my hand. "Believe it or not, I'm not always in control. I would like to be, but that don't always happen."

"Well, you put up a good front," Candi said, standing, then bending down to pick the game pieces up off the floor.

"I gotta put up a front. It wouldn't be any fun if you could actually read me and tell what I was thinking."

"Oh, I can read you well, Kiley," she said, standing up again and switching the game pieces from one hand to the other. "So well that I can tell what you're thinking right now."

I smiled, went up to her and put my arms around her waist. "And what am I thinking about now, Candi?"

"You're thinking about how you're ready to get out of here since you can't have no loving tonight. You're thinking about what if your baby's mama knew you were over here spending all this quality time with another woman tonight. And, I'll just bet, you've thought about Jada tonight."

"One out of the three ain't bad. But you got some work to do trying to figure me out." I took my hands from around Candi and opened up the closet to get my coat. "I had a nice time tonight, Candi. I'll give you a holla sometime this week." I leaned down, gave her a kiss, then left.

Candi was so wrong trying to figure me out. And no matter how hard I tried to enjoy myself by chilling with her, I really couldn't stop thinking about what Rufus told me. It had been on my mind all damn week, and since I hadn't heard back from him yet, I was starting to think I was wasting my damn time thinking about it.

The house was empty when I got there. Kareem and Quincy must have stayed with their ladies for the night, so I chilled all by myself. I went upstairs to the entertainment room, smoked another blunt, and just as I started to doze off on the couch, the phone rang at two o'clock in the morning and alarmed me.

"Hello," I said softly.

"Hi," Jada said.

I slowly sat up. "What's up?" I asked.

"You."

"Naw, couldn't be me. If it were me, you wouldn't be trippin' like you do."

"I know, but, I just wasn't prepared for you to tell me I couldn't move back into the house. And now that you've had over a month to think about it, does your decision still stand?"

"I'm afraid so, Jada. I miss the hell out of you, but this ain't going to work out between us."

"Okay, so let's say I don't move back in. Will you at least be willing to come visit me sometime?"

"Where are you?"

"I'm in L.A. with my aunt right now, but a job opportunity came through for me in St. Louis. I'll be moving back there in a few weeks. The only thing I'm waiting for is to hear from a rental office about this apartment I had a friend of mine cosign for. As soon as they give her the go-ahead, I'll be back."

"Sounds like a plan, but honestly, I can't make you any promises. I got some other shit on my mind right now and any other distractions from the outside might fuck things up for me."

"I understand. I'll call you in a few days and let you know how things go. Please don't give up on us yet, okay?"

"Yeah, Jada. Call me when you get settled."

"I will. And, baby?"

"What?"

She paused. "I love you."

"Uh-huh."

"You can't tell me you love me back?"

"Jada, I don't know what I'm feeling right now. Just call me in a few days, all right?"

"Sure," she said, hanging up with attitude since things didn't go according to her plan.

Here I go again, I thought. Everything with the ladies was going smooth, and then she calls. There was no way I was going to let this be a setback for me. No way in hell. Jada was just going to have to move on without me. And me the same.

By morning, I was in the kitchen when Quincy came through the back door high as hell.

"Man, is that all you do around Veronica is get high? She really seems like a nice gal and don't seem like the type who would be interested in a dopehead."

Quincy ignored me, pulled out a container of orange juice from the refrigerator, and stood there gulping it down. After he finished, he pulled up a stool and put it in front of the counter next to me. "If you must know, Dr. Phil, I don't usually get high around Veronica. After

I dropped her off last night, I went over Kim's house because she's my getting high, 'smack it up, rub it down' buddy. Veronica and me don't go out like that."

Since he was breathing all over my food, I took my plate over to the kitchen table and sat down. "Do you even like Veronica? I mean, you tell me she's cool but then she's always in your company."

"She is cool. Cool as a fan, but since she ain't really that spectacular in bed I have to make other arrangements. For a sista, she kinda on the stiff side. When I try to adventure and do wild shit with her, she be acting funny. Act like it's too nasty for her. Other than that, she's definitely a good listener, she can cook her ass off, and she knows how to cater to me when I'm at her place."

"Yeah, a bad sex partner can fasho turn you off. Trust me, though, I didn't mean to pry. I was just wondering."

"You ain't prying. Feel free to ask me anything. You're the one who always keeping secrets and shit. Kareem and me were talking about your secretive ass the other night."

I laughed. "Do I act like my shit is that private?"

"Act? It ain't no act. That's just you."

"You know where it comes from. I can't open up to everybody like you brothas do. Never know who the fuck I'm running my mouth to."

"You can usually tell who can or can't be trusted."

"And how's that?"

"You get this feeling inside when the ones you can't trust are around," Quincy said, holding his stomach. "It's a funny feeling that makes you feel all queasy and shit."

"Sounds like gas to me."

"Exactly. And that's what it feels like. Makes you feel like you just want to go shit on yourself or something."

"Let me end this conversation. No need for me to be sitting here talking to a man who ain't even in his right mind."

"Naw, straight up. I'm serious."

"Well, why didn't you get these feelings when Donovan was around? I had a feeling, but it was nothing like what you mentioned."

"If you think about it, he didn't snake me, he snaked you. Therefore, I wouldn't have had those feelings. But as soon as that fool stepped in here with Marcus, my stomach was rumbling like a muh-fucker."

"Mine wasn't rumbling, but I did have a funny feeling inside."

"Our feelings might be different, but that's what I mean when I say something inside just don't feel right. Like with the ladies, you said yourself you felt something wasn't right with Jada. And you were right. Now, you're saying the same thing about Candi."

"Yeah, but I think it's just the fact she's been with Donovan that bothers me."

"Maybe, maybe not. All I can say is, observe, my brotha. Observing a woman will tell you things about her she might not even know about herself."

"Trust me, I do. All the time. Sometimes I think I'm too observant. They start complaining, talking about how nosy I am."

"You are nosy. Always up in a brotha's business, but it's cool. Kareem and me know you just be trying to have our backs." Quincy gulped down some more orange juice then looked at me. "Remember, though, we got yours too."

"You don't even have to tell me. I know y'all do. That's why I need to tell you something. I'm not going to tell Kareem because I don't think he'll be able to handle it just yet."

Quincy looked puzzled. "Tell me what? What is it?"

I hesitated, then spoke. "I . . . I think I'm going to have to make plans to get rid of Donovan."

Quincy scratched his head. "Why is that?"

"There are a few reasons. First, in my heart I truly believe the incident with Marcus is going to come back and haunt us. Second, I really feel like he's plotting against us with his new boys. And mainly, Rufus called and said he'd heard it through the grapevine that Donovan had something to do with Papa Abrams's death."

Quincy cocked his head back. "Are you serious? Now, give or take, I've been feeling the same shit about them retaliating, but do you really think Donovan had something to do with Papa's death? You know everybody in the hood loved him like he was they daddy."

"If that was the case, then he wouldn't have been killed. I know everybody was pretending to love him. You of all people know how some niggas are. Be hating like a muh-fucker, laughing in your face one minute and plotting behind your back the next. Keeping that in mind, I'm doing everything in my power to find out the truth. My gut instincts tell me he did. I just want to be sure before I do anything."

Quincy took a deep breath. "Yeah, you're right; but we need to tell Kareem. I don't think it's right to keep something like this from him. I know he's going to want to go handle it his way, but once we talk some sense into him, he'll chill."

"Quincy, I'm telling you he won't. I know him and I'm not going to take the risk of him leaving this house going over there getting all shot up 'cause I fed him the wrong information."

"Kiley, he's going to be more upset with you if you don't tell him. I'm a bit upset myself right now since you're just now telling me. We're supposed to be in this together. All this confidential bullshit with you is starting to drive me crazy."

I chewed on my food and thought about it for a while. After Quincy convinced me, I went against my gut and agreed to tell Kareem as soon as he got home.

Quincy and me were upstairs playing cards when Kareem came home with the chick he had over the other night and her friend, Stephanie, who I vaguely remembered fucking. She'd called me several times to talk but I played her off and told her I'd call her back. Before they could remove their coats, I quickly hopped up and pulled Kareem to the side. "Say, would you mind asking them to come back some other time? I need to get at you about something personal."

He pulled his coat off and laid it on one of the barstools. "Damn, can't it wait?" he whispered. "I told them they could chill with us for the night."

"No, it can't. They can come back tomorrow. Besides, I ain't in the mood to be entertaining."

"Shit, you ain't never in the mood to be entertaining. You the most wishy-washy-ass nigga I know," he said, walking away. He whispered something to the ladies and they got up and left. After he walked them to the door, he jogged back up the steps, picked up a cigarette, and lit it. "This better be awfully damn important," he said, sitting down at the card table with Quincy and me.

I looked at Quincy. He could tell how hesitant I was, so he started talking to Kareem.

"Don't you get tired of fucking, playa?" Quincy said, playfully hitting him on his arm.

"Never. And since you cock-sucking fools interrupted my booty, this better be good, so shoot."

"All right," I said, clenching my hands together. "Here's the deal. But you gotta promise me you won't go jumping the gun, Kareem."

"Nigga, come on with it," he said, blowing the smoke out of his mouth. "You and Quincy sitting up here fucking around and I got bigger and better things to do."

Quincy looked at Kareem. "Rufus told Kiley rumor had it that Donovan had your pops set up. He ain't sure, but—"

Kareem's mouth dropped. "You playing, right?" he said, staring at Quincy. Right then, the phone rang, but we all ignored it.

"Naw, man," I said. "He ain't playing. Before I do anything, I'm waiting to hear from Rufus so he can confirm it for me."

"Confirmation!" he yelled, then quickly stood up. "You waiting on some goddamn confirmation!"

I stood up. "Kareem, calm down. If it's not true, I don't want to jeopardize—"

"Nigga, who in the hell are you to decide if the shit is true or not? You know wouldn't no shit be floating around like that if it wasn't true. You sit your pussy ass over there if you want to. I'm going to go do away with this son of a bitch myself!" Kareem hurried over to get his coat, then pulled his gun out to make sure it was loaded.

I cut my eyes at Quincy; after all, it was his idea to tell Kareem. We both tried to stop Kareem from leaving.

"Get your goddamn hands off me, partna!" he yelled, aiming the gun at Quincy. "Touch me again, fool, and I'll kill you."

Quincy backed away as he saw fire burning in Kareem's eyes.

"Kareem!" I yelled. "Calm the fuck down. I promise you we gon' take care of this shit. You know we will. Don't be trippin' like that."

"Take care of it, huh?" He aimed the gun at me. It trembled in his hand, and when the phone rang again, he quickly snapped his head to the side. He bit into his lip then turned to me again. "How long have you known about this shit, Kiley, huh? Just how goddamn long have you kept this shit from me?"

"Not long. I swear to you, not long."

"What's not long? Two days, three days, what?"

"A little over a week. I'm giving Rufus time to see what he can come up with for me."

"Time!" he yelled shaking his head. A tear rolled down his face. "We talking about our damn father, Kiley. Not some chickenhead nigga in the streets. This muh-fucker played us, man. Lived off our shit for years and you can sit there and wait?" He stuck his gun inside his pants and started running down the steps. Quincy and me ran after him and as he opened the back door, I grabbed him by the back of his coat.

"Sit your ass down!" I yelled.

He gathered up some spit in his mouth and shot it directly in my face. "Fuck you, man!" he yelled. "I loved my father; I don't know about you!" He took his fist and punched me hard on my face. As my jaw burned, I slung him by his coat and threw his ass into the stove. He fell hard on the floor and when I lifted my foot up to karate kick him in the chest, he took his foot and kicked me right in my damn balls. I grabbed my goods and fell to the floor. Quincy was yelling something but I wasn't even trying to hear him. I felt as if my balls were bleeding, and by the time I looked up, Kareem had gotten up and run out the back door.

I limped up the steps to the bathroom to check my dick. Quincy followed behind me apologizing for suggesting that I tell Kareem. "Get the fuck out my face," I spat. "I knew I shouldn't have listened to your high ass."

I headed back up the steps. When we reached the top, Quincy went down the hall to his room and slammed the door. And I went into my room and did the same. After I lay back on the bed, massaging my package, I got up and ran some bath water to relax.

While I was in the tub I could only hope that Kareem wouldn't get himself into any trouble. I wasn't too worried, because he hadn't a clue where Donovan lived. I was sure he was on his way to Tricia's place looking for him, and hoped she wouldn't tell Kareem where to find him out of anger. But the more I thought about it, I got severely worried. Kareem always had a way of finding out shit when he wanted to, and if it meant pulling the gun out on Tricia to find out Donovan's whereabouts, I knew he would.

I dried myself with a towel, trying to take my mind off the situation. I thought about calling Ginger, but I wasn't sure if she and Desmon made it back from Chicago yet. The phone rang twice as we argued, but no one had answered. I checked the messages: one was from Ginger and Candi called too. Before I called Ginger back, I called Candi. The caller ID must have revealed who I was.

"Hello, handsome," she answered.

"What's up?" I said, dryly.

"What's wrong? You sound bothered."

"Nothing, really. I was just returning your call."

"Well, I wish you could be a bit more enthused about it."

I snickered. "Trust me, I am."

"How can I trust you when you say you're excited and don't sound it?"

"Okay, so I'm not excited. I was just calling back to say hello. I'll hit you back later."

"No, no, no. You're not going to get rid of me that easily. If you'd like, I can come perk you up. Mother Nature still bugging but I got other ways of making you relax."

"Say you do, huh?"

"Yes, so can I come over?"

"Are you on your way?"

"Uh-huh. Already walking to my car."

"Then good-bye," I said, hanging up.

I quickly called Ginger back before Candi came over. She answered the phone sounding like she was out of breath.

"Damn, did I catch you at a bad time?" I asked.

She laughed. "Yeah, sort of. I just had to beat your son's butt for painting my couch with fingernail polish."

"You shouldn't be having that shit lying around where he can get to it."

"Kiley, I can't keep everything away from him. He's so damn curious it drives me crazy. Besides, he should know better."

"I know, but don't be hitting on him. Just buy yourself a new couch. You need one anyway. Not only that, he's only four years old. What do you expect?"

"I know how old he is. And if you think I need a new couch, you buy me one. In the meantime, if you called here to give me a lecture about how to raise him, don't. He's going to be disciplined and I don't care who likes it."

"All right, hot mama. I didn't call to argue with you. I just called to see how y'all trip to Chicago went."

"It was cool. We stayed at my aunt's house most of the time, and last night I went to a club with one of my cousins."

"You didn't let nobody touch on your ass like you did at the club a few weeks ago, did you?"

"No, not as long as you didn't fuck that bitch Candi while I was gone."

I laughed. "And if I did?"

"If you did you know I'm gonna hurt you, don't you?"

"You can't hurt me any more than I'm already hurting."

"Why? What's wrong? I thought you sounded kind of funny."

"Naw, I'm cool. Kareem and me just got into an argument and he left. I'm worried about him."

"He'll be all right. Just pray that everything will be okay."

"Sure. I hope so."

There was a long pause before she cleared her throat then continued the conversation. "I was going to ask if you wanted to come see me. But since you're sounding kind of blue, I guess my timing ain't right."

"No, it's not. I'll probably get by there tomorrow. Kind of wanna chill for the night. Let me talk to Desmon, though."

"Sorry, but he's in timeout right now. I'm sending him to bed in a few, and I hope he learns to get his act together."

"When I get there tomorrow, I'm putting you in timeout too. And don't be so hard on him, all right? He's just a kid."

"A hardheaded kid who should know better. As for your timeout, I welcome it. See you tomorrow."

"No doubt."

Ginger told me she loved me and hung up the phone. Trying not to stress myself thinking about Kareem, I went down the hallway to Quincy's room to apologize to him for going off on him. After twenty-one years of knowing him, I'd never talked to him like that. I knocked on his door. "Quincy," I said, yelling through the door.

He unlocked the door and stood in the doorway with his shirt off. "What?"

"Listen, I know you're upset, but I'm sorry for dissing you like that. I was just pissed off with how the situation turned out, so don't take it personal."

"I won't," he said, slamming the door in my face. It took everything I had not to put my foot on the door and kick it down, but I figured he needed more time to cool off. And after I heard the doorbell ring, I just walked away.

I opened the door for Candi and followed up the steps behind her, checking her out as she walked directly up to my room. She took her coat off and wore nothing but navy blue silk pajamas. All I had on was my boxers, and after I took those off, we pulled the covers back and got right into bed.

She massaged my sore muscle for a while, but when I tried to open her pajama top to suck her breasts she stopped me.

"Roll over on your stomach," she whispered. I did and she eased over and straddled my back. She rubbed something on her hands and started massaging my shoulders. As her hands worked down my back and she grazed my ass like she was rubbing lotion on a baby, I was in la-la land.

"Damn, that feel good," I moaned, closing my eyes as she pressed deeply into my back and shoulders with her hands.

"Told you I could make you relax. Now be quiet and concentrate on sleeping. You know you need it."

"You're damn right I do," I said, already dozing off.

I turned my head sideways on my pillow and faded. By the time I woke up it was after five o'clock in the morning. I rolled over and looked at Candi; she was cuddled up with my body pillow sound asleep. My eyes scanned her sexy body; I damn sure wanted to fuck her. But with Kareem being heavy on my mind, my thoughts quickly shifted to him. I tossed the covers back and got out of bed to see if he'd made it in. When I saw his bedroom door was open, I suspected that he hadn't. I went upstairs to the third level to see if maybe he was chilling up there. Instead, Quincy was up there by himself, asleep on the couch.

I tapped him, asking if Kareem had called. He shook his head and went right back to sleep. Fearing the worst, I went downstairs to the living room and sat up in the dark. I called Kareem's cell phone several times but got no answer. Then I called the number Donovan gave me to reach him, and when some other brotha answered sounding like he was asleep, I hung up the phone.

I thought about how angry Kareem was when he left. I hadn't seen him cry since Daddy's funeral, and to see him like that just tore me apart. As I thought about how I threw him on the ground, I couldn't do nothing but get choked up. What damage had I done? I thought. And how in the hell was I going to fix it?

When I saw Candi coming down the steps looking for me, I squeezed my eyes to hide my emotions. I called her name as she headed for the kitchen.

"Kiley?" she said, coming into the dark living room. "Is that you?"

"Yeah, it's me."

"Why are you sitting in the dark?" She reached for the lamp on the end table, turning it on.

"Thinking."

She sat down on my lap and wrapped her arms around my neck. I leaned back and put my arms around her waist. "Why do you have to think in the dark?"

I didn't respond.

"I think you really need to tell me what's going on with you. I can tell you're upset, so tell me. I'm a good listener."

I shrugged. "It's really nothing. I just had a fight with Kareem last night and I'm kinda worried since I haven't heard from him."

"Why you so upset about that? Siblings fight all the time. As close as you and Kareem are, everything will be okay."

"I know it will, but he left out going after Donovan. I won't be able to live with myself if something happens to him."

"Donovan? Why would he leave out going after Donovan?"

"Because we think Donovan had something to do with my father being killed in L.A. I told Kareem about it and he got angry."

"Why would you think Donovan had something to do with it? He was your friend, wasn't he?"

"Yeah, but someone who I trust with my life told me Donovan set everything up. Thing is, I just don't have proof yet."

"And what if Donovan did have something to do with it? You aren't planning on . . ."

I moved forward and eased Candi off my lap. I stood up and took her by her hand. "I don't know what we're going to do. All I can say is that it won't be pretty." I walked up the stairs with Candi and could tell she was kind of frightened by what I said. When we got back in bed she lay on my chest and rubbed it up and down with her hands. As it was starting to feel good she stopped.

"Kiley?" she said, looking up at me. "Would you ever really kill somebody?"

I hesitated for a moment. "Who wouldn't? I think when it comes to the ones you love, anybody would."

"So did you kill the guys who killed your father?"

I hesitated before answering. "Let's just say they got what they deserved."

"By you, Kareem, or Quincy? Who?"

I just looked at Candi and didn't respond. She laid her head back down on my chest and continued to rub it. "I guess that's why you shake in your sleep like you do, huh?" she asked.

"Shake?"

"Yes, I touched you and stopped you from shaking several times throughout the night. Were you having a bad dream or something?"

"I guess. I have those from time to time. That's why I like to sleep alone."

"Hmm," Candi said, continuing to rub my chest. As her hands slowed, she started to fade.

I couldn't go back to sleep until I knew Kareem was safe. And after ringing his phone until nine in the morning, he finally answered.

"Why you keep calling me?" he yelled.

"Why haven't you been answering your phone?" I asked calmly.

"Because I didn't feel like it. I knew you would be up pacing the damn floors, so I wanted you to suffer thinking something happened to me. Hopefully you'll stop keeping secrets from me and start telling the truth about shit."

"I didn't want to tell you because I knew how you were going to react. I promise you, if Donovan is responsible, he will suffer the consequences."

"I think we need to go see Rufus, personally, and find out more about the shit. I don't want to sit around waiting on him to call us back."

"Rufus is the most reliable nigga I know. He'll call back, trust me. Meanwhile, just cool out. We don't need to be making no more unnecessary trouble for ourselves right now."

"I'm giving him one week to get back with us. After that, I'm sorry, I'm going to meet with Mr. Donovan to see what he has to say about it."

"I already talked to him. He said he had nothing to do with it. Told me I'd gotten rid of the muh-fuckers who did."

"Yeah, we'll see. After all the shit that's happened lately, I can see him saying some shit like that."

"Me too. But just how we planned the last one, we're going to have to plan this one. I don't want no fuckups."

"Me either. I'll be there in a bit. After I left last night I drove around looking for that fool. Then I realized how stupid it would be for me to go out like that, so I stopped by Felicia's house for a li'l relaxation."

As Kareem and me continued talking on the phone, I looked in the mirror at Candi still lying on my chest. When I moved her hair away from her face, I could see her open eyes in the mirror.

I ended my conversation with Kareem and told him I would holla at him when he got home.

She lifted her head off my chest and stared at me. "Kiley, should I be worried about you?" she asked.

"Naw, Candi. And please don't be afraid of me. I can tell by the look in your eyes that you are."

"I'm not scared. I just don't want anything to happen to you."

"Nothing's going to happen to me. I take care of myself very well."

"How can you be so sure? It really sounds like you're playing a dangerous game."

"Look, don't worry. Everything will be cool. All you need to worry about is getting rid of Mother Nature so I can get at you like I want to."

"Two more days. That's all I got left. After that, I'm yours."

CHAPTER 14

I was on the phone listening to Jada as she broke the bad news telling me she decided to stay in L.A. since things didn't work out between us. Deep down, I was kind of glad. Didn't have time for her in my life, since I was fucking Ginger whenever I wanted to and making plans to get down with Candi. She called after her period ended a few days ago but I'd gotten so messed up with Quincy and Kareem, I didn't feel like any company. She sounded disappointed, but I wasn't in the mood.

"Kiley, did you hear what I just said?" Jada shouted into the phone. "I don't have any reason to come back there, do I?"

"As a matter of fact, you don't. We can't seem to get our shit together, and all this 'fuck me, fight me' shit is driving me crazy."

There was silence, then Jada spoke up again. "I agree. Our relationship has been toxic, so maybe a long break is what we need."

Break my ass, I thought. As far as I was concerned, this shit was over. But just to keep down the noise, I continued a cordial conversation with Jada and then wished her well.

"If you need anything," I said, "holla."

"You know I will."

After we ended the call, I felt closure. A real sense of relief came over me, and as I released a deep sigh, my eyes shifted to the monitor. I saw the mailman drop the mail inside the door and went downstairs to get it. There was a big brown envelope on the floor, and when I picked it up I saw that the return address showed it was from Rufus. I ran upstairs to my bedroom, dropped the rest of the mail on my bed, and opened the envelope. When I unfolded his letter, there were several pictures inside. Some showed Donovan with his arms around two of the niggas I killed in L.A. They held up peace signs. The other pictures showed them at a nightclub in L.A., clinking glasses together and laughing.

"Damn!" I yelled out loud. "I'll be muh-fucking damned!" I threw the pictures on the floor and plopped down on the bed. I was angry with myself for not killing that fool when I had the chance. Wouldn't even be in this situation if I would have let him lie on the kitchen floor and bleed to death. I took a deep breath and opened Rufus's letter to read it.

Playa, playa, playa. Sorry it took me awhile getting back with you but I wanted to make sho when I provided you with info about Donovan it was legit. I hate to be the one to break the bad news, but Donovan was, without a doubt, the mastermind behind Papa Abrams's death. I didn't want to call to tell you on these fucked-up phones because I know they be listening in on our conversations, but after I doubted Ricky he mailed those pictures to me to back up his accusations. After seeing the Black Stallion in action, when he clearly said he didn't know the fools, I'd say it's time to shake, rattle, and roll. I wish I was there to blow his fucking brains out for ya but I'm sure you'll have a good time doing it yourself. Thanks for the money, and since they just slammed three more years on me for being a menace to society, I'll see you when I get out. Sorry it had to be like this for ya. I know you were hoping for a betta outcome.

Love ya,
Killer

I balled up the letter and tossed it in the trashcan. I felt like somebody had stabbed a dagger in my chest. Since I promised Kareem I wouldn't keep anything else from him, I went to his room to break the news. When I woke him up I tossed the pictures on the bed for him to see. He sat up looking at them with his mouth wide open.

"This shit here just pisses me the fuck off!" He yanked the covers back and got out of bed. "How did you get these?"

"Ricky mailed them to Rufus and he sent them to me."

"I knew it! I knew he was behind that shit the moment you said he might be!"

Quincy stood in Kareem's doorway yawning. "What's all the yelling about?" he asked.

Kareem gave the pictures to me and I handed them to Quincy. He looked at them and shook his head. "Man, he played all of our asses like some fools."

"Naw, he didn't," I said. "He played himself by having those damn pictures taken. I guess he thought the chance of us seeing them was slim."

Kareem opened his closet and pulled down a jogging suit. "It's time to get this show on the road. Tonight." He looked at me with his face scrunched up. "I'm not waiting a moment longer, Kiley."

"I told you, all I needed was confirmation, and since I got it, I say let's roll."

"Don't leave me out," Quincy said. "I can't wait to hear what that fool got to say."

We made plans to leave the house around ten o'clock. Feeling a slight bit nervous, I called Ginger and told her I was on my way to see Desmon. On the drive to her house, Candi called and said she wanted to come see me.

"Not tonight, baby. We'll have to make plans some other time."

"Kiley, you promised. I knew you were going to put me off."

"Look," I said, loudly. "I'm not doing it intentionally. I got some business I need to tend to."

"I don't like the way you're sounding, Kiley. You're not about to get yourself into any trouble, are you?"

"Candi, stop asking questions. I know you're worried but this has nothing to do with Donovan. Besides, you and me will have our time together. Just not today."

"But—"

I wasn't in the mood to explain myself so I just hung up on her.

Desmon was in his room playing with the train set I bought him a few weeks ago. Worried, I didn't leave his side. Ginger came in a few times and talked to us, but since I finally opened up and told her what was going down tonight she left us alone.

At eight o'clock I called Kareem and Quincy and told them I was on my way. Since Desmon fell asleep while I was there, I had a chance to have sex with Ginger before I left. She cried the whole time. Said she had a bad feeling about tonight and made me promise to call her when I got home. As I headed out the door, she pulled me by the arm.

"Baby, please just let it go. I know I'm asking a lot but what about your son? What if—"

I placed my fingers on her lips. "Shh, that's why I didn't want to tell you. You worry too much. It'll all be over with tomorrow. I'll call you tonight when I get in."

Ginger walked me out to my car and continued begging me not to do it. Feeling as if I wanted to change my mind, I drove off knowing that I couldn't.

On the drive home, I talked to Daddy silently in the car. I explained to him how different it was going to be for me this time because I had someone in my life to live for: Desmon. I swore I heard his voice telling me not to do it, but I wouldn't listen. I reminded him if it hadn't been for him I wouldn't even exist. There would be no Desmon and I wouldn't have the finer things in life I'd always dreamed of having. I also reminded him of how much he warned me about Donovan, and always taught me not to let anyone step on his family and shatter his legacy. Knowing that he left it up to me to carry on, Donovan had to die tonight. No questions about it.

Kareem and Quincy were standing outside waiting for me when I pulled up. A car they'd gotten from Al's was parked behind the house, so we drove that instead of mine.

As we neared Donovan's place, I called his crib to see if he was there. When he answered, I told him I found some clothes of his in the basement and was on my way to bring them to him since I was close by. I told him that when I got closer, I would call so he could come to the car to get them.

When we parked in front of the house, I called Donovan again and he said he'd be right out. Kareem and Quincy seemed relaxed in the back seat, but I sat, tapping on the steering wheel with my fingers, thinking about the consequences.

Donovan finally came out of the house jogging down the steps with his hands in his pockets. I unlocked the door for him and he opened it, then leaned down looking into the car.

"Get in," I said.

He sat in the car and closed the door behind him. He turned around and looked at Kareem and Quincy. "How you brothas doing? I didn't know y'all were coming to see me too." He smiled. Kareem and Quincy didn't say a word. Donovan looked over at me. "They ain't speaking to me?"

I put my foot on the accelerator. "You in the mood to go for a ride?"

"Not really, but I guess I have no choice since you're already driving off."

I pulled down an alley around the corner from Donovan's house and parked the car. When I turned off the headlights, I could see his hands shaking. I looked over at him. "Do you remember our conversation a few weeks ago?"

"Yeah, I remember. Remember well."

"Well, my connections came through for me." I handed him the pictures. "You remember those niggas, don't you?"

He nodded his head looking through the pictures. "Yep, I remember them."

"I thought you said you had no dealings with them."

"I didn't. I saw them at the club a few times and hopped in the pictures with them. They knew I was down with y'all, man. Besides, pictures don't prove a damn thing."

"They prove to me that you're a lying-ass nigga," Kareem said whistling, putting some bullets into his gun.

Donovan looked back at Kareem and smiled. Then he turned around and quickly opened the car door and rolled to the ground. By the time he got up and started running, Kareem pointed the gun out the window and pulled the trigger. One bullet grazed Donovan's side, and the other two missed since he was running so fast. Quincy, being the fast runner that he is, got out and ran after him. Knowing that there was no way for Donovan to swindle his ass out of this one, I slowly drove down the alley. I pulled the car over when I saw Quincy kicking the shit out of Donovan where the gunshot wound was. Kareem and me got out of the car.

"I would have shot his ass but I didn't want to take the pleasure away from the two of you," Quincy said, taking deep breaths and kicking Donovan in his stomach while he was on his knees bending over.

"Kiley, please, man," Donovan begged. "You gotta hear me out when I tell you I had nothing to do with it."

"I believe you, Donovan. But do yourself a favor," I slid my gun over to him. "Take your life anyway. Might as well, 'cause thing is, even though I believe you, Kareem don't."

Donovan picked up my gun and placed it against his head. He looked at Kareem, "I would have never had Papa Abrams killed, man. You gotta believe me!"

"Shut up talking to me, fool, and pull the trigger," Kareem said, aiming his gun at Donovan's chest.

Donovan took a deep breath, quickly turned the gun on Kareem and fired. As he shot blanks, Kareem fired four bullets right into his chest. Blood splattered and his body fell forward. I kicked my gun away from his hands, picked it up, and we got in the car and left.

There was silence on the way home. When we got in, we all went into our rooms, closed the doors, and didn't come out until morning. There was nothing to talk about when shit had to go down the way it did. But it had to be done, and I had no regrets. Still, I felt ill inside. Wanted to throw the fuck up, and scream at the top of my fucking lungs. I hated to be betrayed. I hated backstabbing niggas; Donovan was just that. There was no way, whatsoever, that I could let him off the hook. He'd fucked up too many times. Regardless, this shit hurt. It stung. Stung so bad that I had to shed some tears. I smacked them away, especially when I thought of my father. And while thinking of him, I couldn't help but nod my head and feel as if I'd done the right thing.

I started to fade, and as I drifted off into a deep sleep, the ringing phone awakened me. I snatched it up and held it close to my ear.

"Why didn't you call me?" Ginger asked.

"I'm fine," I said, rubbing my eyes. "Can I call you back though?"

"Take all the time you need. I just wanted to be sure you were okay."

"Thanks for checking on me. Kiss Desmon for me and I'll get at you later."

Ginger told me she loved me and hung up. I appreciated her words, but at this time, love didn't mean shit to me.

CHAPTER 15

For the next couple of weeks, I stayed cooped up in my room. The only time I came out was to get something to eat or to talk to the fellas for a minute or two. Things seemed back to normal for them; they were already running the streets, going to the clubs, and entertaining females. I just wasn't quite ready for that yet. My mood was calm, but I was paranoid as hell. Definitely couldn't find it in my heart to trust anyone else again. I stayed up many of nights, trying not to fall asleep, in fear of having nightmares that I often had when murder was on the mind.

It took me another two weeks just to get out and go see Ginger and Desmon. And the only reason I did that was because she had the flu and said she needed a break from him. She sounded a mess over the phone, and when I got to her place, she looked even worse. The whole time I was there, she stayed under the covers. I tried to climb in bed with her, but she insisted she wanted to be alone.

Respecting her wishes, I took Desmon home with me and let her get some rest. By now, he was getting used to being with me and was getting into everything around the house. My nerves were kinda bad and I found myself yelling at him for every li'l thing he did. After I took a chill pill, I cooled out. We played with the pinball machines and video games, and sat around watching movies all day until I got tired.

I'd fallen asleep with Desmon, and when he woke me up and told me the doorbell was ringing, I looked at the monitor and saw Candi standing outside on the porch.

Upset about her sudden visit, I rushed to the door and opened it. I released a deep sigh with a frown displayed on my face. "Look, baby, I'm really busy right now. Can you come back later?"

"Looks to me like you've been sleeping," she said boldly walking into the house. "I just came by to find out why you haven't called me. I'd say you owe me an explanation, wouldn't you?"

I slammed the door then grabbed her arm as she proceeded to walk toward the living room. "Didn't you hear what I said? I would like to be alone right now."

Candi snatched away from my tight grip then massaged her arm. "You don't have to be so rough. I just came by to see how you were doing. Is that a crime?"

I gazed at Candi, who I suspected was there to do me no harm. Being on edge had me this way, and maybe it was a good thing that she was here. "No, it's not a crime, and I apologize for the attitude. I'm upstairs chilling. Follow me."

When we got upstairs, Candi saw Desmon sitting on the couch and she sat next to him. "Kiley, he is so cute. What's your name, sweetie?"

"Desmon Jermaine Abrams," he said, looking at her and kicking his feet against the couch.

"Desmon," I said. "Do Daddy a favor and go to my room and put your pajamas on. I'll be down in a minute to tuck you in bed." I held my arms out and he gave me a hug.

"I didn't know you had your son today, Kiley. I can come back if you want me to."

"You really should have called first, Candi. You just never know who I might be entertaining."

"Sorry, but every time I stop by you don't ever have any company. It would really surprise me if you are seeing someone else. And if you are, I know it's not anything serious."

"Well, you're right about that. I don't get serious anymore."

"That's your choice, but are you at least having sex with anyone? I mean, since you ain't having it with me, are you giving it up to anybody?"

I leaned back on the couch and looked at my dick that had been deprived for almost three weeks. I touched it and looked at Candi. "Who I have sex with ain't your business. Let's just say I don't suffer without it unless I choose to."

I wanted to fuck Candi, no doubt, but there was something about her that sent off bad vibes. Then again, maybe it was just me. There were very few people who I trusted, and it was imperative for me to watch my back. In order for me to calm down my dick, I excused myself from our conversation then went downstairs to check on Desmon. If my dick was still hard when I returned, then maybe it was time for me to handle the ongoing urge I had of being inside of Candi.

Desmon was sitting up in bed flipping through the channels with the remote.

"What you doing?" I asked then sat on the bed.

"Trying to find something to watch." He rubbed his eyes. "But I'm getting sleepy now."

He laid the remote down then yawned. I kissed him on the forehead, turned down the lights, and then went back upstairs to finish my business with Candi. She looked bored as she remained on the couch with her legs crossed, displaying a fake smile.

"Would you like something to drink?" I asked, and then walked over to the kitchen to get myself a beer out of the fridge.

She turned around on the couch. "Yes. I'll have what you're having. If it's a beer, I'll take a light one, please."

I got Candi a Bud Light then handed it to her. I sat on the couch and picked up a joint Kareem or Quincy must have already rolled up sitting on the table. I lit it then passed it to Candi.

"No, thanks. I don't do drugs."

"Why not? It's only marijuana. Relaxes the fuck out of you when need be."

"I usually have sex when I need to relax. And trust me, weed is doing more to your mind than just relaxing it."

I took several hits from the joint and kept smiling at her. Then I picked up my beer and eased over next to her on the couch. I put the tip of the joint out with my finger, laid it in the ashtray, and looked at her. "I need to know what's up with you. I play you off, treat you like shit, and you still coming by. The same routine been going on for months. Most women would have told me to go fuck myself. What's your purpose?"

"Oh, trust me, I've thought about telling you to go fuck yourself many times. And your question is a good one because I was wondering why I put up with your shit myself. The only conclusion I can come up with is I guess I just don't give up that easily. Not only that, I think the wait is going to be worth it. So, you keep acting funny all you want to. I'm not giving up until I get what I came here for."

"And what's that?"

"You."

"I don't come that easy."

"Who you telling? I already figured that out. And since you don't, that's what drives me."

"So, you like a challenge?"

"Love it. It's what I live for."

Candi lifted up her legs and laid them across mine. I scooted back on the couch and she hiked up her dress and straddled my lap.

"Are we finally getting ready to do this?" I asked, looking up at her while holding her hips.

She leaned forward and whispered, "Why keep putting it off until tomorrow when you can for damn sure have it your way today?"

We started kissing, and when the phone started ringing, I ignored it. This time, there were going to be no interruptions. I dimmed the lights, took off my boxers, and stood in the middle of the floor with my jewels in my hand, looking at her. She smiled, and before coming my way, she slid her black dress over her head. After kicking her heels over to the side, she stood naked across the room. She parted her hair with her fingers and moved it away from her face so I could see her.

"Are you coming over here, or must I walk all the way over there?" she asked with her hands on her hips.

"Naw, I thought you were coming over here to get it. You've come this far, so a few more steps ain't going to hurt you."

"Oooo, so unfair. You can meet me halfway, can't you?"

I stepped forward until I was face to face with her. I moved her back to the wall behind her and pressed myself against her. I rolled my tongue up and down the side of her neck, then I held her breasts and sucked. As I felt her body trembling, I lifted her up, leaving her against the wall, and rested her thighs on my shoulders.

She looked down at me, as her hair draped down the sides of her face and snickered. "I hope like hell you got me," she said, holding my head.

"Just relax. I promise I won't let you fall."

I leaned in forward, moved her cushiony soft hairs away from her goodness with my tongue, and went deep inside her. As I vibrated her clit with my mouth, she rubbed my head and let out soft moans. And as soon as I started to get more into it, I heard Kareem and Quincy coming up the steps talking. I stopped and looked up at Candi. She whispered for me to put her down, but I shook my head. As they came into the room laughing, I looked over at them and smiled.

"Say, do you brothas think I can have a li'l privacy?" I asked.

Kareem covered his mouth. "Damn, big brother. Let me get out of here and let you get back to business. Sorry for the interruption," he said, looking at Candi.

Quincy cleared his throat. "We just gon', uh, leave. Right now, so, y'all have y'all selves a good time."

They walked slowly out of the room, and when they got to the steps they ran down them yelling and laughing like complete fools.

I looked back up at Candi. "Sorry about that. I didn't think they were coming back this soon." I slid her down to my hips and she wrapped her legs around me.

She held on to my neck and looked me in the eyes. "I have never been so embarrassed in my entire life. Knowing them, they're going to talk about this forever."

I nodded. "Yeah, no doubt about it, they most certainly are. We can try this another time if you'd like."

"No, no, no. It took me this long to get you and I'm not about to let you go that easily. Put me back where I belong."

"Naw, I got a better idea. How about I put my package where it belongs?"

"That sounds even better."

Candi continued holding on to me with her legs around my waist. I eased myself inside of her while holding her against the wall, and taking deep strokes. As I found myself getting so into it, I moved away from the wall and stood with my arms holding her legs, pounding her body against mine. She was enjoying every bit of my loving. Had already come once, and by the warm feeling on my dick, I knew there wasn't nothing fake about it. I walked her over to the couch, laid her on her stomach, and straddled her with one leg resting on the floor. Before I went in, I took a look at her from behind and could only think about how lucky I was. I hoped that nigga Donovan was looking up at me from hell, 'cause one man's trash was definitely another man's treasure. I slid my goodness inside her again and took deep, fast strokes to make her come again. Shivering, she cried out, closed her eyes, and gripped the couch with her fingernails.

Soon, she fell to the floor then turned to her side looking at me next to her, smiling. "There has to be a word better than satisfied, isn't there?"

"Sure, there's plenty. There's pleased, fulfilled, gratified, mollified, content; take your pick."

"I like overly pleased. More pleased than I've ever been in my entire damn life."

I kissed her and got up off the floor. I smacked her ass to watch it jiggle then helped her up. "Damn, that ass is soft," I complimented her.

"But that hurt. You didn't have to smack it so hard, did you?"

I wrapped my arms around her. "Sorry. You know I wouldn't do nothing to hurt you."

"I hope not. And you know I wouldn't either."

I lay back on the couch and Candi rested in between my legs. As I combed through her hair with my fingers, I kissed her forehead.

"And what's that for?" she asked, rubbing my legs.

"It's for helping me relieve some of this stress I've been feeling lately."

"I'm glad I can be of assistance. You've been kind of distant lately. My purpose was to come over here and cheer you up."

"Well, now that I'm back to reality, it's going to take a lot more than just loving you to cheer me up."

"I can stay for as long as you'd like. Or at least be here for you when you need me. But you got to tell me something."

"What's that?"

"Does your mood have anything to do with Donovan?"

"A li'l bit. Why?"

"Because when I read the paper the other day I saw a picture of him. The paper said his name was DeAndre McPhearson and said he'd been gunned down."

"I wouldn't know nothing about that. I wanted to hurt him myself but I just couldn't do it. Besides, he was hanging around with some shiesty-ass fellas so that doesn't surprise me at all."

"Did you read about what happened?"

"Naw, but Kareem told me. I feel sorry for that fool, but you just can't trust everybody."

"I know. I feel kind of sorry for him too. Seems like he was doing okay when he was living here with y'all. Why did he leave anyway?"

"He left on his own free will. Now, I don't want to talk about it anymore. It upsets me just thinking about the shit."

She turned and looked up at me. "I'm sorry. I didn't mean to upset you." She kissed me and pressed her head back against my chest.

I rolled my hand around on her belly for a while then moved it up to her left breast. I licked my hand and shaved her nipple with the palm of it.

As it hardened, she grabbed my hand. "Uh-uh, you're finished with me today." She grabbed my hand tighter so I would stop. When I took my other hand and did the same to her other nipple, she grabbed that hand too.

"Please." I smiled. "Just one more time before you go."

"No!" she yelled, standing up, looking for her clothes.

"Come on, you know you want it."

"I do, but I need a break after what you just did. My stuff is still sore."

"Let me cool it down for you then." I said, rising off the couch.

She backed up and tried to run for the steps. When she got there, I grabbed her and we eased to the floor. She rolled over, opened her legs, and I crawled in between them.

"Where are you going without any clothes on?" I asked, holding her hands down above her head.

"Nowhere. I just wanted to see if you could catch me. Nothing wrong with having a little fun, right?"

"I thought you were having fun."

"I am. More fun than you will ever know."

CHAPTER 16

Things were slowly but surely getting back to normal. My paranoia was starting to ease, and even though I said I wouldn't, I was starting to trust females again. Candi and Ginger both helped me get through what I was going through. They comforted me, cooked for me, and were fucking my brains out every chance they got. More so Ginger. I felt a better connection with her, I guess because I'd known her longer and she was the mother of my child. I still played Candi off every once in a while, but I was definitely keeping her "overly pleased."

Summertime was just around the corner, and the cold weather was finally behind us. Many more niggas were hanging out in the streets, and the females had all kinds of body parts showing. Kareem and Quincy had a reputation for being the male hoes in the hood. So many females were running in and out it was ridiculous. I had to pull them aside, several times, and ask them to chill; but as usual, they kept shit on the down low for a while, then were right back at it.

I guess I really couldn't complain since they seemed to be enjoying themselves, and it was good to finally see things back to normal again. And if we had the ladies in our lives to thank for that, so be it. Pussy had a way of making things better for a brotha anyway.

Memorial Day weekend I picked up some steaks from Saveway while shopping with Ginger and planned a barbecue for the fellas and me. They'd invited a few ladies, and since I had to make a choice between Ginger and Candi, I chose Candi. Ginger said she was cooking for her family, so what the hell, I thought. But when I slipped and told her Kareem and Quincy was bringing somebody she knew what time it was.

"Who is she, Kiley? And I hope it's not that thing you left the club with that night."

"Ginger, baby, please. Everything been going so well with us, don't go trippin' with me now."

"It's been going well because you're getting everything you want from this relationship. All I'm getting is a big dick and a smile."

"Come on now. I've taken you out several times. Don't even sit here and pretend like I haven't."

"Once or twice in the last month. That's it. And you seemed to be rushing me so we could get back here and screw."

"See, this is what I've been trying to avoid. You promised me that you wouldn't be trippin' like this with me. I see other people occasionally, but most of my time is spent with you."

"You didn't answer my question. Did you invite that thing over to your house for the holiday?'

"Yes, I did. Only because you said you were cooking for your family. If you'd like to come over instead, I'd be more than happy to tell her not to come."

Ginger rolled her eyes and spoke with attitude. "Naw, that's okay. Don't be doing me any favors."

She hurried to grab her bags from the front seat and got out of the car. I didn't want to get into an argument with her, especially since I had offered to change my plans. With a smile on my face, I popped the trunk to get the rest of her groceries. I followed her as I carried the bags into her apartment. As I set the groceries on the kitchen table, I heard her on the phone, laughing and talking to someone. She said "baby," so just to fuck with her, I went to her room and stood in the doorway with my arms folded. I really didn't care who the nigga was, but I pretended as if I did. As long as I was getting mine, I was good. "Who are you talking to?" I asked.

She grinned. "Okay, Theodis, I'll see you around six. And for the holiday, if you can pick up a few packages of hotdogs for me I'd appreciate it."

She hung up the phone and tried to walk by me. I held my arm across the doorway.

"Move, Kiley. I'm not going to play your damn game anymore. I'm tired of putting my life on hold for you and you screwing around with who the hell you want to." She pushed my arm. "Now, move, goddamn it!"

"Don't curse at me. I told you if you wanted to come over you could. Why you still trippin'?"

"Because I was a second choice for you. Maybe even third or fourth, who knows? But don't worry about it. I made plans just like you did."

"Plans with Theodis, huh? You still got that fool running around here?"

"Yes. He's there for me when you ain't, just like I'm sure you got somebody there for you when I'm not around."

I was upset, but I couldn't bring myself to argue with her. I went in the kitchen and unpacked her bags. After I put everything up for her, I got in my car and left. She called me while I was driving, but I didn't answer my phone.

When I got home and listened to my voice mail, she apologized and asked me to call her back.

I lay on my stomach across the bed and started dialing her number. Just before I hit the last number, the doorbell rang, and when I looked at the monitor, I saw two police officers standing on the porch. I scrambled around the room, looking for the keys to unlock the front door. After taking deep breaths, I slowly went to the door. I wasn't sure if they'd seen me pull up, and I knew if I didn't answer the door they'd think I had something to hide.

"Yes," I said, standing in the doorway with my arm resting against the door.

"Hello, sir. May we come in?" one of them asked.

"Sure," I said, backing away from the door to let them in.

The other officer pulled out a notepad. "I'm Officer McBride and this is Officer Jackson. If you don't mind, we'd like to ask you some questions about a gentleman by the name of Donovan Dukes, alias DeAndre McPhearson."

I nodded. "Well, come on in, Officers. Have a seat," I said, getting ready to walk into the living room.

"No, we won't be long Mr. . . . ."

"Aw," I said, shaking their hands. "Kiley Franklin."

"Right, Mr. Franklin." McBride wrote my name down on his pad. "Anyway, Mr. Franklin, when is the last time you saw Mr. Dukes?"

I shook my head. "It's been awhile. A friend of mine told me what happened to him and, actually, I really wasn't surprised."

"Why is that?"

"Well, Donovan and me used to be very good friends. He lived here for a while with a few other fellas and me. But he started hanging around with the wrong crowd, and when I came in one night and saw them doing drugs I asked him to leave. Shortly after, he packed his things up and left. He'd called me a few times after that. One time he told me a dude named . . ." I pretended like I was thinking. "Uh, Marcus, that's it. He told me Marcus and him had a fight and Marcus shot him in the shoulder. So, when I heard about what happened to him, I felt bad for him, but I really wasn't surprised."

"Yeah, we talked to Marcus. He gave us your address and told us to come talk to you. Said that you and a gentleman by the name of Quincy jumped on him and beat him up real bad."

"Officer, that isn't true. He was one of the fellas who helped Donovan move his things out. Yes, he argued with my friend Quincy and me after calling us some faggots, but it went no further than that."

"So, are you a faggot, Mr. Franklin?"

I laughed. "That's really none of your business. The fellas and me like to keep things on the down low if you don't mind, and it really has nothing to do with this case."

They looked at each other. "One last question, Mr. Franklin. Several months ago, a young lady called the police and said a Mr. Kiley J. Abrams assaulted her. Are you Mr. Abrams?"

"Look. I go by my mother's last name, which is Franklin. My father's last name is Abrams and I haven't used that name since I was born. He wasn't never no daddy to me so it would be stupid of me to keep his name."

They looked at each other again. "Thanks, Mr. Franklin. We're not going to take up any more of your time, but if you can think of anybody else who might have had it out for Mr. Dukes," he said, handing me his card, "give me a call."

"Will do, sir. Sorry I couldn't be much help to you."

After the officers left, I closed the door and wiped the sweat from my head. I closed my eyes, knowing that deep down they could see right through me. Thing was, there was no proof of anything. There was no evidence anywhere that I knew of. I went back upstairs to my room and watched them as they sat in their police car talking. I'd have given anything if I could tell what they were saying. And after a few more minutes, they jetted.

My palms were wet and so was my forehead from the beads of sweat that dotted it. There was a tight knot in my stomach because I wondered if the police knew more about what had gone down. What if somebody was talking in L.A.? Could Jada be there running her damn mouth?

I was paranoid as fuck, so I made a quick call to one of my police connections in L.A. He didn't answer, so I left a message for him to hit me back. I then called Quincy and Kareem to tell them what was up. Neither of them answered, so I left messages to warn them about the police and about Marcus possibly running his mouth, too. I also wondered if the police had been talking to people like Ginger, or even Candi. And even though I was in no mood to hear Ginger's mouth, I called to see what was up with her. When I asked if the cops had been snooping around, she said they hadn't. I was relieved and was glad to hear her sound like she wasn't trippin' anymore. Because of Desmon, I had to keep Ginger on my good side. A little smooth talking definitely helped to keep things with her calm.

"Who are you, Dr. Jekyll and Mr. Hyde?" I asked in a joking manner.

"No. But you know you be pissing me off though, don't you?"

"And purposely doing so."

"Anyway, I wanted to tell you I'm coming over Memorial Day."

"What about all that meat and stuff you bought at Saveway for your family?"

"I'll cook it some other time. Besides, I don't want no other woman over their digging her claws into you."

"Digging? The only digging I feel like doing is into you."

"Why have you gotten all nasty all of a sudden? You didn't use to talk to me like that."

"Maybe because I wasn't fucking you like I'm fucking you now."

"It's loving me, Kiley. Not fucking me."

"Yeah, well, whatever you want to call it, it's all the same thing."

"Well, since you seem not to be lying to me when you said I could come over for the holiday, I ain't coming."

"What?"

"I just wanted to see what you were going to say. I'm not going to cancel plans with my family all because of you. Besides, I'm going to call you around the clock to make sure ain't none of that 'fucking' going on."

"Hey, feel free. Call all you want. I take my barbecuing seriously. Besides, how you gon' be calling here when Theodis will be keeping you occupied?"

"Fool, I haven't seen Theodis in months. I was talking to the dial tone. Don't believe everything you hear and use your brain sometimes, okay?"

"I do be using my brain. Y'all women just play too many games. Once we got one game all figured out here y'all come with another one. Then always talking about us. Y'all invented the games; we just copying off y'all."

"I beg to differ, but I just called to hear my bookie-boo voice since him was all upset with me when he left," she said, talking baby talk to me.

"Bookie-boo? What in the fuck is a bookie-boo?"

"It's the name I give you when I'm talking to my girlfriends about you. I be telling them how my bookie-boo be putting it on me."

"That don't even sound right. Why can't you call me Tarzan or Amistad? Give me a more masculine name—you know what I mean?"

"Because, I like bookie-boo. If you don't like it, too bad. It's not for you to hear anyway."

"All right, Big Gulp, you keep telling your friends about your bookie-boo if you want to.

They gon' be trying to get a piece of the action in a minute, then you'll be all mad."

"Wait a minute . . . Big Gulp? What kind of damn name is that?"

"It's the one I use when I talk to the fellas about you."

"Oooo, Kiley. You know you ain't right. That is terrible."

"I'm just playing with you. Can't you take a joke?"

"You'd better be playing. If not, you better come up with a better name for me than that."

"Okay, I will. Let me get off the phone and think about one for you." I hung up and in a few minutes called her right back. "Okay, got one."

"What?"

"Deep Throat." I laughed and she hung up.

I called her back. "Sharkey?" She hung up again.

I kept this up, and when I finally called saying what she wanted to hear, she stayed on the phone and laughed.

"I love you too, bookie-boo."

When I woke up the next day, I went downstairs to the kitchen to spice up my meat. I was worried because I still hadn't heard from

Kareem or Quincy, so I called them again to see what was up. Both of them said they hadn't been approached by the police, and they got in my shit about being too paranoid. Maybe I was, so I did my best to chill and enjoy the day.

"I'll be home within the hour to help with the food," Kareem said. "Do you need me to stop and pick up anything?"

"Nah, I think we're good. Holla soon."

I got down on seasoning the meat, and then headed to the backyard and fired up the grill. I laid a few pieces of meat on it, then ran upstairs to change clothes.

By the time I came back down, Kareem and Quincy were pulling into the garage. Quincy got out, strutting with a joint dangling from his mouth and a blue bandana tied around his head.

"You just about done with that meat yet, bro, or what?" he asked.

"Naw, fool. I just got started. Why don't y'all go upstairs and change so y'all can help me finish up."

"Change?" Kareem said. "Change for what? This cool what I got on, ain't it?"

I looked at Kareem and Quincy with their dirty sweat suits on from playing ball. "Come on now, fellas. We can't be around the ladies looking like that. Kareem, I know your da—"

"Yeah, yeah, yeah. You're right. My daddy didn't raise me to look like this." He walked up the steps with Quincy. "Did anybody call?"

"Yeah. Jackie."

"Jackie? Jackie who?"

"Aw, sorry, that was for me."

Kareem and Quincy laughed and went into the house. We waited for our guests to arrive, and to no surprise, Candi was the first female to show. Shortly after, Felicia and her friend, Chris, who Quincy was talking to, came by. I asked Quincy what happened to Veronica and he said he'd finally given up on her. He insisted she was a waste of time and he couldn't put up with her shy-ass ways anymore.

While I was outside cooking the meat, Candi was inside making some potato salad and baking a German chocolate cake. Quincy and Kareem wasn't doing shit but drinking up most of the alcohol and grabbing the hotdogs off the grill as soon as they were done. When I complained about it, Felicia and Chris stepped up and offered to help Candi out in the kitchen. I thanked them, and as I turned my head to continue cooking, I watched a cop in his car slowly drive down the alley, looking around. When he waved, I waved back, dropped my head, and went back to barbecuing. I started getting really paranoid when I saw two police cars, and alerted Quincy and Kareem of their presence by nudging my head. We all played it cool by waving again, and we were sure not to display any of the weed we'd smoking. Seconds later, the police cars were out of sight, putting me at ease.

The food was done, so we all sat down at the picnic table to eat. My legs straddled the bench and Candi was sitting down right in front of me. She wiped my mouth with a napkin, as sauce got on it from grubbing like I hadn't eaten in ages. And when she got some sauce on her lips, I leaned over and licked it off.

Kareem was biting into a rib and threw it down on his plate. "Y'all some good horny muh-fuckers. All this wiping and licking bullshit starting to get on my nerves."

I laughed. "Nigga, you just jealous. You might want to work on those drips on Felicia's chest, instead of worrying about what I'm over here doing."

Felicia looked down at her chest, picked up a napkin, and wiped the sauce off her shirt. Kareem looked at her, "Baby, you know I would have taken care of that for you."

"I'm sure you would have, honey," she said, puckering up her lips. "You just too busy right now smacking on that food like you ain't never had nothing that good to eat, when I feed you good every time you come to my house."

"Not like this though, baby. You don't be feeding me this good," he said, pointing at the ribs, and smacking as he put it back into his mouth.

"This is pretty good, Kiley," Quincy said. "And, Candi, the potato salad is off the hook."

Felicia put her hands on her hips and looked at Candi and me. "They didn't even get it. Did y'all get it?"

Candi and me both shook our heads. "I got it, Felicia," I said. "You have to excuse Kareem. He a li'l slow sometimes."

Kareem chewed his meat, nodding his head up and down. "I got it too. But like I said, I ain't never 'ate' anything this good." He looked at Felicia. "Now, if you think you taste better than this meat, I got news for you, you don't. By all means, baby," he said, patting her on the leg, "you're good, but just not this good."

"I'll be sure to remember that when you're laying there crying like a baby when I don't give you none. And the next time you come running to my house after you leave the club, knowing that those other hoochie mamas can't do the job, I'm going to leave you standing outside in the cold."

"No, you won't, baby. You know how I know you won't?"

"How?" She smiled.

"'Cause it ain't cold outside. You can't leave me out in the cold when it ain't cold no mo'."

Felicia playfully punched Kareem in the arm and we all laughed.

When I heard the phone ring, I hopped up and went inside to get it. I looked down at the caller ID and it was Ginger's cell phone number. I wasn't going to answer, but since I knew she would be trippin' if I didn't, I went ahead and picked it up.

"Are you having yourself a good time yet?" she asked.

"Of course. How about you? Did Theodis show up yet?"

"I told you he wasn't coming over here. I really didn't want anything. We over at my mother's house, and since I just laid Desmon down for a nap, I thought I'd give you a holla."

"Well, kiss him for me, and if you act right, I just might come see you later."

"Good-bye, fool. And call if you decide to come over. My mother and them over here running their mouths. Ain't no telling how long we're going to be."

"It must run in the family," I joked, heading to the downstairs bathroom, while talking dirty talk to Ginger. When I heard the back door squeak open, not knowing who it was, I quickly slammed the door and ended my conversation with her. After I washed my hands, I opened the door and Candi was standing there.

"Did you need something, baby?" I said, wiping my hands on a paper towel.

"Yeah. I got kind of lonely outside without you."

"Say you did," I said, pulling her into the small bathroom, closing the door behind her. As she backed up against the door, I held her hands over her head and stood in front of her, looking her in the eyes. She released one of her hands from mine and rubbed it on the side of my face.

"I'm falling in love with you, Kiley. This, without a doubt, was definitely not in the plan."

"So, you got plans for me now, huh?" I reached for the light and turned it off. I slowly pecked down her neck. "Did you plan on coming in here to give up some of that sweet pussy?"

"No, no, I didn't."

"Well, you should have, especially since you came over here with this short-ass flimsy dress on so I can have easy access to everything." I gripped the edge of her dress to raise it up. Candi turned around, pressing her hands against the door as I moved her thong over to the side and slid inside her. After sinking into it, she bent farther over. Her moans started to sound more like cries. Curious, I stopped. She turned around and held one of her hands with mine. I turned on the light and saw tears trickling down her face. I mean, what in the fuck was going on here? Something wasn't adding up today, and it caused my paranoia to resurface again. My mind traveled back to the police cars casing the place earlier. Now this. Was Candi afraid of telling me something that she knew? My face twisted as I stepped back a few inches away from her.

"What's up? Did the police say something to you about me or did . . . did I hurt you?"

She started to cry harder and moved her head from side to side. A light no escaped from her lips, and then she gave me a quick peck on the lips. Afterward, she opened the door and ran out.

I quickly pulled up my pants and ran after her. By the time I reached her, she was opening the door to her car. I grabbed the door so she wouldn't get in. "What in the fuck is wrong with you?"

"I just need to go, Kiley. Please just let me go. I'll call you later."

I was trying my best to figure out what had upset her so quickly. "Did the police say something to you, or was it the phone call from Ginger?"

Her eyes fluttered and she nodded. "It was the call from Ginger. I didn't appreciate the disrespect, but I don't want to talk about it right now. I need to go."

I didn't buy that bullshit for one minute, but trying not to act a fool about the situation, I moved away from the car so she could drive off. She jetted so fast that if I blinked, I missed her.

With my head hanging low and my thoughts all over the place, I made my way to the backyard. Candi's actions had me fucked up. I knew women did crazy shit like that, but, damn; to stop me in the midst of things and to start crying worried the hell out of me. I didn't think she'd heard my conversation with Ginger, but there was a possibility that she had. Then, what if the police had gotten to her? What if they'd told her about my past, but she didn't want to tell me? I didn't know what the fuck was up, but in order to calm my nerves, I finished up the night getting high with Kareem, Quincy, and their lady friends. When they inquired about what had happened to Candi, I told them that she had an emergency and had to go. I didn't think Kareem believed me, and after the ladies left I told him and Quincy what happened. They laughed about it.

"What the fuck is so funny?" I asked

"It ain't funny, dog," Quincy said. "Sounds kinda scary to me."

"To me too," Kareem said, leaning back on the couch cracking up.

"Y'all lost me. What's so funny about her leaving like that?"

Kareem sat up and folded his hands together. "First of all, big brother, if you're laying it down like I saw you laying it down against that wall right there," he said, pointing to the wall, "she probably scared of you. Some women just ain't ready for that type of action."

"I agree," Quincy said. "Prime example, if I would have done some shit like that to Veronica, she'd probably be scared of my ass too."

I stood up and went over to the bar to pour myself a drink. "Naw, that ain't it. She never seemed to have a problem before. Why now?"

"Well, you said yourself she heard you on the phone with Ginger."

I took a sip of the cognac. "Yeah, I'm sure she did. And since I was getting a li'l freaky deaky on the phone with Ginger that probably pissed her off. Either way, I'm not going to call her. She told me she'd call me so I'll wait until she cool off."

I tossed and turned all night thinking about Candi. Last thing I wanted was to hurt her. She'd been so good to me, and the thought of upsetting her like that just frustrated me. I picked up the phone several times, only to lay it back down, not wanting to pressure her since she'd backed off when I asked her to. So instead, I watched my James Bond collection, not feeling good about what the days ahead would bring.

CHAPTER 17

I didn't hear from Candi for almost two whole weeks. When she finally called, she told me that since she'd fallen in love with me it was difficult for her to accept the fact that I was still seeing Ginger. I was happy to hear from her, but I reminded her she was free to see whoever she wanted and so was I. She said she didn't want to see anyone else and was ready to take our relationship to another level. Feeling for Ginger, I couldn't agree to that. I told Candi if she wanted to call it quits that was fine with me. But after telling her how much she meant to me and how my life wouldn't be complete without her, she agreed to take our relationship one day at a time. The police hadn't been back, and I'd barely seen any police cars casing the streets. I had also spoken to my connect in L.A. He told me everything was all good, and that no one had been looking for me. With that tad bit of information, I decided to put these crazy thoughts to the back of my mind and tried my best to forget about that had been transpiring. I went to the strip club to ease my mind, worked out more often to keep my body in shape, and spent more and more time with Desmon. Being with him helped to ease my mind.

Later that day, Kareem, Quincy, and me tossed a football around on the porch while making plans to take a trip. Desmon was riding his new 4x4 Power Wheels car that I'd bought him for his birthday up and down the street.

As the heat started to take its toll, I went inside and grabbed some ice-cold bottled waters from the refrigerator. On my way out, I handed Kareem and Quincy one, then sat down in a lawn chair leaning back with my foot resting on the rail in front of me.

"Shit," I said. "This is the fucking life. Chilling out here with you fellas and watching my son get older beats going to Jamaica any day of the week."

"I'm sorry, big brother, ain't nothing about sitting on this hot-ass porch, trying to cool off by drinking muh-fucking water beats going to Jamaica," Kareem joked. "Then again, when you went before, you did go with Jada, didn't you? Probably didn't even get a chance to enjoy your poor self."

We laughed.

"Naw, I really didn't. We argued so much it was crazy. Do you know that heifer accused me of lusting for some women on the ship? White girls, too. I don't have no problem doing 'em but I very rarely will lust for them."

"Man," Quincy said. "Jada would accuse you of lusting for her dog, if she had one. That was one crazy bitch." He looked at me. "Aren't you glad she's finally out of your life?"

"Somewhat," I said. "Sometimes I think about her and sometimes I'm glad she's history."

"Besides," Kareem said, sitting down on the first step of the porch, "what's there to think about when you got women in your life like Candi and Ginger? You hit the jackpot with them, man, straight up hit the jackpot."

"I wouldn't say all that. They can be a pain sometimes too. Especially when shit don't go how they want it to." I laid my water down on the porch and headed down the steps to help Desmon, who was stuck in some mud. By the time I reached the bottom step he had gotten himself out.

"He don't need your help, fool," Kareem said. "Stop treating him like a punk and let him handle his own shit."

"Like I let you handle your own shit, huh?" I said, tapping him on his face with my hands.

"You want some of this, big brother?" He put his water down, stood up, and made fists with both hands. "Spssss," he said, moving side to side like a boxer.

"You silly, man. You can float like a butterfly and sting like a bee, but Muhammad Ali you definitely can't be."

We all laughed again and when Desmon car got stuck in the mud again, I went to go help him out. When I pulled his car out of the mud, I proudly watched him head down the street like a big boy. Suddenly, a car skidded around the corner. When I saw how fast the car was moving and a semi-automatic pistol come busting out the back window, I yelled at Kareem and Quincy on the porch and ran to catch Desmon. I dove on top of him, we hit the ground, and my head smashed against the concrete. With blurred vision, I looked up and saw Kareem pull his gun out from his pants and fire shots at the car. Then I saw him fall backward and his blood splash on Quincy's white T-shirt. Quincy was firing bullets too, and I flew down the street like a marathon runner, firing behind the car. I couldn't catch it, so I hurried back up the street to see about Kareem. Quincy was on his cell phone pacing back and forth, calling for an ambulance. I walked up the steps, saw Kareem lying flat on his back, and fell down beside him. I lifted his head up and held his trembling fingers as he tried to touch his chest where the bullets went in.

He took deep breaths as he looked at me with tears in his eyes and blood dripping down the side of his mouth. "Did you . . . get them fools, man?" he stuttered.

Tears streamed down my face as I squeezed his hand. "Yeah, I did. I got 'em. But hold on for me, li'l brother!" I yelled. "Help is on the way."

Kareem grinned and tightly closed his eyes. After I yelled at him, he opened them. He started shaking his head slowly. "I . . . I can't hold on much longer. You gon' have to . . . handle yo' shit without me." He grinned, closed his eyes again, and his body started shaking even more. Shortly after, he started coughing up blood.

I held him in my arms to stop him from shaking and looked up at the sky, "God, please!" I begged. "Not now, man, please not now!" I looked down at Kareem as my tears started to fall harder. "Don't you do this to me, man! Don't you leave me like this!" I yelled louder.

Kareem squeezed his eyes tighter and placed his bloody hands on his chest. With the little strength he had, he forced his eyes open, grinned, and closed them again.

His blood had stained my clothes and it was all over the porch. I knew it was over for him. My heart dropped and I screamed so loud I could hear my voice echo. Quincy tried to put his arms around me, but when Desmon started crying, he ran down the steps to grab him.

Just that fucking fast, my li'l brother was gone.

When the ambulance came, the paramedics pronounced Kareem dead at the scene. They covered his body with a white sheet, and shortly after, the place was swarming with cops. They questioned us over and over about what happened, and since I was too messed up to talk, Quincy did most of the talking. I dazed off, hoping to wake up from this badass dream I'd seemed to be having, but this time I couldn't. Just last night I had one about Kareem and during my dream, he died. Not thinking much of it, I kept it to myself.

As I watched them finally take his body away, I knew it was real. He was gone. The same way Daddy had left me, and there was nothing in my power I could say or do to get neither one of them back.

Before the police left, they made it perfectly clear they'd be back. I sat in the living room in a daze. Quincy came downstairs to tell me Desmon was upstairs asking for Ginger. I tried to strengthen up to go see about him, but I fell back on the couch and continued to sob.

Eyes just as swollen as mine was, Quincy sat down next to me and pounded down on my leg. "I know, man. Ain't nothing I can say to make this easier for you but we gotta be strong. Kareem probably upset with the both of us for acting like this."

I sat up and covered my face with my hands. I wiped my tears, then gripped my hands together in front of me. "You know who that was, don't you?" I said, looking over at him.

"Yeah, I got a pretty good look at him. It was that fool Marcus."

"Yep. So here's the plan. You know the cops coming back for us, right?"

"Yeah, I kinda got that feeling."

I nodded. "Okay. First, I'm going to take Desmon home. After I drop him off, I'm going to the hospital to get things situated with Kareem. Hopefully, they'll hook me up with somebody I can talk to about having his body cremated like he always wanted. When I get back, we gon' shake, rattle, and roll."

"Sounds like a plan to me," Quincy said, drying his eyes and standing up.

"Cool." I stood up too. "While I'm gone, gather up whatever you need, because after tonight, I don't think it'll be safe for us to stay here. Come on, follow me." I unlocked the basement door and Quincy followed me downstairs. When I punched in the code to open the wall, he looked at me like I was crazy.

"What in the hell?"

"Not now, Quincy. I don't have time to explain."

We went into the private room and when I opened the safe, I showed Quincy the money and told him to pack it up with the rest of his things. He stood with his mouth open, while looking at thousands of dollars I had stashed away.

When I got to my room, Desmon was sitting on the bed crying. I hugged him and told him to put on his jacket so we could go. His face had been skinned from hitting the ground when I jumped on him, so I put a bandage over it to cover it up.

On the drive to Ginger's house, I punched out the radio with my fist, thinking about Kareem. I couldn't stop crying, all I could think about was blowing that muh-fucker Marcus and his partnas to pieces.

Desmon dashed out of the car and started banging hard on Ginger's front door. When she opened it, she started to yell, but then she saw the bandage.

"What in the hell happened to him, Kiley?" she asked, as he cried holding on to her. "What happened to my damn baby!" she yelled.

"He fell," I said softly, standing by the front door.

She took the bandage off his face and looked at it. "Fell?" she yelled. "This damn scar on his face look worse than just having a goddamn fall!" She stood up and darted her finger at me. "Why are your eyes so red? Are you high or something? I knew it was a big mistake letting him spend time with you, I knew it!"

"Ginger," I said. "Calm down."

She looked down at Desmon. "Baby, go to your room. Mommy will be there in a minute, okay?" Desmon went to his room. She turned back around, lashing out at me again. "I truly didn't want to disrespect you in front of him, but how in the fuck could your stupid-ass let something like this happen?"

Burning inside I wrapped my hands around Ginger's neck and started choking her. We fell backward onto the living room floor, and when Desmon came running in, crying and hitting me on my back, I raised up off her.

"Desmon!" I yelled. "Go back into your room!"

He ran back in his room, still crying.

"You stupid bitch!" I said, looking down at Ginger on the floor as she tried to catch her breath. "I lost my fucking brother today! Could have lost my damn son but I covered him up to protect him! If you stop bitching all the god-damn time, maybe you would have listened before jumping to fucking conclusions." I got up, opened the door, and slammed it behind me.

She came running out after me. "Kiley! I'm sorry. I didn't know! Please don't go," she cried.

I got in the car, slammed my door, and sped off.

When I got to the hospital, I talked to the lady who was in charge of assisting people with the deceased, but when I told her I wanted Kareem's body cremated she directed me to someone else. Before I left, they asked me if I wanted to see him again, and since I didn't want to remember him with bullets riddled in his chest, I declined.

On the way back home, I sat in the car thinking. Life without Kareem just wasn't going to be the same, and I knew it. If it weren't for Desmon, there really wasn't no reason for me to live. And since he'd seen firsthand what went down, I wasn't sure if me being a part of his life was the best thing for him.

Suicide was definitely an option for me, but then again it wasn't an option because somebody was going to have to pay for this. I would make sure of that, and when it came to my little brother, there would be no fucking regrets.

CHAPTER 18

I could see the lights a mile away. Helicopters were circling the air, and the closer I moved in, I saw about twenty police cars parked outside the house. I didn't want to get too close, so I turned the car around and kept on driving. I'd turned my phone off after I left Ginger's house because I knew she was going to be calling, trying to apologize. When I turned it back on, Quincy had left me three messages. He told me the police was outside and he was trying to find a way out of the house without them seeing him. He wanted to hide downstairs but said he didn't know the code to close the wall. He told me he loved me and then let me listen to them pounding on the doors. I was crushed. I pulled the car over, got out, and pounded the roof with my fist. I screamed out loud, got back inside, and aimed a pistol at my head. As the tears started to fall again, I closed my eyes tight, then I thought about how I refused to leave this earth with unfinished business.

After driving around for a while, I parked down the street outside the house Donovan had lived in with Marcus and his partnas. I must have watched the house for hours before I finally saw somebody walk out and get into a car. When I drove down the street, I saw it wasn't Marcus; it was some other nigga. I circled the block a few more times, then parked my car again.

Anxious to know if he was home, I called to see if he was there. When someone answered, I asked to speak to him and they told me to hold on. I hung up, then called Candi's house. It was almost midnight, but she sounded like she was wide awake.

"Hey, are you sleeping?" I asked, knowing she wasn't.

"No, I was sitting up watching a movie. Where are you? I've been calling you all day."

"I'm out taking care of some business. But, uh, I need you to do me a favor."

"What?"

"When I dial this number, I need you to ask for Marcus. When he answers make up a fake name and tell him you're outside waiting for him."

"Who?"

"Marcus."

"Kiley, what are you up to?"

"I'll tell you about it later. Just do this for me, please."

"I don't know; this sounds like a setup if you ask me. Where are you? I need to talk to you about something."

"Not right now, Candi. Just trust me. I wouldn't ask you to do this if it wasn't important."

"All right. Dial the number."

I dialed, and when Marcus got on the phone Candi told him she was some chick named Angela who he'd met and she was outside waiting for him. He insisted he didn't know any chick named Angela and hung up the phone.

"Damn!" I said. "Call him back for me."

"Look, Kiley. I don't know what's going on but you're scaring me, baby. Where are you? Is everything all right?"

"No, it's not but I'll hit you back in a minute." I hung up, but she kept calling me back. I didn't answer, because I was trying to figure out a way to get Marcus to come outside. I thought about just shooting through the house but I wasn't up for no innocent people getting hurt. So I did what I knew best and just waited.

By morning, I was still scoping out the place. I was slumped over in the car so no one would see me from the cars that passed by throughout the night. Finally, around eleven in the morning, Marcus walked out of the house. He was with this other fool, getting into a black Cutlass Supreme.

As they drove off, I followed them. They stopped at a convenience store right around the corner from their house and the other dude got out to go inside. I didn't waste any time. I went right up to the car, and tapped on the window. When he turned his head, I smiled at him, pulling the trigger five times and blasting his head wide open.

I sped off the lot, and as I was heading for the highway the cops flew right past me. After driving for about an hour or so, I found a cheap motel where I could chill at until I figured out what to do. Going back to L.A. was out of the question. And staying on the run was out as well. Life didn't even feel worth it anymore, but I still had Desmon and my main man, Quincy. I was curious to know what happened, and if he managed to swindle himself out of this mess, I wanted to be around.

Feeling the urge to talk to my son, I called Ginger's house to speak to him. She answered and told me how sorry she was.

"Don't worry about it, Ginger," I said dryly. "Just put Desmon on the phone."

"Baby, please don't be mad at me. Where are you? I can hear the pain in your voice. Please tell me so Desmon and me can come be with you."

"Ginger, bad idea. Just put Desmon on the phone."

She put the phone down and Desmon picked it up. "Hello," he said softly.

"Hey, my man," I said, swallowing as my throat ached. "I'm sorry about yesterday. You know your daddy loves you, don't you?"

"Yes."

"Are you sure?"

"Yes."

"Daddy gotta go away for a while, but I'll get back to see you as soon as I can, okay?"

"Okay."

"Put your mother back on the phone."

"Daddy?"

"Yeah, man," I said, as my eyes watered.

"Did Uncle Kareem die?"

I closed my eyes and busted out in tears. I held the phone to my forehead and turned it off. I didn't even have the guts to answer him. In a while, I called Ginger back and told her to tell him the truth for me.

At that moment, I realized that if I stayed I couldn't be the father to him I wanted to be. He'd never look up to me like a son should look up to his father. I had nothing for him to be proud of, no good footsteps for him to step into, and no good examples for him to follow.

As I lay across the bed with my eyes closed, my cell phone rang. Finally, it was Quincy.

"Q, where are you?" I asked.

"I'm in jail. Where do you think? And before you start running your mouth, I'm cool. Everything's taken care of."

"What do you mean?"

"I mean, I told them what happened."

"Everything?"

"Yeah, everything. They know I was the one who killed Donovan. And they're aware of the drug transactions I was doing behind you fellas' backs."

"But, Quincy, you don't have to—"

"Listen, it was only fair to y'all that I came clean. I'll be here for a few days, so when you get a chance, come tell them the truth so you can move on with your life."

"I'm coming to see what's up now. Man, I don't want you—"

"Listen, my time is up. They want to talk to you but make sure you tell them the truth about me, okay? I know how much you care for me, and I don't want you taking the blame because you want to go down with me."

"Yeah, whatever, but—"

Quincy hung up and I had to go see what was up. I cleaned myself up a bit and rushed to the police station to find out what the hell Quincy was doing. Sounded like he wanted to take the blame for everything that had happened, but why? Especially when he didn't have to. If I had to suffer the consequences for trying to protect my family, so be it. There was no way in hell I was going to let him take the fall all by himself.

When I got to the station and told the police who I was, they took me into an interrogation room. According to them, Quincy's confession had too many holes in it. He'd come up with some shit, and until I figured out what to do, I really didn't say much, but, that whatever he told them was the truth.

After holding me for almost sixteen hours, they finally let me go. They promised me I'd be joining Quincy, and there was no doubt in my mind that someday soon I would be.

CHAPTER 19

Quincy and me stuck to the same story for months. After his court date, he was sentenced to fifty years in prison without the possibility of parole. I was devastated. We talked almost every day up until his sentencing day, and since they never found any evidence against me, I was a free man.

After I left the courthouse, I drove down Highway 40 and pulled my car over to the side on the Poplar Street Bridge. I kissed the container with Kareem's ashes in it and held it in my hands.

I wiped the tears that fell down my face. "Life ain't the same without you, li'l brother. And the ladies, whew, don't know how they're going to manage." I looked up at the sky. "Do you know they're still calling my phone asking for you? You must have left a good damn impression, but, uh, that doesn't surprise me. You're an Abrams, right?" A few more tears fell down my face as I slowly opened the container. I looked

inside it. "I know, I know, you love me, so take
your hands off your chest." I smiled and let the
ashes drift off into the Mississippi River. "I love
you too."

Several cars drove by blowing their horns at
me. A white man in a truck called me a stupid
motherfucker for holding up traffic. Instead of
making more trouble for myself, I got in my car
and left. I found another cheap motel outside St.
Louis and stayed there until I figured out where I
was going to run next. I wasn't sure if the police
were looking for me or not, but I was so damn
paranoid. It felt like I was going crazy, and I
even thought about Quincy snitching and telling
the police everything he knew. My thoughts then
turned to Desmon. My only son. What would
he do without me? Feeling like a deadbeat, I
decided to never call Ginger's place again. She
called almost every day and left messages, but
as soon as I heard her voice, I deleted the call.
I knew if I listened, she'd convince me to come
back to her, but staying in St. Louis wasn't in my
plan.

As for Candi, she still hadn't given up either.
Called me day after day, begging me to call her
back. I planned on calling her but I needed more
time to figure out what to do.

Once Quincy got settled he called and told
me I could come see him in jail. We kept our

conversations short on the phone 'cause Rufus already gave us the scoop about them listening in on people's conversations.

Anxious to see him, I sat in a chair behind the glass, waiting. I tapped my foot on the floor, knowing the sight of him behind bars would kill me. Finally, he came out with handcuffs on, and shackles on his feet. The guard took the cuffs off him, and he sat down in the chair in front of me. He smiled, picked the phone up, and so did I.

"You look like you should be in here," he said, laughing. "I mean, the beard, your fuzzy hair; don't ever think I've seen you look that rugged."

I looked down at the ground as I tried to catch myself from tearing up. The sight of Quincy being on the other side wasn't a good feeling. After I got myself together, I held my head up. "You didn't have to do this, you know?"

"Yeah, but what the hell? I ain't got nothing to lose anyway, right?"

"Yeah, you do. You've lost your life, your freedom; and why? Because of your muh-fucking love for me." I dropped my head again, fighting my emotions.

"Come on now, playa," Quincy said, shaking his head. "Don't go doing that shit." His eyes watered. "You gon' have these fools up in here thinking I'm soft."

"Naw, if anybody up in there thinks you're soft," I said, pointing my finger at him through the glass, "you tell them to come see me. You the hardest muh-fucking colored man I know."

Quincy blinked the water from his eyes and laughed. "So, uh, have you seen Desmon?"

"Naw, man. I'm leaving him in the past. Ain't no telling when I'll make it back his way."

"Naw, playa. It ain't going down like that. He's the reason I decided to do this. He needs you, man. It's not about the money; it's not about the beautiful women and fancy cars. It's all about just being there for him. You couldn't do that if you were cooped up in here, so please, do the right thing."

"I don't know, Q. I don't think I'm cut out for the daddy bullshit."

"Bullshit, man, and you know it. Papa Abrams taught all of us about the important things in life. He'd be disappointed in you for walking away from your own son. I know for a fact he taught you better than that."

I rubbed my hands across my face, gave Quincy a stare, and then shook my head. "You're right. He would be disappointed, but he'd for damn sure be proud of you."

"Man, please. I just did what I had to do. Now, you go do what you need to do."

"I will, bro. I promise you I will."

Quincy and me reminisced about the good times with me, him, and Kareem and he had me cracking up. I couldn't understand how he managed to put up such a good front like everything was cool, but deep down I knew the thought of him being there for fifty years was killing him.

"Well, my time is just about up," he said. "They be straight up clocking a brotha up in here, so keep your phone available and send me a li'l something when you get a chance."

"No problem. Anything you want, my brotha. Any damn thing you want."

Quincy held up the deuces sign, pausing before hanging up the phone. He placed his hand on his heart and mouthed that he loved me. I whispered it back, and after he got up and walked away, I stayed there for a moment, thinking about how wrong I was for letting him take the fall. I knew his intentions were good, but I couldn't live with myself knowing he would be locked up for almost the rest of his life. Last thing I wanted was to sit back and watch him go down, especially when I knew that I was the one behind this madness, not him. I dropped my head in shame, and could hear my heart pounding hard against my chest. My eyes watered, and when I looked up again, Quincy was gone. I felt a serious need to go turn myself in. Something about this didn't seem fair. I knew that Desmon needed me too, but what kind of father could I be to him under these conditions? There was no doubt that he would be better off without me.

When I got back to the motel, I called Ginger to let her know I was coming to see her and Desmon that night. I told her everything that happened, and told her that after spending one last night with them, I was turning myself in. She disagreed with me.

"No, Kiley. Please don't do it. Don't you understand that we need you?"

"Yes, I do understand, but I can't let my boy go out like this. This shit is eating me alive and I already feel guilty as fuck. Desmon will be okay. He got you, and I know you'll continue to do right by him. Promise me that you will."

There was a long pause before Ginger answered. "I know I'm not going to be able to talk you out of this, but I wish I could. And you know I'm going to be the best mother I can to Desmon. That's a promise I can keep."

"Good. And one last thing. Don't bring him to prison to see me. I'm ashamed of some of the things I've done, and there's no way for me to explain this shit."

"You have no right to be ashamed. You did what you had to do. I will make sure that your son knows that you're a good man, Kiley, and a damn good father."

I took a hard swallow and massaged my aching forehead. Hurt was all inside of me, and I couldn't wait to wrap my arms around my son and tell him how much I loved him. I told Ginger I would be there as soon as I showered and changed my clothes.

The second I got out of the shower, Candi hit me up on my cell phone. Since I hadn't talked to her in a while, I finally answered it. She sounded excited to hear my voice, and knowing that I would probably never see her again, I told her I wanted to come by and say good-bye.

I knew I would probably be all night at Ginger's place so I stopped by to see Candi first. When she opened the door, seeing her put a serious smile on my face. She hugged me tightly and didn't want to let go.

"Damn, you miss me that much?" I asked then removed her arms from around my neck.

She nodded. "I've been so worried about you, Kiley. Why haven't you called me?"

"Baby, I'm sure you know there's been a lot going down."

"I know. I've been hearing all kinds of things on the news, and reading shit in the papers. Why didn't you tell me what was going on?"

"Because I didn't want you judging me, Candi. That's why. You never would have understood."

"Yes, I would have. I'm not like that and you know it."

"Well, it's all over with now. Kareem's dead, Quincy's in prison, and I have no idea where I'm headed."

"Are you leaving town?"

"Maybe. That's why I wanted to come see you and tell you good-bye."

Candi took my hand and walked me into the bathroom. Why? I didn't know. She closed the door and stood in front of it. "Take me with you," she whispered, as tears started rolling down her face. "Let's leave tonight. I'll go anywhere you want me to go."

I cocked my head back and displayed a puzzled look. "Why are you rushing me into the bathroom to say all of this?" I reached for the knob to open the door.

She grabbed my hand, "I'm in here because I want to finish what we started in the bathroom at your place that day. But before we do, I have so much I want to tell you, but I can't right now. Let's go and—"

I placed my fingers on her trembling lips. I was eager to finish what we started in the bathroom that day too, especially since the only reason I'd stopped by was to get my final fuck on. "Shhh, we will. Just let me hold you for a while."

I pulled the bathroom door open, took Candi's hand, and walked her into her bedroom. I pulled my shirt over my head and lay back on her bed. She straddled herself on top of me. When I started to undo her silk black robe, she grabbed it with her hands and looked at me.

"Kiley, please tell me you didn't kill anybody. I'm afraid for you and it's just something I have to know."

I moved her hands away from her robe, watching as it fell to her sides. I put my hands on her breasts, massaged them together, and watched her nipples harden. "Don't ever be afraid of me, Candi. I only hurt those who hurt me."

She grabbed my hands again and stopped me. "Did you kill Marcus, Kiley? It's time that you open up and tell me the truth."

I hesitated before answering, but decided to come clean. "Yes, Candi, I did. But please know that I did what I had to do."

She busted out in tears and fell down on my chest. "I'm sorry," she sobbed. "So damn sorry I—"

I tried to calm her but she wouldn't stop crying. I lifted her face up and held it in my hands. "Baby, relax. This has nothing to do with us."

Just then, I heard a loud crash then footsteps running through the house. And when I looked up, the cops were coming through the door. About fifteen of them surrounded us in her bedroom, aiming their guns at me.

"Officer Campbell!" one of the cops yelled, holding his gun steady. "Read him his rights!"

After the cop yelled at her again, her body shook and she mumbled in a soft voice, "You have the right to remain silent. Anything you say or . . ." She stopped, lowered her head, and couldn't continue.

One of the officers came over, pulling her off me. He hugged her, as she cried on his shoulder and he continued reading my rights to me.

Shortly after, Veronica came into the room. She embraced Candi, telling her it was all over with and what a great job she'd done. Candi slowly nodded and the two of them left the room.

The officers cuffed me, and that's when everything started to make sense. Candi and Veronica had been at the game for a long time. Candi must have thought Donovan was the leader of the pack and Veronica must have thought the same about Quincy. When they realized it was me, Veronica backed off Quincy and Candi continued working on me like no other woman out there could. Thing was, deep down I'd known something wasn't right. But as usual, pussy got the best of all of us and we lost focus. I wasn't mad, though. I knew Candi had hurt herself as much as I'd hurt mine by trusting her. And not as if it really mattered that she'd fallen in love, but she was going to have a tough life ahead of her trying to forget about me.

The officers grabbed me off the bed, stood me up, and led me through the living room. Veronica sat next to Candi on the couch, holding her and giving me a fake smile as I passed by them. Candi held her head down, and as soon as they were about to take me out the door, she yelled for them to wait.

"Please!" she yelled, looking at me with puffy red eyes, sniffling. "It's the least you all can do for me!" The officers stopped and two of them held my arms tightly from behind. She came over and stood in front of me. "I was really hoping that you were innocent. You made my job very damn difficult and I'll never forget you, Mr. Kiley Jacoby Abrams."

"I am innocent. Killing somebody for hurting the ones I love doesn't make me a criminal; it only makes me human. But I'm sure you know that, Officer Campbell, and I'll never forget you either."

The cops snatched me away from her, and as they put me in the back seat of the cruiser, she stood in her doorway and watched. When they drove off and I looked back, our eyes continued to connect until the car faded out of sight.

The thought of hopefully being with Quincy again was the only thing that kept me calm, and even if they found out about what I'd done in L.A., and sent me to prison there, I'd at least get to see Rufus again. But either way I looked at it, Kareem and Daddy were probably much better off than I was. I closed my eyes, leaned my head against the back seat, and thought about what I'd thought about many, many times before. Kareem and me used to sit on the porch as kids, watching the drug dealers roll by, and always ask ourselves: "How can I be down?" wishing like hell we had what they did. Well, at this moment I finally had my answer. One thing was for sure: it couldn't possibly get no downer than this.